I0602589

# VEGAS RUN

# VEGAS RUN

## THE RICK KELLER CHRONICLES
### BOOK TWO

## RACHEL A. BRUNE

Copyright ©2025 by Rachel A. Brune

Cover Design by Natania Barron

All rights reserved.

No part of this book may be reproduced in any form or by any electronic or mechanical means, including information storage and retrieval systems, without written permission from the author, except for the use of brief quotations in a book review. No part of this book may be used to train LLM systems or artificial intelligence.

*This book is for my fellow women in uniform, kicking ass and taking names.*
*Proud to serve with you.*

1

---

Outside, the night wallowed deep in the dark well of early morning, but Dr. Gratusczak had long ago ceased to mind the artificial strictures of time. Inside the calming monotony of MONIKER's concrete underground, he could work in silence for days with only the buzz of the fluorescent lights to accompany his meditations.

The centrifuge whirred to a halt. Gratusczak frowned. The three vials settling in their slots were the last samples he had gleaned from Rick Keller, and none of them displayed what he searched for. No matter. He would ask again, and the agency would get him more. A moment of wry pleasure twisted his lips at the thought of Keller's reaction. For all his attempts at Teutonic stoicism, the wolf wore his buttons on his sleeve, and in such a case, how could one help but press them?

The first delight would be to show him he was not as far removed from MONIKER's reach as he believed himself to be. The second...

Dr. Willet reminded him of a granite precipice—unyielding, hard-faced, and dangerous if you got too close. A delicious, rare adrenaline thrill wormed its way through his veins at the thought of her under his knife. He had come close once or twice, and then she'd slipped from his grasp, but exquisite opportunity continued to knock down here amongst the agency's delectable toys.

Gratusczak plucked one of the vials from the machine and twisted off the plastic plug. He sniffed, almost absent-mindedly, and flicked his tongue, snake-like, at the narrow opening. He smelled and tasted copper and dirt.

"Grabbing a snack?"

Gratusczak didn't jump, even though the question came from behind. It took a lot to startle him, and Dr. Willet's alto voice did not come close.

"Dr. Willet." He placed the vial upright in a stand of test tubes. Removing a pen from behind one pallid ear, Gratusczak scribbled the date on a small label. "Thank you for coming by. I need more samples."

"Rick's living furry in the north country." Karen pushed past Gratusczak, not meeting his gaze, another invisible victory for his tally sheet. "Good luck."

She opened the door to a mini refrigerator in the corner of the room and grabbed one of the bottles of water Gratusczak kept stacked there. Twisting off the cap, she sat down on the fridge and swigged straight from the bottle.

Gratusczak carefully pulled the label off its backing and stuck it on the vial. It went on slightly crooked. He frowned, pulled it off, and scratched at the residue with his fingernail. "I'll need you to get in touch with him."

Dr. Willet didn't answer right away. She drank the entire bottle of water as he waited.

The scientist wasn't bothered by the delay or the silence. The lack of small talk relieved him more than anything. He wrote out another label, peeled it up carefully, and spent an extra second making sure he placed the small rectangle correctly and evenly on the vial.

The buzzing of the fluorescents grew louder until it almost echoed off the walls. Dr. Willet crumpled the empty water bottle as slowly and noisily as possible, screwed the cap back on, and tossed it on the floor.

"I'll see what I can do."

Gratusczak waited until she left before walking over and picking up the discarded bottle with long, spindly fingers. He tossed it into the low, round trash receptacle. The good Dr. Willet had been more agitated tonight than normal; the nerves she usually hid so well filtered through the edge of his senses like finely ground cinnamon.

His lips twisted. He meticulously labeled and stored the remaining vials, placing them in the tall specimen refrigerator. Casting one last glance around the room, he headed for the door and knocked. The ever-present security guards opened the door for him, one keeping his less-lethal shotgun trained on the scientist at all times.

"I am ready to return to my cell."

The first security guard keyed his radio. "This is Bandit 8. On the move with Old Spooky." The guard waited for his hail to be acknowledged, then used his handcuffs to fasten Gratusczak's wrists behind his back. "Let's go."

Gratusczak clasped his hands as the first guard slammed the door to the lab. The lights clicked on before them, then off behind them as they moved, a technological quirk meant to both disorient an unknown entity and highlight his movements. They thought it was effective and were proud of their ability to avoid lapsing into complacency regarding the scientist's secure confinement. He'd had the path memorized since his first trip down the hall.

Their footsteps fell softly on the concrete floor, the click of the lights following them with soft echoes. As he moved into the shadows, Gratusczak did not smile. Only the slightest hint of anticipation lit his eyes, completely unseen by the foolish men who matched him stride for stride.

## 2

The pack was restless and had been all day. The mothers started snarling at me two days ago, snapping and growling anytime I got too near their cubs. They knew what the night brought, even without calendars and clocks.

Old Grandfather finally ran me off around mid-afternoon. If I'd been in human form, I would have been aware enough to take myself away. But after six months in wolf form, I'd lost some of my higher-level critical thinking skills. Some would argue I'd never had an over-abundance anyway.

The older wolf harried me away from the pack, unyielding and stubborn without being vicious. Every time I turned around to try to run back, he would simply plant himself in front of me, blocking the path. Whimpering, groveling, begging, trying to sneak around when his back turned—nothing worked.

Finally, he grew impatient with my attempts to make an end run back to the pack territory. As I darted by him yet again, he opened his jaws and bit down hard on my haunch. My hind end landed on the ground, and I rolled on my side and whined. This time, he gave a little shake before he let go.

Once he released me, I turned on my paws and trotted away. Sparing one final backward glance, I caught a glimpse of the old wolf, his graying fur catching the last light as the sun started down the horizon behind him. He growled perfunctorily, and I kept going.

Up in the North Country, even the summer nights come with a chill as the light fades. I rarely feel the cold, but this night brought something with it. Strange. Tasted like metal. My tongue lolled, and I panted, drooling, trying to rid myself of the taste. The first hints of the Change unfurled inside, yawning and stretching, grinning as the part of me that exists beyond the wilderness prepared to emerge.

For years, I'd lived hostage to the full moon, hiding underground or removing myself to the wilderness in turns. The twentieth century brought me to the attention of MONIKER. The organization's scientists had, in the midst of their needles and experiments, unlocked the key to the change, allowing me to run free outside the endless cycle of the moon.

After MONIKER, I'd retired to a place in Vermont. And by retire, I mean left one day without telling anyone where I intended to go, found a place with some hefty acreage for cheap, and then spent a few months digging traps and setting tripwires around the place to keep out unwanted visitors. Slowly, I'd let myself forget the MONIKER-enhanced abilities and allowed the change to come naturally, hiding myself away in a silver-enclosed sanctuary.

But the organization has a long reach, and I'd found myself back in its snares, at first an unwilling participant—and then I'd met Karen. Dr. Willet. A badass in combat boots and a mind like a laser knife. Sure, sign me back up!

I loped at a steady pace, aiming my steps away from the pack. These days, I had the change back under my control, thanks to MONIKER and its machinations. But the Change—that's capital "C," and it stands for something I thought existed only in legend—grips me in its claws for one night every month. The devastation when I come out of it is…it's something I don't want to try when I'm around people or wolves I care about.

The wolfpack could always sense it coming. I'd been furry for so long by then I'd started to lose some part of my human side, but Old Grandfather kept me in line, as he did every other wolf in the pack.

The pain started in the center of my body. It began as a tweak, like a nerve pinch in the wrong place. I shook it off, but the irritation returned.

It spread through my body, an itch I couldn't reach to scratch. The wolf I wore tried to rub off the pain, scratching my whole face along the ground, whimpering and whining as I rubbed back and forth, trying to escape the inevitable.

All this time, I kept moving forward, putting as much space between the pack and me as I could muster. My steps began to falter. I couldn't quite get the muscles to do what they're supposed to. My hind legs went first, collapsing to the snow. Throwing back my head, I howled, a long, low cry.

The next spasm grabbed me in its fist. Crunch. Snap. The bones broke, flexed, elongated. My vision blacked out, then flashed red. Then black. Limbs stretched. The ends of my legs cracked and curled, forming the half-hand, half-claw horror prostheses the Change gifts me with.

My heart rate soared. I whimpered. The heat I push out with the Change melted the snow beneath me through to the tundra below.

This is the *Überwechsel*, the Change I can't escape. Yes, I think of it with a capital "C". I'm German, and we love our proper nouns. The regular *wechseln*—the change I can call to me without much thinking these days—is the form my mother gifted to me. But the Change is different. With it, I'm more powerful, faster, and more vicious. And no matter my control, when the full moon rises, I can't dodge it or force it down and away. No matter how I try.

The pain built and built until I couldn't stand it anymore, and then intensified some more. My body spasmed, shuddering, building to one final convulsion. I leapt to my feet. Raised my arms to the sky. Stretched. Screamed. It came out as a half howl, half something else.

Then—silence. Blinking back the film that the Change leaves across my vision, the landscape cleared before me. Throughout my sight, a subtle change, almost unnoticeable, revealed a final gift of the Change. For one night a month, the dark grays and blues against the white snow of the North Country glow in all their chromatic brilliance.

Above my head, the aurora borealis undulated in all its jade and emerald glory. The pain vanished, leaving in its place a renewed energy, the knitting back of my psyche, the excitement and vigor and joy, the memory of what it means to truly be more than human, more than wolf.

I leapt, hanging for a split second in the air where it felt like I could almost touch the northern lights, and then I fell back on the snow, running just for the love of motion over the ground. Under my path, small creatures darted away. I snapped after them, but my heart wasn't in it. I wasn't hungry for prey. I thirsted instead for the cold air and the night and the full moon to guide me on my path.

Just for fun, I reared up, arms back, claws extended in classic werewolf horror movie pose. Laughing. No one was here to get the joke. I howled again, just between me and the moon, who pulls this Change from me. In answer, I expected only silence or perhaps the harsh whisper of wind over snow.

Instead, the steel and diesel chop of a helicopter answered my call.

I froze. A second bird quickly joined the first. They were painted white, with a black and green corporate logo on the side. Not MONIKER. It read: "Черная Гора."

I perked my ears, extending my senses as far as they would reach, stymied by the roar of the engine and blades.

The night air froze the tips of my ears, but the helicopter doors were locked open. As they passed overhead, I caught glimpses of men bundled tight in thick arctic parkas. They sat along the edge of the open door, casually cradling rifles with long sights in their laps.

The helicopters slowed, sweeping over where I crouched, mottled gray against the snow. They made a lazy circuit, then peeled off, heading further north.

What the hell?

The realization hit me. I leapt back in the air, and this time when I hit the ground, I ran for all I was worth. Legs churning, powerful limbs grabbing the ground, I had no time for joy or revel. Only the absolute certainty I would be too late.

---

The screams of pups and the smell of blood hit me before I reached the wolfpack. The path I had just walked with Grandfather nipping at my heels seemed to stretch out, taking me forever to retrace my steps. Overhead, the helicopters circled, the rifles barking spouts of flame from their barrels.

The men inside laughed and joked as they painted the ground with blood and fur. I scrambled to close the distance to the pack. My powerful back legs launched me up and over the final tuft, and I landed, limbs splayed, in the middle of carnage.

The wash of the rotors beat against me. The noise deafened my ears but did nothing to my sight or the fact that at this range, I could smell each hunter, and what they'd had to eat for breakfast.

Red painted itself against my vision. The color glowed, drowning out all others, until my sight misted crimson.

I howled and leapt at the machines hovering side by side, high enough to escape my grasp but low enough to ensure none of the men could miss a shot. I wanted to weep, but the Change twisted it into rage.

The corpses of the pack lay strewn about. A mother had tried to shield her pups with her body, but the high-caliber rounds had gone through them all. A few of the males had run, snapping, but they had been ripped apart like an afterthought. One, barely out of his juvenile growth, pawed weakly as if still trying to run at the untouchable enemy.

I threw my head back and howled in rage. Where was Grandfather?

The helicopters still hovered. None of the men had taken a shot. I didn't know why, didn't care, as I frantically searched the ground. I found nothing except more dead and dying friends. Finally, toward the edge of the clearing, I smelled the unique scent that signaled Grandfather.

He lay on his back, a short skid in the snow indicating he'd been hit so hard the force had thrown his body along the ground. In front of him, the bodies of several wolves and a few juveniles littered the clearing. He'd been trying to chivvy them along. Perhaps he'd heard the danger approaching and tried to get the pack to run. He'd been too late.

Perhaps he'd been late because he'd been trying to get me away.

I dropped to my knees beside him. For once, I took no joy in the chromatic sight the *Überwechsel* gifted me. The red streaking the ground around Grandfather burned itself into my memory. His body was warm to the touch, but already death set its stiff fingers in his side.

A snarl welled up within me.

The crack of a rifle echoed even as the rounds stitched their way across my side. I guess the men in the helicopter gave up trying to figure out what I could be and decided to proceed with the next step of the plan, trying to kill this thing that snarled like a wolf but walked on two legs.

The snarl turned to laughter. I couldn't save my pack. But I sure as hell could make sure their blood wasn't the only life spilled on the snow.

Another set of rounds hit my side, burrowing through skin and fur. They wouldn't leave so much as a mark in the morning, but for now, they hurt like hell.

For most of my existence, I've been the leap-before-you-look type of tactician. This has mostly worked out for me. Crouching, I got as much coiled spring in my stance as I could. I leapt straight into the air, faster and further than I expected. Certainly faster than the men in the helicopter thought possible.

Reaching out with my teeth, I pulled the first man clear from the helicopter. He screamed as he fell, but I was already slashing my way into the bird. My claws met flesh and metal and rent them both the same. The blood splashed across my face and tongue. It tasted sweet as copper.

The men tried to bring their weapons to bear, but they were long-barrel rifles, more suited to shooting helpless prey from a distance. I lunged in close, slashing and panting and biting. The pilot banked and swung, trying to throw me off balance. He succeeded in shaking loose another of the men, who fell to the snow below. I tossed pieces of his comrades after him.

The pilot tried one more gambit, pushing the craft until the hydraulics whined. I ripped his throat out and left him gurgling and choking to death on his own blood as I jumped free of the crashing bird.

The second pilot should have taken off as fast as he could, but instead, he came in hot, canting the bird, aiming for me with the whirring blades, Hollywood stuntman style. I darted to the side, faster than he could track.

As the helicopter passed me, I launched myself after it. Grasping for purchase, I climbed through bodies, hacking and slashing. Again, I threw the men out of the bird piece by piece.

This pilot came well-armed. From his side, he pulled a pistol and began firing back into the cavity of the helicopter. His rounds landed in his own aircraft, in various soft tissues of the men in the back, and a few in my shoulder and thigh.

I swung my claws, leaving the end of his arm a bloody, mangled ruin. He screamed and cried. The bird swung wildly. It canted on its side. Using a strut for purchase, I leapt straight in the air, my momentum taking me out the open door, now facing up. The helicopter continued forward as my leap took me up, out, and back down to the ground.

Where the bird hit the snow, the metal crumpled and sparked. The spark hit a fuel line, and the entire aircraft vanished in a ball of fire. The explosion emanated a thick, oily smoke over the ruins of the former hunting party.

The once-refuge of the wolfpack had become a charnel ground. Human and wolf blood mixed in rivulets, melting the snow and salting the ground. Predators would come calling. Some of the men's hearts still beat. After a moment's deliberation, I tore their throats out.

They were probably dead soon anyway, but I'd left the enemy to my back before, and I wouldn't be making *that* tactical error again.

The first aircraft had crashed and crumpled but not burned. The pilot slumped over the controls, still bleeding, although life had left his sightless eyes. I dug around the cockpit and his pockets for any kind of papers or identification, a task made more complicated by both the Change distorting my hands and the fact I streaked gore over everything I touched.

In the log book, I finally found something. Enclosed in a plastic sheet protector, a single piece of paper displayed the specifications of this particular helicopter model, as well as the registration number, pilot, and license numbers. The black and green logo told the name of the holding company that apparently owned the craft.

Black Mountain Holdings and Subsidiaries.

I flipped it over. The same information, only this time in the Cyrillic alphabet. Interesting. Or maybe not. A Russian-owned outfit ferrying weekend warriors to sport hunt defenseless wolves wasn't the weirdest thing I'd ever encountered.

Another howl started in my gut, working its way to my throat and erupting in a primal scream of rage and sadness. Yet another refuge, yet more friends, ripped away from me by men bearing rifles.

Caught in a wave of anger and blind fury, I savaged the fallen men with teeth and claws until they were no longer recognizable as human beings. My vision became one long, solid panorama of blood.

Pausing, I searched the sky. The full moon cast her light without mercy or judgment over the tableaux below her. She had not even reached her midnight position overhead.

Gathering my feet below me, I stood over the bloody ground. The sweet taste of liquid copper in my mouth had gone slightly sour. There would be time later for revenge and hatred and whatever decisions I would make. Perhaps it was time for me to go back to my human half.

But for now, the Change called. It sped the wind under me as I took off into the darkness.

I ran and ran, and this time those small creatures erupting under my path did not make it far. I snatched and crunched and chewed, flinging bones and small bodies as debris littered my route.

I would run and run and run under the moon until the Change spent itself. And then, it would be time to leave the North.

3

As always, the *Überwechsel* left me about ten pounds lighter and one hundred percent meaner. I usually spent a few solitary days afterward hunting, waiting until I made a kill and eating most of it before returning to the pack.

Now, I didn't have much choice. The Change left me strung out and twitching like a junkie, but I had to return to civilization, or whatever approximated it this far north.

I'd left a cache for myself when I decided to spend some quality time with me, myself, and my furry id. Packed in a weatherproof container, hoisted up in a tree, I found the stash intact. Thankfully. Pair of pants, flannel shirt, and jacket. Hat. Gloves. Wool socks and waterproof hiking boots. Key. I travel light.

Wish I had thought to pack a protein bar or something. I was half-tempted to go back furry and find another pack. My stomach growled, and bile rose at the idea of having to be human. Or at least pretend to be. I wasn't sure which side I wanted to be on these days.

The hike to the nearest town took the better part of a day and a half. I broke down halfway through, slipped through the change, and handled the hunger with a few small kills. I used the snow to wash myself off, got dressed again, and headed back to the trail.

I didn't want to go back. But every time I slowed down and thought about turning around and living out the rest of my life with a tail, the image arose in my mind of a black-and-green logo and the men who laughed as they killed from above.

The joy of the Change had turned to hatred, and it stopped me from retracing my steps.

The signs of the city appeared as grumblings of traffic and light furrows of small Cessna-type planes as they circled and landed at the narrow airstrip on the edge of town. It wasn't a huge place, with a population not much over nine hundred, but it had built itself up as a hub for transportation in the area.

As I trudged down the road, I checked out the aircraft dotting the fields along the strip. Most were the lightweight, fixed-wing craft I expected. But now, there were several of the Black Mountain craft. I wondered how good the airport security might be. Might be worth checking out. At the least, I could cause some damage and be gone before they realized it.

A passing vehicle almost hit me from behind, swerving at the last minute. A large, bearded man cussed me out as he wrestled with his vehicle.

"Fuck you, too, lumberjack." I indicated my feelings with a one-finger wave, then realized I'd been the asshole. Lost in observation, I'd wandered and was now walking in the middle of the road. Fucking civilization.

Down the road, a place in town rented storage lockers on both a short- and long-term basis. I dug in my pockets for the key from my cache and used it to retrieve a few more belongings—my St. Jude's medal, a backpack, change of clothes, razors, a certain notebook I probably should have burned when I found it, a paperback book I was in the middle of reading—and a good deal of cash I hadn't wanted to leave out in the cold. I turned the key in to the attendant and spent a few minutes canceling my account. I wasn't coming back.

The next order of business—food. Metric fucktons of food. My mouth started to water at the thought of meat that someone had cooked and seasoned before I shoved it in my mouth, and I could swear I heard a cup of coffee call me by name.

"Hey, asshole, over here."

*Aw, crap.* That was not actually a cup of coffee. Rather, the voice speaking to me in such a loving tone belonged to a big, burly, red-flannel clad jackass by the name of Randall Tso.

"Yeah, jerkoff. I'm talking to you." He strode across the street, ignoring the honking horns around him. A giant pickup truck almost clipped him as he hopped up on the sidewalk, but it didn't faze him. "You got that twenty you owe me?"

Tso loomed over me. He only stood at five-ten, but he was wide. And I'm short.

"Ask your sister for it, fucker," I told him. My voice came out raw. Rough. Hadn't used it much in over half a year.

His mouth split open in a huge grin, and he laughed, pounding me on the back. "Don't worry, I already got it from your mom." His final pat on the back caused me to stumble forward with its enthusiasm. "She said I was the best she ever had. Gave me a tip."

I forced a smile in return. My mom...let's just say, more violent men than Randall had met her and not lived to tell the story. Just the thought of her had me breaking out in a cold sweat.

He finally finished laughing at his joke and settled. "Seriously, man, where you been?" Stamping his feet, he tucked his hands under his armpits. For all his girth, Randall was originally from New Mexico, and he still felt the cold easily if he wasn't moving around. "One moment, we were heading out on a job; the next you fell off the face of the earth."

I shrugged. He wouldn't believe me if I told him to his face.

"Ah, whatever, man." He put his arm around my shoulders and started walking. So I started walking, too. "What's twenty bucks between friends, especially one who leaves without telling the other one where he's going. Let's get lunch. Your treat."

We settled into a booth at the end of the long diner. I found an electrical outlet under the table. My old battered cell phone had been part of the package I picked up from the storage unit, and I plugged it in to charge before the waitress even brought our first cup of coffee.

"What are you, a teenage girl?" Randall nodded at the phone. His straight black hair was longer than I remembered, pulled back into a ponytail. "Gotta check your Instagram? Maybe send a Tweeter?"

"I'm sending a dick pic to your mom," I told him. "She must be lonely with me gone this whole time."

He rewarded me with a guffaw and called the waitress "babe" when she waddled up. Her name tag read "Lara H." She poured us mugs of thick, steaming coffee, and when she walked away, he slapped her ass.

Guess he noticed my raised eyebrow. The woman had to be at least four months pregnant. Barely showing, but I could sense the extra heartbeat and see it in her wary gait, a sort of hunching self-protectiveness.

"You and her?"

In the space of a heartbeat, Randall Tso went from gruff poster boy for lumberjack masculinity to a puddle of puppy love. "Yeah." He grinned, displaying the results of a new dental hygiene habit. "We started dating after you left. Getting church-married in the spring. Gonna do it up real nice with her family and everything."

"Mazel tov." I raised my coffee cup and surreptitiously checked the battery on my phone. A little green charging light blinked on and off. Hooray.

"You should see the place I'm building," Tso started. He began telling me about it—a little cabin right outside of town, she could walk to work, sister would watch the kid, blah blah blah. If Randall were the same guy I'd known before I wolfed it out of there, he could hold up his end of the conversation for a few hours, requiring nothing out of me except the occasional grunt and nod. He was my favorite conversational partner. I hate conversation.

The phone chimed, the battery finally full enough to stay powered up. I expected maybe one or two calls. Maybe Randall trying to figure out where I'd gone to.

Instead, my entire voicemail was full, and a series of texts filled up the tiny, ancient device's memory. Should have canceled my data plan.

Tso kept talking even as Lara came back around again. I simply pointed to the menu. Biggest combo I could find. He paused to kiss her cheek and kept going. The coffee tasted strong and rancid. Either it had to be leftovers from yesterday, or I'd forgotten what coffee tasted like. Still, it helped keep me focused.

Who the fuck had been calling me and blowing up my phone? I briefly considered deleting my voicemail box at one go and possibly breaking the phone and burying it in concrete somewhere.

"Yeah, and then after you left, we got this new dude who took your shift," Tso was saying. "Really off kind of dude. Like he wasn't all there, you know?" He shook his head. "He didn't last long." He paused as the waitress came and set down our food. "Darlin', you remember that dude's name? The weird one—worked with the crew for a bit."

She thought for a moment, and when she spoke, her voice was flavored with just a hint of Eastern Europe. "John something. Mell or Fell."

I flinched, and the coffee splashed across my hand. The lukewarm liquid didn't scald me, but I paid it no attention in any case.

"Yeah, he was a skinny blond dude," Tso said. "Didn't think he was going to last. And he didn't."

"You boys enjoy," Lara said. She twisted away from Randall's embrace. "I got other customers waiting." She gave him a kiss before she went off to pour coffee.

Randall didn't notice my reaction, he just went back to his soliloquy about his woodland retreat.

"This John guy, he stick around town?" I asked, interrupting him mid-syllable.

He took the interruption in stride, not missing a beat. "Yeah, man. Pretty sure I saw the dude the other day. Got a job working for that outfit that moved in. Chern-ey something. Russian outfit. Name means 'Black Mountain.' They're doing some kind of surveying or whatever. Taking rich dudes out on hunting parties, that sort of thing." He shrugged. "They tried to hire a bunch of guys off the crew, but man, nobody wants to work for a bunch of rich fuckers coming up here to trophy hunt, now they lifted all the regs. Fuck those guys."

I grunted in agreement, which he took as his signal to return to his original topic.

The food was good, and Lara brought out a lot of it. By now, the insides of my stomach were twisting from hunger. The hearty biscuits and gravy tasted like heaven, and the bacon…well, let's just say, if I hadn't been eating in public, I would have shown a lot less self-control.

The only sour taste leaving an acid burn in my insides was learning that a skinny blond man by the name of John Last-Name-Rhymes-With-Tell had followed me up north. Last I'd seen or heard of a man fitting his description… Well. I'd keep an eye out. I thought our mutual enemies had killed him. It wouldn't take much to correct that oversight.

Scrolling through the phone, eating my way through the mountain of food, with one ear tuned to any break in the conversation requiring me to grunt, I checked out my calls. The vast majority of messages were from one number. There were a few from spam numbers, the ones that fake you out with faux toll-free numbers, but the last one caused me to almost vomit everything back up.

Dmitri. Holy shit. I must have gone pale because Randall stopped his word spew.

"What's up, man?" he asked. "Look like you just farted, and it came out solid."

He came closer to the truth than he realized.

"I…need a ride to the airport." I shoveled more food in my mouth and spoke through the hash browns and sausages. "Like A.S.A.P." Choking, I coughed, dislodged a piece of whatever, and kept shoveling. "Or after we eat."

"Yeah, sure, man," he said. "You sure are a strange one." He shook his head.

Randall Tso was not a complicated man, but he was a good friend, and I don't have too many of those. I wasn't about to clue him into my past. I hoped by not telling him about it, it wouldn't touch him.

Vain hopes.

The airport wasn't actually so far away I needed a ride. I'd literally walked by it on my hike into town. But I wanted to get there with no interruptions and no chance meetings with anyone else I hadn't prepared myself to meet. If MONIKER had sent John up here looking for me, it would be in everyone's best interests if I slipped quietly out of town before they knew I'd come back.

Once out of the wilderness, gunning for Black Mountain, I'd wanted nothing more than to come and lay waste, but spotting Randall and then meeting his pregnant girlfriend had put an end to my original trajectory. Rage—red-hot and vision-blurring rage—still filled me when I thought of what those men had done to my pack. But I wasn't willing to risk the lives of friends and family just for a bit of revenge.

Besides. MONIKER and this Russian outfit, hanging out in the same town together—coincidence? I think not.

Yeah. Slip quietly out of town. Let's see how this works out.

I borrowed a ball cap from Randall with a vague promise of returning it if I ever made it back up north. He broke off his one-sided conversation long enough to ask when I planned on coming back. I shrugged. Really no idea. He accepted it. Before meeting Lara, back when we were both working together, we were the same—moving from place to place, working and drinking until we got bored, then moving on.

I liked Randall. He'd spent some time in the Army, which had decided in its wisdom to take a Navajo farmer from the southwest and assign his ass all the way up in Alaska. After four years driving trucks, he'd gotten out of the military but stayed in the north. One of those guys who took life as it came, he could see that something was eating at me and, for all his rambling, didn't ask a bunch of dumb questions or try to convince me to stay.

By this point, my face hadn't seen a razor in well over a year, I wore a sweaty ball cap, and none of my identification had anything like my real name on it. Still, I couldn't hide the fact I'm a short, blond, German-looking dude traveling by myself. MONIKER likely had people stationed behind the counter of every mode of transportation out of town. Whatever. They could follow me. I'd lose them back in civilization—or else, they would disappear.

I travel light at the best of times, and this was no different. The man behind the counter didn't give it a second thought. Most of the flights out of the tiny airstrip were commuter runs down to Sea-Tac, and people traveled there for all sorts of reasons. I still had a good deal of cash from the pile in the storage locker, which I used to pay for my flight. Once I got there, I'd figure out my next move.

The next flight left in an hour. There wasn't any kind of a security line to go through. The airport was so tiny they would shuffle us through a quick check during the boarding process. I sat on one of the hard, plastic chairs, pulled down the brim of the cap, and flipped open my phone.

The line of voicemails and texts waited for me. Grimacing, I decided to go for broke and find out what Dmitri had to say. Scrolling down with the tiny arrow keys—yes, kids, that's what you had to do with these old-fashioned devices, now get off my lawn—I pulled up the notification with his name.

Well, shit. It wasn't a voicemail. Just a missed call. From about three days ago. Crap. Making a mental note to call him back, I then made another mental note to avoid doing so for as long as possible and to not answer the phone if he called again.

I am an ancient creature of blood and magic, but Dmitri is an old Soviet spook who scares the fuck out of me.

One number still appeared—one that wasn't programmed into my machine. The same number filled my voicemail and text messages. I scrolled to the first message they'd left, selected it, and put the phone to my ear to listen.

The voice on the other end clenched me up inside. I pulled the ball cap lower over my face and hid my reaction with my hand. I couldn't help the wave of heat and emotion her voice spurred in me even after all this time.

"Rick. Call me back. I know you still have my number." Click.

Scrolled up to the next one. Hit play.

"Rick. I need you to call me back. This is Karen." Pause. "I know you know who this is. Call me back." Click.

Okay. Weird. Figuring the rest of the messages went more or less along the same lines, I tap-scrolled back up to the very last message she had left.

"Rick, you fucking prick." Uncharacteristic, but not out of the realm of possible Karen reactions. "I don't know where the fuck you are. I don't care if you're out on some communing with nature in Canada bullshit." Well, that answered the question about whether MONIKER still tracked my whereabouts. "You better get your ass to Vegas by Monday, or I swear to God I will hunt you down and make you into a rug." Click.

Damn. Even the click at the end sounded extra unhinged.

Under the verbal abuse—not her normal M.O., but not necessarily out of the ordinary where I'm concerned—I could hear strain and nerves. Something had her rattled.

Even more than her words, the tone hidden in her voice signaled something had gone wrong, and if I counted her a friend, I would be there yesterday. I checked the date and time of the message. It had been left a few days ago. What the hell day was it today?

Karen's number was programmed into the first position on my speed dial. (Look it up on Wikipedia, smartphone generation.) I pressed the key and waited for the ringing to begin. The phone picked up on the other end, and my mouth went dry. What the hell should I say?

It wasn't her, though, but her voicemail.

"Karen, it's Rick. I'm on my way."

Guess I was going to Vegas.

4

Over a century on this planet and more than fifty years working for a secret strategic organization, and not once had my travels ever taken me to Sin City. Hollywood owed me one, with all their visions of secret agents tearing around the strip in fancy cars.

I landed in Vegas at high noon, seated on the wrong side of the plane for anything like a good view as we came in for a landing. Once I'd called Karen from a known cell phone, I'd broadcast my whereabouts to all the world. She'd fixed my flight status, bought me the ticket, and texted that she would meet me at the arrivals gate when I hopped off the plane.

The only luggage I had was a gym bag I'd borrowed from Randall. With that slung over my shoulder, I made my way through the strangely dingy airport. The route toward the exit wound around several open areas of electronic slot machines that pumped a cacophony of noise into the air.

Most travelers at this time of day looked like they were just passing through—with the exception of two bros who saw the lights, screamed, "Vegas, baby!" and chest bumped. They smelled like they were already having a good time. I shook my head. Hollywood had made it seem like I had been missing something. Maybe it was just bad timing on my part.

I sensed her halfway down the corridor—her rosemary-and-rain scent mingling with another indefinable marker.

She waited for me at the end of the security gate, holding up a sign that said: "Keller." Guess we weren't operating with fancy code names or shit.

I looked and felt like crap, but Karen—I barely recognized her. She had lost weight, and not in the way you're thinking—this was the kind of weight you lose when you're under too much stress and not getting enough nutrition—the kind of weight loss I had to make up for every month after the Change.

The woman standing next to her drew my notice before I even laid eyes on her. She smelled of chocolate and cinnamon, with a subtle, bitter aftertaste that rolled around like copper on my tongue. She stood behind Karen, slightly to her right, and she towered over me— about the same height as my friend. Tension ran through every sinew of her body, although she projected a calm, relaxed demeanor outwardly. If an active shooter situation broke out, she would be the one to respond immediately and put it down—or be the one perpetrating it.

"Rick."

"Karen." I nodded. "Like the sign."

She ignored me, turning to her friend. "Calix, this is Rick."

Calix barely acknowledged the introduction, just squinted at me with her dark eyes. I returned the gaze. Like I said, she was tall, with black hair slicked back into a braid, and she darted her glance around even as she gave me the once-over, hyperaware, as if she were looking for a threat. Finally, she nodded.

Karen continued. "He's an asshole but a friend."

That's me in a nutshell. I went to make some wisecrack, but the tension I'd heard in her voice on my phone hummed off her in person. She vibrated, like a knife when it landed in its target. I did not want to be said target. "Sounded pretty bad on the phone. Why don't we walk and talk?"

"Fine by me." Karen shrugged and turned, tossing the sign in a garbage can as we headed out of the airport.

When I followed them out into the sun, blinking against the glare, the heat punched me in the face with the force of a furnace. How was it this hot this early in the year? Hell. Las Vegas was hell. And I had landed smack dab in the middle of it.

Calix fell into step beside Karen, a few inches apart but close enough to confirm a suspicion that had begun to grow as I'd made my way toward them. By the way their scents mingled and danced with each other, I might as well tuck any last remnants of the torch I'd been carrying far away.

Figures. I'd never had a chance with Karen's grandmother when we were at O.S.S. together; it stood to reason history would go ahead and repeat itself.

<hr>

Karen drove well, but she had a lead foot. Calix sat shotgun—fine with me because I preferred the center back seat. They had put up the roof of the Mustang convertible—great for security, but I struggled to breathe, dying in the heat.

"Are you...panting?" Calix turned and glared, even as Karen cornered the vehicle.

"I'm not used to the heat." Understatement of the year. Hell, I missed the snow already, and I'd grown sick of snow.

I waited for her to keep the conversation going, but she wasn't one for small talk, either.

"Up here?" Karen didn't have to elaborate.

"Yep." Calix nodded. They had one of those couple moments where something unspoken passes between two people. Ugh. Please.

Yeah, I hear you asking, but Rick, what's the matter? You're trapped in a car with two good-looking women. Well, first, at least one of those women is completely capable of kicking my ass. Repeatedly. And the second one, I'm willing to bet, is just as proficient.

Second, here's the thing with wolf nature—when someone mingles their scent with another person, it's game off. I could sit and be disappointed about it all day long, but anything Karen and I—mostly I—might have once thought about having was gone. And Karen and Calix had mingled their scents pretty well.

I wasn't sure if Karen had explained me to her friend past the asshole part, which was and is completely true. If not, I looked forward to discovering how this new person reacted to surprises. Heh.

"Hang on, we're almost there." With a squeal of the tires, Karen landed us in a spot I'm pretty sure didn't actually count as a parking space.

The building we parked outside of seemed pretty normal. Only when you walked around to the front did you realize the hotel opened onto Fremont Street. I had never been there, and I hope never to go back. The sights and sounds of hundreds, maybe thousands, of people bowled me over in a riptide of humanity.

From the flashing of various signs and lights to the smoke ripping through my senses and the constant aural barrage, I started to lose some calm. The change perked up, feeling the stress, flexing its claws at a possible opportunity to surface. I clenched my fists until my nails bit deep into my palms.

"We have to hurry." Karen led the way into one of the hotels, threading a path through the crowd with ease. Calix followed her. The people almost instinctively stepped back from the two Amazons, subconsciously giving them their proper respect. Then they stepped forward, and I had to fight my way through to keep up.

I stopped. Something reached my nose. Something that remembered blood and copper but tasted old, like a stack of Buffalo pennies. Then it disappeared, and I realized I'd turned in the wrong direction, so I hurried to catch up.

The women waited for me by the elevator.

"What the hell is going on?" It came out more forceful than I intended, but the claustrophobia had started to close in. Wolves and enclosed spaces and crowds—not a good mixture. And the old people smell. Jesus.

"I'll explain when we get up there." The elevator dinged, and Karen held the door. Two more patrons attempted to follow me on. She held up a hand. "Get the next one." They didn't even argue.

My stomach growled. I needed to eat again. I'd hoped we would stop for food, as the flight attendants had served us exactly one cookie and one cup of coffee. I hadn't wanted to spend cash on the inflight menu out of principle. So now I kept getting distracted because I couldn't stop smelling buffet.

I white-knuckled my way up in the elevator—still didn't love the enclosed death traps—until it stopped at the top floor, and we got out.

"This is the penthouse," I said in my starring role as Captain Obvious. "How did we get up here?"

Karen ignored the question. "Follow me." The floor was deserted, just a hallway with three double-doors past the elevators. "We don't have a lot of time, but the agency was able to pull some strings to get us in here before they sent in the cleaners."

I tried to pretend I understood but got stuck on "agency" and "cleaners." Karen bent over the locking mechanism for the center set of doors and worked some kind of magic. The lock light flashed green and clicked. She pushed it open, just a crack, then laid her hand on Calix's forearm. "You going to be okay?"

Calix nodded. "Let's get this done."

Karen opened the door the whole way and beckoned me in. I had smelled the blood all the way from the elevator.

---

The room beyond stood empty; the dried stains painting the décor had faded to a dry, dingy hue. I stopped at the door and looked back at the two of them.

"This would be easier if I were furry."

Karen and Calix exchanged glances. Karen shrugged. "Go for it."

Okay, then. I started stripping down.

"Whoa, wait, what the hell?" Calix demanded.

"Just wait." Karen put an arm around her waist. "Watch."

Honestly? Watch? I'm not a fucking circus freak. The change, which had been circling, waiting for a moment to rear up, fed my anger.

"Rick. We're going to be working together. This is the best way."

I hesitated.

"And you owe me."

Karen was right. I owed her big time from our trip overseas and how I'd ducked out on her in New York. On the other hand, if she and MONIKER hadn't fucked me over, I wouldn't have been in a situation to need her to get me out of it in the first place. So, there was that…

In the end, I simply shucked my clothes, tossed them to the side, and allowed the change to roll back in on me. By the time I'd achieved total furry, I no longer cared what Karen and her girlfriend thought or did. Instead, my nose led me to the room of death and violence, now uncanny in its shroud of silence.

I closed my eyes, letting the change subside now that I had acquiesced to it. It left me in a state of heightened awareness, more than just the signals my senses could sniff out, but with a seventh sense which performed some kind of calculus, making all the sensory feedback more than the sum of their parts.

Here in the hallway is where the trouble began. Three men entered. Their boots left scuff marks on the perfect parquet floor. Their weapons had been newly oiled, fully loaded. One of them chewed a piece of salt licorice.

They faced off across the room. Another man, this one older, who indulged in expensive cologne. An old man sat in a comfortable chair, flanked by two women much his juniors in age.

Ranged around the room—more flunkies, all of them armed. More women, all of them not.

Pausing in my information intake, I opened my eyes, trotting around the room. There were other scents there. Latex and plastic, metal and starch. The dark plastic of zippered bags. The responders had carefully criss-crossed the aftermath, teasing out their own version of what had happened. I concentrated, and those tracks faded. No sense in getting distracted.

By the front of the door, I could sense rather than see Karen and Calix getting restless. They shifted stances, moving their balance from foot to foot without losing their alertness. I wasn't sure who they expected to try something, but it was time to figure out the rest of this puzzle.

Ah. Found it. Over in the corner. Almost an afterthought. Certainly, those who responded to the scene wouldn't have spent much time over it.

You've seen this scene before, in Hollywood or Grade B straight-to-video flicks. The gangster and his archrival face off. They each bring plenty of guns to the showdown. They trade barbs and insults, escalating the situation until one person pulls his weapon.

Then, the bullets start to fly. The main gangster might get hit right away and go down, or maybe he just gets winged as his henchmen return fire.

The intruding gangsters spray the room with automatic fire. They don't bother to take cover, relying instead on their rapid-fire shooting. A few members of the home team take aim and let them have it. They duck and cover, shooting back and forth, deafening everyone in the room and painting the walls with blood.

And then, of course, there are the obligatory shots of half-naked—or all-naked, depending on whether this is network TV or Cinemax—women. They've only been invited to this party as arm candy, serving up nose candy or whatever. And when the bullets start to fly, they are the least prepared of any in the room. They run, but the flying rounds cut them down. The camera captures the moment but then rapidly pans back to the men, to the main action.

In this show, the main gangster—remember him? He only got winged in this scenario, and so he crawls under cover of fire toward a back corner of the room.

He finds a young woman, a beautiful young waitress who smells of cinnamon and chocolate, cowering behind a bookcase. The gangster doesn't know who she is—just someone there to serve drinks. He pulls her in front of him, shoving her from her hiding place, pushing her toward the rounds.

It doesn't matter. The intruders shoot them both, and the rounds pierce right through their bodies and deep into the wall behind them.

Yeah, I've seen this movie, too. In it, someone will find the evil gangsters and make them pay, but there's no question about who the main characters are. Those men with the guns who take the lives of everyone in the room—even those who were, by any standards, innocent.

Karen's hand on my back brought me back to myself. I caught myself standing, four legs splayed, growling at the spot behind the bookcase. I let her calm me, stroking my back. Her touch lay on me like a livewire, but its intensity soothed me.

Reaching out for the change, I slipped back into human form, stepping into my pants, which Karen held out to me.

Calix had come up behind us. She, too, stared at the spot behind the bookcase.

"Your sister?" It was a guess, but the scent tasted familiar.

"Yes." She gave no sign she had witnessed a werewolf getting naked and doing his thing. Made of stern stuff. "She and I were very different. She loved Vegas."

"Younger sister?"

"No. Twin." Calix's hand drifted to her side. It gave the impression she was used to being armed. She and Karen were a well-matched pair. Both were tall, Amazonian. Carried themselves with a military posture indicating they knew their way around the business ends of a wide variety of weaponry. While Karen was a green-eyed brunette, Calix reminded me of the Asian women I'd met in the former Soviet republics, although her skin had a darker hue.

With the flight and energy drain of changing twice, I was about to implode from hunger. "Karen, I'm not sure what you want me to do with the nightmare I just sniffed out, but I need to eat."

"Of course you do." She tossed me a shirt. "Get dressed. You got the scene in your nose?"

Now I was offended. I had this scene stuck permanently in all my senses. It would linger there for a long time. Still, my head and arms were fumbling around with my shirt, so she couldn't see my offended face. I mumbled an assent.

"Good. We'll eat, and then you help with what we brought you here for."

---

Karen, always good for her word, took me to a place far from both Downtown Las Vegas and the strip before I went crazy and sank my teeth into the next asshole who walked by smoking weed. That shit burns my nose and blinds me to everything. She and Calix pulled up at an old-fashioned diner, where they served large burgers for cheap. I ordered two and then ordered two more. The grease in the joint lay thick on everything, and I suspected my digestive system was going to have no plumbing issues in the next day or so.

Finally, I swallowed, pushed the plate away, and belched. Rude, yes. Satisfying? Also, yes.

"So, how long have you two been together?"

Calix started, but Karen only rolled her eyes.

"Long enough to nunya." She ate a fry.

"Nunya?"

"None ya business."

I used both middle fingers to show her what I thought of her joke. She rewarded me with a ghost of a grin. What the hell was going on? "You still with MONIKER?"

"Yes. And no." She shrugged. "It's complicated."

"Jesus Christ." I debated telling her what I'd heard from Randall—about the possible sighting of John Tell and the subsequent possible connection between him and the Black Mountain murderers. But no, there were other issues at stake here.

Speaking of steak, I really wanted another burger.

"My sister, Arista, was working at the hotel," Calix began. Guess she'd gotten tired of waiting for me to eat. What the hell was with their names, anyway? Parents play too many video games? "She was a waitress. Trying to be a showgirl. That was her— She— It was..." She paused, and Karen squeezed her hand. She pulled it away. "Last night, one of the whales was ambushed and killed in the penthouse. Arista was there."

Calix shook, her fury boiling up inside her. I could feel it emanating in waves from her. And yet, it was barely perceptible to the human eye. I'm not, however, human. Mostly.

"My sister did not carry a gun," Calix said. "She was not a slut. She was just trying to make a living, and nobody gives a shit that she's dead."

There was something else going on here. Something Calix wasn't saying. Maybe something even Karen didn't know. I couldn't get at it, so I let it go.

"The local LEOs have been giving us the runaround," Karen added. "Mostly, they're looking into the whale, trying to figure out who wanted him dead, focusing everything they have on his business and partners. Meanwhile, they don't give a shit about the girls who were there."

I grunted. "They know who did it?"

"You know how it is," Karen said. "They know. But they can't say. And frankly, the perps wore masks and used generic weaponry. They were smart. Knew how to cover their tracks." I could almost hear the teeth grinding in her jaws. "So, no, the cops can't tell us who did it, and even if they did, they can't make a single move on them."

Grinning, I let a little of the change into my eyes. Tracking and hunting those who had betrayed and murdered innocents was my favorite task. Karen knew me well, and knew I would be more than willing to deliver as soon as I found out what she needed. And if I did, perhaps we could work a little *quid pro quo*. Maybe she could help me tease out the links between MONIKER, Black Mountain, and Tell.

"Maybe they can't." And now the change chomped at the bit, begging to be let loose. "But we can."

5

Karen had a good idea of where to start looking, thanks to a few well-placed contacts with the Vegas P.D. Still, they were less than specific and less than willing to spend any more time than necessary, especially when they realized that—in this case anyway—she was working on behalf of the sister of one of the ancillary victims. Any assistance provided would be off the books and unlikely to be of much use.

After the diner, we stopped at a gas station. Karen filled up the car, and I filled up on bags of beef jerky and pork rinds. Usually, when I return to my non-furry form, I go through a period of hunger and the shakes. It wears off in a couple of hours. But now, I couldn't seem to get clear of it. Maybe it was the six solid months I had spent furry. Maybe it was the new gift of the *Überwechsel*. Maybe it was just that human food is so delicious.

Holy crap. I *am* part dog.

After we finished fueling up, Karen took me on a rolling tour of Las Vegas. This wasn't one of those fun ones where we cruised the strip and ate cannoli at Caesar's Palace. Instead, we headed out into the bright sunlight, out past the strip to where it became clear that Las Vegas is a city built on the back of a desert.

*Now* they decided to put the top down, and the sun and heat punched me in the face as the air beat around us. At least out here, the scents became cleaner. The sand and scrub and stone tasted dusty in my mouth, but still a marked improvement from the teeming mass of humans and their bodily functions and heightened emotions that overcrowded the tourist areas.

I pulled on Randall's ball cap and tugged it down over my eyes. Should have bought some cheap sunglasses.

Karen turned down a wide, four-lane residential road. On one side, a curly-haired woman jogged, headphones in, oblivious to the world. Somewhere, a dog barked, brave behind a wood-slat fence.

Calix drummed her fingers against the car door. "So what, we just roll around here until your old partner turns into a dog again?"

"Just wait." Karen put her turn signal on, came to a complete stop at a four-way, and then looked both ways before turning left.

My old partner obviously hadn't really told Calix anything about me. Fine by me. Also, it's a wolf. Bigger than a dog.

She circled the neighborhood a few times. It consisted of a couple of gated communities, pine and palm trees peeking over tall stone walls. Who plants pine trees in a desert? The pollen crawled up my nose. I sneezed. We weren't going to find anything around here except suburbia and soccer moms.

I caught Karen's eye in the rearview mirror and shook my head. We were wasting our time.

We hit a few more of these neighborhoods. Each time, Karen would catch my eye, questioning me silently. Each time, I would shake my head. Nothing. I mean, Las Vegas had its fair share of whatever goes on behind closed doors in suburban sprawl. And believe me, some freaky things were definitely sprawling here. But none of it smelled like anything I had caught a glimpse of in the execution chamber at the top of the hotel.

We stopped around five o'clock. The sun had begun to dip under the mountains in the distance, throwing streaks of darkness over the valley. I briefly thought of the times I'd witnessed the northern lights under the spell of the Change, when the larger, deeper transformation had widened the spectrum of my eyesight for a night. Maybe I'd get a chance to catch a sunset at some point when I could see all the colors.

At the thought, the other, smaller change stirred, rearing its head, stretching. We were still close enough to the full moon for it to call to the other part of me. I hoped with the coming of the night, the heat would give us a break. Pretty sure I'd gotten sunburned.

By this time, I had no idea where we were, except far away from where we started, and I wanted to eat again. The breeze had picked up, bringing with it a cool moisture heightening the smells it carried.

I hadn't realized the change lingered so close to the surface. It had me in its grips, and I had turned halfway from human before I could even think to stop myself. Something in the breeze burned like sulfur, and I recognized the licorice and gun oil signature. Faint. Unmistakable.

My clothes briefly tangled me up as the change crashed over me, sweeping me in a crunching pain that rearranged my spirit and anatomy in half the time it normally took. Karen barely had time to slam on the brakes before I launched myself in my full gray wolf glory out of the car. A few horns honked.

Darting through traffic, I came close to getting clipped once or twice. No matter. I would heal in less time than it took me to regain my footing.

Finally, I darted clear of the road, cutting through a fence and across well-manicured, drought-proof yards. Out here, the expanses were more vast. The gates enclosed not communities but massive stucco mansions.

The scent of oil and licorice grew stronger. Now, it warred with other strains in the wind. Blood. Concrete. Birthday cake. Somewhere near, a couple was having sex. I could hear one of them crying.

All these scents and more passed over me, through me. I tasted them on my tongue, and felt the long fingers of their ghosts pass through my fur. I'd landed in stone and mulch, the rocks still hot enough to warm my paws as I loped along, even as the evening cooled quickly.

Somewhere behind me, I heard the distinctive rumble of the

Mustang. Karen tracked me. I spared a thought for her, then forgot about them. Maybe they would show up on time. I hoped not. She always got judgmental when I wreaked havoc, even when it was her idea.

Then, I found it. The colossal mansion loomed over the lawn; the lush, full grass smelled sweet and wet. Clearly, whoever lived here dwelled in denial that they were located smack dab in a desert. I leapt soundlessly over the fence bordering the property and belly-crawled under a short row of shrubs. They had been cut low to deny any intruders a hiding place. But I liked too-small places and the shadows that came with them.

The movement over the fence triggered a motion sensor light. I froze until the timer went off and plunged the area into darkness. Couldn't tell if anyone had noticed. Probably wrote it off as a squirrel or other wildlife. Sometimes, our own security measures inculcate self-defeating patterns of habit. Yes, I know words of more than one syllable.

Five, ten, twenty minutes dragged out. From my vantage point under the bush, I spent time taking in as much information as I could. Off to the back of the house, the owner of the mansion had installed a giant pool—and not just a simple inground with a fence. This monstrosity turned out to be a multi-pool, irregularly-shaped affair, perfectly landscaped, with fountains and fire features, and whatever other kind of shit rich people need when they go swimming.

Usually, it would take me a matter of seconds to tear across the lawn, slip my way inside, and start tearing through some evil men. And women. I'm an equal opportunity body counter. But three things kept me under the bush, plotting.

First, the children's toys scattered around the backyard by the pool. They were expensive—like the big car with a doll logo on the side, probably some little kid's favorite toy one Christmas. Then, there were the discarded flip-flops and towels scattered around the pool in child sizes and cartoon images.

Finally, the scent that came to me with the breeze. Mingling with the salt licorice and the gun oil I had followed there, I now tasted popcorn and vanilla ice cream, chlorine, and the fresh, new scent humans retain until they lose it under the onslaught of chemical serums American commercials insist people need so they won't smell bad or dare to look their age.

Fuck.

A low whine escaped me. I wasn't ready to go all avenging angel in a house with kids. Flashes of fur and blood popped across my vision in blooms, the color of red in my memory.

The rumble of the approaching vehicle interrupted my hesitation. Karen and Calix stopped a good distance away. I wanted to jump up and away, warn them of what they were walking into. I couldn't move. If I stirred, I risked hitting the lights again, possibly warning the men inside the house of their approach. If I did nothing…well, Karen's the best shot I've ever met, but I wasn't willing to bet any kid's life they wouldn't get caught in the crossfire.

I was going to regret this.

Abandoning my hiding place, I darted to the middle of the lawn, sat my furry ass down, and started to howl at the moon.

Lights flooded on. Commotion crowded the windows. Men stirred and spilled onto the lawn. Howl after howl erupted. Scents flooded around me, bowling me over. I lost track of Karen and Calix. Surely, they wouldn't approach but I couldn't tell.

The first bullets whined toward me. Seriously? This is the approach they were taking? Not even call the dogcatcher? Okay, straight to the shooting portion of our program. Keeping up a steady stream of howling, barking, and growling, I ran in a circle, chasing my tail.

A few rounds came close to nicking me, but these men were lousy shots. They were nervous, too. A couple of them tried to get the others to stop shooting and made as if to catch me, but they didn't come close.

I caught no sign of any of the kids. But the smell of salt licorice came to the fore.

A tall man, white guy with sharp features and salt and pepper hair cut close to his head, stood framed against the door. He turned back inside and shouted to someone. "Keep the kids inside. I don't want them out here."

That accomplished the first part of my plan I was totally making up as I went along.

The bullet entered my rear, tore a long furrow, and exited my stomach. Don't worry. All part of the next stage of my plan. My howl cut off into a yelp, and I went from running in circles to writhing in pain on the ground.

This made them all a little braver, and they crept closer. My teeth and claws still worked though, and they didn't get too close. Instead, one of them fired another round into me, this time into my chest.

The wound burned like hellfire. I tried to scream, but it came out a strangled whine. It wasn't going to kill me, but the thought was cold comfort as the shock hit my body. I snarled and shook and snapped at anything I could.

"Hold your fire." The tall man with the salt and pepper hair approached. He chewed a piece of licorice. The juice and saliva mingled as he hawked and spit. "Gimme your gun."

One of the men standing in the circle over me handed him a large pistol. I tried to scramble out of the way, but none of my limbs were working.

"Where the fuck did this guy come from?" The question was rhetorical and met with a bunch of shrugs. The man raised the pistol and placed it right in the center of my head, ignoring my feeble attempts to snap at him.

Well. I guessed I was going to learn if I could come back from a direct shot to the brainpan.

A rifle cracked. The man nearest the tall man fell without a word.

Another shot rang out. Now the men scattered, trying to discover where the fire came from. I took advantage of the man's microsecond of hesitation to roll back to my feet. The furrow in my backside— assholes—had started to heal, and while the pain in my chest wasn't fading, I forced myself around it.

I launched myself at the tall man, throwing my weight against him, snapping at any exposed flesh I could find.

"Daddy!"

The one word rang across the lawn. The man's attention shifted from trying to pry me from his body to stumbling back across the lawn.

"Mackenzie! Get back in the house!" He shouted and waved at the little girl clutching her doll, staring wide-eyed at the pandemonium turning her playground into a bloodbath.

I let him go, jumping away. Whipping my head from side to side, I found myself someplace I'd never been—frozen in indecision in the middle of a firefight.

The tall man dragged himself to his knees, then to his feet, moving all the while toward the house where his daughter waited.

An older woman swooped from behind, picking up the little girl and disappearing into the house as the child screamed for her father. At least, no matter what happened, she would be one less witness.

Another round hit my side. I snarled and leapt. The man who shot the bullet fell to the ground, throat hanging open. I spent an overindulgent few seconds savaging the wound, then raced to the next closest man.

Meanwhile, the targets fell steadily, victims of the two women who shot from cover and concealment. They would fire, move, pop up someplace else, fire again. Even I couldn't tell where they were from moment to moment. Every round was judiciously aimed, and every time one of their rifles cracked, another man would fall.

Before I knew it, I was the only one left alive, bleeding into the finely manicured grass. I lolled back, embracing the fire stitching itself across my chest. Just my body healing itself. In another ten minutes, I'd be good as new.

Soft footfalls announced the arrival of my partner and her girlfriend. Karen squatted next to me. She reached out with one gloved hand, gently ruffling the fur. I winced when she found the entrance wound. With deft movements born of experience, she massaged the area. I howled again from the pain, but within seconds she had coaxed the round out, and the flesh started to close and heal around it.

"The leader's inside," Karen said. I nodded, but she wasn't talking to me.

"Thank you." Calix slung her weapon. I wondered what she was about to do, but then the woman—and I kid you not—drew an honest-to-God Japanese samurai sword from a sheath on her back. Not a cheap mall version of a katana, either. The binding smelled dusty and old, maybe older than me. I'd found the source of the scent of old blood and metal I kept catching from her.

She nodded at me. "Thank you." Then, sword at the ready, she disappeared into the house.

I scrambled to my feet, trying to shuck the change off my body. My words came out as a garbled whine. Surely, they had seen the little girl. She knew who she would find in the house. I had to stop Calix, get her back out.

Finally, I stood, reclaiming my human form. "Karen." My mouth filled up with blood. I spat. "We can't let—"

"I'm sorry, Rick."

Startled, I caught her eye. The dead look inside them stopped me. This wasn't Karen, the woman I'd fought beside only a year ago. What the hell had happened?

And then I forgot the question, forgot about the tall man and his daughter, forgot about Calix and her freaky sword, and pretty much forgot my own name. Karen stepped back, syringe in her hand, plunger depressed. A small bit of blood clung to the end. My blood.

And then the silver haze hit me. The Change cried out, but it warned me too late. Darkness came rolling in and took me along with it.

6

Snow fell in big, fat flakes, wet and sticky. I was back up in the North Country. Closing my eyes, I reveled in the silence. Snow and pines and loneliness.

Wait. No. This wasn't the arid plains and scrub of my most recent trip. These trees were older, and the soil under me held foreign memories from before I was born.

*"Guten Morgen, Herr Wurst."* Alexsy thought he was funny. "I trust your sleep was to the finest of accommodate?"

"Jesus Christ, Alexsy. Pick a language and learn it."

Alexsy shouldn't be here. Alexsy had never been here, dug in shoulder-deep in a foxhole somewhere cold. When had I been here? I couldn't recall specifically. I knew that it was wrong for Alexsy to be with me.

But I missed him. He laughed, head back, shoulders shaking.

I looked around nervously. Now I recognized it. The listening and observation post. I'd spent three days there, hiding, sleeping, and shitting in this foxhole with a member of the Republic of Korea Army. The war had just begun, but I'd been there since earlier that year.

They'd pulled me from post-war activities behind the Iron Curtain. Said I'd become too close to the mission. I think they'd simply panicked after I got rolled up by Dmitri's troops and moved me as far away as possible.

I'd hooked back up with Gunny's unit as a sort of extra-service attaché. No one really knew who I was or what I did, except Gunny, but it was the age of agencies with lots of acronyms and money and not too many questions asked of either. Nobody could figure out my mission, least of all me, so most of the time, I'd grab one of the ROK soldiers and head out to take a look.

This time, I'd had a ROK Army kid we all called Shin. I don't think he even had a rank or ever told us his full name. Just Shin. I liked hanging out with him. Tough, smart, and adaptable, he could see things in the trail even I would miss. I don't know if he felt the same—he didn't talk much—but he would share his pickled vegetables with me, and I'd give him part of my rations, so I think it worked out.

"Alexsy, you're not supposed to be here." He'd been staring at me throughout my inner walk down memory lane. "This is Korea. Where's Shin?"

"You tell me, Sausage Breath," he answered. "This your dream. I'm just riding along with."

Okay, then. I wasn't going to complain.

"You back in with those MONIKER fucks?" Alexsy could speak passable English if he wanted to. He had the cuss words down, anyway.

"What are you talking about?" I had a hard time wrapping my brain around everything. The scenery smelled so real; I could taste the snow and feel my toes numbing in my boot. "I'm not in with them. I'm just helping out a friend."

"A friend?" He leaned back in the foxhole, resting his rifle up against the muddy side. In addition to our rifles, we both wore a pistol at our sides and carried a good number of grenades. Never knew what you would find out in the wilderness, and both Shin and I believed in being prepared.

"Yeah, a friend. Karen's a friend." As I said it, I realized something dark and bitter had taken root, flavoring the words with a gentle irony. I bit it back. "Karen saved my ass and my life more than once. I trust her."

"She's not her grandmother, you know." Aleksy pulled out a smoke from his ubiquitous pack. He offered me one, but I declined.

"You think I don't know that?"

He shrugged. "We are men of blunt words and violent actions."

When alive, Alexsy had rarely indulged in his serious side. I knew he had one, but he never revealed it on a mission, preferring to joke his way past the danger of death and torture and anything else the Soviets might have in store. Everything about this conversation was weird.

We sat in silence for a while after that. Alexsy smoked. I leaned forward, enjoying the feel of the cold snow against my face, the wind as it whipped around the trees.

Off in the distance, a low rumble started. It gradually grew louder, working its way toward us. The wind blew at just the right angle to our position, and I caught wafts of fermented cabbage and explosives. Lots of explosives.

"Keep an eye on the trucks." I grabbed my rifle, hunkering down. Alexsy extinguished his smoke and followed suit. "I'll keep an eye out in case they have scouts covering their path."

I radioed in our position, as well as the number of trucks and direction of travel. After the kid on the other end of the line acknowledged and signed off, I returned to scanning the woods. My nose told me this convoy had flankers out to protect its travel, and I didn't want to be caught unawares.

I couldn't tell you exactly what happened next.

A shot cracked out. I turned to track where it had come from. No luck.

"Alexsy?"

He sprawled face-down at the bottom of the foxhole.

"Shin?"

I rolled him over, knowing already what I would find. Alexsy stared back at me, eyes wide. A thin line of blood ran down between them from the bullet that had caught him perfectly in the center of the forehead.

No. This wasn't Alexsy. This wasn't how he died. He died in Poland. This is Shin, sitting here beside me, and I didn't catch the sniper in time, and he died.

Shouts came from a few meters off. One of the men running toward our position stopped. He took a knee, drew something from his side, and almost lazily lobbed it in my direction.

The grenade exploded right outside of our foxhole. I stood half in-half out, leaning forward to aim and fire. The force of the explosion blasted me back. I caught the hole's edge and rolled backward, peppered with shrapnel. My body clenched in a firestorm of pain.

I ended up flat on my back, spread-eagled in the snow.

In these situations, you're supposed to see your life flash before you, but all I remember is how beautiful the sky looked.

One of the North Korean soldiers approached, slowly, pistol out. I lay there. My body convulsed, still in the first stages of pain before it started trying to heal.

I turned my head to the side. The North Korean soldier should have shouted something to the others. I should have scrambled to my feet, unlimbered my grenade, and tossed it at them where they had clumped into an easy target.

But it wasn't the North Korean sergeant. Instead, Karen stood there, pale as ice. She wore her combat gear, looming over me. I couldn't move. What the hell?

She walked over to me, kneeling on one knee beside me.

Drawing her weapon, she placed the barrel against my forehead.

I couldn't move, not even to struggle against the inevitable.

Karen looked over her shoulder at someone I couldn't even see. "Now?"

*No, not now, stop; what the hell are you doing?* The words stuck in my throat.

"Yes."

Holy shit. I knew that voice.

Now Karen looked down at me, and I found myself caught in the intensity of her gaze. She nodded slowly and pulled the trigger.

---

I awoke to full consciousness a fraction of a second before the bullet left the gun. I immediately regretted it.

First came the pain. Then next, a wave of rage. My vision blacked out, and I launched myself, reaching for the change.

And ended up snapped back, the chains at my wrists and ankles burning into my skin. *Holy crap, that stings.* They cut into furrows already burned deep by the silver manacles.

I rocked back, attempting to stand, but the chains were attached to the wall in such a way that the closest I could get was a pissed-off crouch. Just in case I did manage to slip myself out, a wall of bars coated in silver blocked off a nice little cage area for their now-resident werewolf. Only in one place did I have a habit of waking up like this. At least this time, I wasn't completely naked.

"Welcome, Mr. Keller."

I knew I had recognized his voice. Reaching again for the change, denied again by the silver, I settled for throwing myself against the chains. Snarling tends to be less effective when I'm not furry, but I gave it all I got.

The man standing just out of reach—Dr. Gratusczak—had put me in chains once before, poking and prodding and infecting me until he had unleashed the forces of the *Überwechsel.*

"I thought you were dead." The words came out with a glob of spit that landed short of the tall, slender man in his white lab coat.

"Really, Mr. Keller." Gratusczak brushed at his lapel. "You know MONIKER makes the best use of its resources, even those that come to it under…coercion."

His voice came out as flat and dry as I remembered. He left a curious scent void that I remembered as well—as if there were something missing in his physical existence. And yes, I did know what MONIKER did with its resources—they had long counted me amongst their number. From my current circumstances, it looked like they still had me listed on their books. Keller, Rick. Werewolf. One each.

"Ah. Good. You are understanding." The doctor nodded, clasping his hands behind him. "My presence is required elsewhere for the moment, but I look forward to renewing our acquaintance."

Uh…what in the hell? No. This time I stepped backward; the cold concrete behind me gave me no place to retreat.

Gratusczak smiled, thin-lipped, without any real sense of amusement. He turned and, as he moved out of my field of vision, revealed two guards in MONIKER uniforms. They fell into step next to him as he exited the room. Clearly, the agency took no chances with this particular resource. And yet, I wondered if they truly understood who —what—he was.

Probably not. Because if they did, he would join me here in this cage.

"Rick."

I sat down on the floor, mind racing, trying to calm my body, which had started freaking out, unable to access the change. Clamping down hard, I tried to stop myself from rocking back and forth, breathing accelerating to almost hyperventilation. On a whim, I tried reaching for the larger Change, desperation lending me delusional hope. Not a whisper of an answer. Going from the complete freedom of the North to returning to a MONIKER cage would drive me insane if I didn't get out of there. And fast.

"Rick."

Karen stepped forward to the bars. Something about her smelled off. The humming tension I had sensed when I met her earlier had been muted. It wasn't so much that it had worn off or that she had gotten herself under control. The silver burned my sinuses, but I could still taste her rosemary-and-rain scent. But now, something else added to the mix. Something sluggish and chemical. I rubbed my nose on my shoulder. My friend was not the same person she had been when I left her in New York.

Speaking of. "This isn't the New York office." And it wasn't. For one, the building appeared much newer, from the fresh paint to the pristine condition of its cells. For two, the dust on her boots was fresh and smelled of desert.

"We're still in Vegas," she answered. "Well, technically, in the desert outside the city."

"Want to tell me what the fuck is going on?" Where was the woman who kicked ass, took names, and would never betray someone she'd fought with side by side?

"It's a long…story." She paused, dragging out her words. Was she stoned? She spoke like she might be stoned. "I needed help. Calix needed help."

"I don't understand." I rested my wrists on my knees and spread my hands, palms up, almost as if in a prayerful appeal. The damned silver rested directly on my wrists. The pain was so acute I couldn't stop myself from sweating. "I would have helped. Once I got your call."

Karen took so long to reply I worried she might have spaced out or lost track or just couldn't follow me. Or maybe she was *really* stoned.

"I tried calling." She thought some more and shrugged. "You didn't pick up the phone."

There wasn't much I could say in reply. My vacation had made me hard to get hold of. "Still. Your next play was to call MONIKER?"

Karen caught my eyes and returned my stare. She didn't blink. Unnerving. "I didn't have to call them. I work for them." A trace of black rimmed her irises. She gripped the cage bars, knuckles white against her skin. "I've been Dr. Gratusczak's minder since you left."

Well. That explains why she was strung out like a junkie. I didn't trust the doctor to give me a flu shot. I certainly didn't trust him not to play the agency for fools while he played the part of one of their "resources."

"Doesn't explain why I'm here." Grunting, I tried to shift the handcuffs just a little more. I regretted not wearing long sleeves. "And what this is all about."

"I needed help from MONIKER." Karen's gaze slid away until she almost looked at me but slightly past. It wasn't any less unnerving. "They promised their help."

"In exchange for what?" Just kidding. I already knew the answer.

"You," Karen confirmed. "They've been keeping tabs on your last known. But now it's time to reel you back in."

"And I thought John Tell was a son of a bitch." The change clawed and dug at me inside; the silver burned from the outside. "What's the difference between what he did and all this?"

Karen shrugged and stood up straight.

"MONIKER wants you, MONIKER has you." She took a step, staggering slightly. "Ramirez wants to meet with you. He's going to offer you a deal. Come back to work with us again and get out of that cage. Or stay there and become another one of Gratusczak's lab protocols." She turned and started to leave, stopping just as she reached the door. "It's really all the same to me."

For a long time after she left, I couldn't move. I simply sat, accepting the pain, unable to accept what she had said.

MONIKER had brought me back in after a long time away. At that time, I'd thought we were heading back to an age of working clandestinely to save the world. Or at least fix small parts of it. Instead, it had been a ploy by Agent John Tell, who'd used the agency's resources—and Karen—to track me down, bring me back, and, finally, sell me to the highest bidder. Who'd turned out to be Dr. Gratusczak.

Tell's betrayal had taken me back to my old stomping grounds in eastern Europe, and then my home turf of southern Germany. Something in the soil had reconnected after so long away. That something kept clawing at me, and once we'd finished the mission, I found it too hard to settle down in one place.

I'd packed up and headed north. Drifted from town to town. I'd met Randall over drinks one night, and we'd knocked back enough shots to beat the shit out of each other and wake up best friends. He'd offered me a job working outdoors. It had been enough for a couple weeks until the first full moon yanked the *Überwechsel* out of me. When I woke up, far out in the north country, stark naked in the snow, I had gone furry. And decided to stay furry for a few days. Then a few weeks. Then I had gone back into town, prepped for a long time away, and slipped back into the wilderness with no intention of returning until MONIKER had completely given up trying to find me. With one exception—a quick trip to New York City to help a friend— I'd become a complete ghost.

*Fuck.*

Shifting position, I tried to find some way to keep the wrist manacles from touching skin. By now, deep welts had formed, blistering and popping. Every time the silver touched raw skin, it felt so painful I wanted to throw up.

When I'd met Tell, I had thought he was a son of a bitch. I'd gone against my instincts and trusted him, and it turned out my initial assessment had been correct. I didn't think too much about what they'd offered him; at the time, I hadn't cared.

But Karen—if she could be turned, if *she* had a price, then I had to ask myself, did I trust myself to fend off the agency? In the end, what would it take to get to me?

"You are an interesting man."

Raising my head, I spotted Calix standing across the room. She leaned against the wall, arms crossed. Seeing she had my attention, she pushed herself up and walked over to the cage.

Calix leaned her forearm against the cage and rested her forehead against her arm, looking down on me. I've been looked down on by better-quality human beings.

"Go fuck yourself."

She stretched, folded her arms, and leaned her shoulder against the cage bars.

"Karen tells me you've worked for MONIKER before." She gazed at me intently.

I swallowed a mouthful of bile. Not only did the silver bite at my wrists and ankles, but the miasma emanating from the silver that laced the bars coated my lungs with every breath. If I didn't get out of here in a timely fashion, I was going to rot from the inside out.

"It's quite fascinating," Calix continued. "I mean, Karen told me about this phenomenon, but I have to say, I didn't believe it until I saw you do…the change, I believe she called it?"

"What the hell do you want?" My speech slurred. I couldn't move. My vision had started to fuzz around the edges. "I promise I won't poach your girlfriend."

Calix didn't react. She just gazed at me steadily. "Karen told me you are friends."

"Were." Pretty sure I should use the past tense.

"She needs friends."

What? "She's got you."

Another shrug. The woman was positively full of them. "I'm new."

I coughed and felt something in my lungs detach. Dark droplets sprayed across my hands.

"This is killing you, isn't it?"

"People have tried in the past," I informed her. "I'm not dead yet." Trying for humor. "I think I'll go for a walk."

"You're not fooling anyone, you know," she answered.

"Didn't know middle-aged badass ninja turtles watched Monty Python."

"Middle-aged? Meee-ow."

"I'm about to bleed to death internally; I have no shame." Shame and dignity get in the way of a good time. So does bleeding to death internally.

"Take their deal." Her voice didn't waver, her gaze didn't flinch. "Take the deal. Get your ass back in the fold. Help me get Karen out of here."

7

I could have held out a little longer, but everybody involved pretty much had my number, so I caved. Yup. I called "uncle" as loud as I could, and they came, took the silver off my wrists, and let me crash in a different cage.

The men who came to take me there were nameless, uniformed, and not very chatty. They approached me with cattle prods, nervous. There was nothing for them to worry about. By the time they showed up, I could barely think straight, let alone move.

One of them put the end of the prod right up against my neck, while the other unsnapped the silver cuffs and replaced them with a pair that still contained enough silver to discourage me from any futile escape attempts and muffle the change. These ones, though, were thankfully coated by a thick enough layer of steel, and they barely burned at all.

When they motioned for me to get up, my legs wouldn't cooperate. Hell, by this point, the silver they'd encased me in had infected my entire body, and I don't know what they expected. Making a mad dash for freedom wasn't an option. Neither was standing under my own power.

One of them grabbed me under the elbow on my right side, the other took up on the left, and they simply frog-marched me down the hall, dragged me down a flight of dingy stairs, and threw me in a free-standing cage in the middle of a concrete basement.

Then they'd locked me in, headed upstairs, and turned out the light before they locked that door behind them as well.

No matter. MONIKER had a habit of throwing me in dark places. Their playbook varied little, if at all. And it hardly ever included feeding me. Bastards.

Somewhere, a water heater kicked on, thrumming for a few minutes before it turned off again. The smell of damp and musty concrete almost masked the scent of old blood.

The last time the agency had snatched me out of retirement and dragged me to New York, I'd woken up in a basement almost identical to this one. The building had been older, more corporate. From what I'd seen of this place, it was not only newer and brighter but also much more specifically designed with someone like me in mind.

This worried me. This worried me a lot.

John Tell had sold me to Gratusczak and whoever bankrolled the creepy doctor's research. They had wanted to replicate the change, take it over, and turn it into a weapon. I'd thought our work had disrupted that train of thought, but now my head started to clear and it became apparent MONIKER had just brought Dr. G on the payroll and decided to make his research *their* research.

This facility would be a pain in the ass to break out of, if not impossible. Not just for me but for anyone else they planned on subjecting to their pet mad scientist's experiments.

Holy shit, I hoped to hell and all the Gods my mother never found out about this. You may laugh, but you never met my mother. If you did, you'd shit your pants and then die because she would eat you. I know I make a lot of wiseass cracks, but this is not actually a joke.

The familiar, normal change stirred again. Four more weeks until the next full moon. I had no idea if the greater Change, the *Über-wechsel*, would triumph over the layers of silver they'd surrounded me with. Maybe? Probably? Likely, it would. And man, I did not want them to know about that.

I've been alive for a long time. Time slows for me every month. The moon works her way through every cell in my body as the change takes me. If you started to look closely, though, I'd begun to age. I'd even begun to see it in my face, feel it in my body. Perhaps manipulating the change had robbed me of the regeneration. Until the *Überwechsel* caught me up in its grasp. The greater, wilder Change that gave me the gift of powerful sight, a stronger form than I'd ever achieved—and a call whispering in the back of my head of the Forest God of my ancestors. And now I'm back, caught in the throes of that inescapable Change that shows me the colors of the night sky every month under the full moon, but I'm also certain I'm recovering the time I thought I lost.

And I had one hundred percent abso-fucking-lutely no intention of spending one moment of the time I had left in the service of this organization.

Sitting in the dark, wondering if they were going to feed me soon or give me a chance to take a piss, I made a decision.

Recent events had proven it wasn't enough to just get out of MONIKER. If I wanted to *stay* out, I had to get Karen to leave. Also, I probably needed to take Calix along; otherwise, Karen would just go back, and that would be the end of *that* carefully laid plan.

Okay, I had a plan. I had a goal. I just needed someone to come and LET ME OUT. So I could get started.

Also, note to self, stay out of Gratuszcak's lab. Dude was creepy, and no matter what controls MONIKER thought they had on him, I was pretty sure they weren't working.

---

After a few days, they got around to remembering about me. A team of two flipped on the light when they came downstairs. Usually, they just shoved an MRE and a bottle of water through the bars, swept up any garbage left from the previous meal, and left without saying a word.

This time, though, they'd unlocked the door to the cage and

motioned me out. The handcuffs allowed my wrists to heal somewhat, although they still sported a circle of raw, swollen flesh where my skin reacted to the muted silver.

When I stood up, one of them pointed at me with the cattle prod, and the other snapped a pair of leg irons on. Same deal. Silver coated with steel. Great. Not only was I not going to change anytime soon, but now I got to do the convict shuffle wherever the hell they were taking me.

The stairs were a fun challenge.

Also, after three days of MREs and a week of no showering after emerging from the wilderness, I got a distinct satisfaction in the fact they had to smell me. Ha. Assholes.

I'd hoped to be able to gather more information about where the hell they'd brought me, but I guess they were going to keep going on the information deprivation playbook. Why fix what works? In addition to the hand and leg irons, they put a blackout bag over my head, then pulled it tight around my neck. Not only could I not see through the thing, but I also couldn't look down to catch a glimpse of where we were walking.

This made maneuvering where the two men flanking me wanted me to go extra annoying. It also signaled my current status. Last time, they'd picked me up because they wanted me to return as an agent. This time, my status was unsure. Until they removed the cuffs and hood, call me Rick Keller, the captive lab rat. Wolf. Whatever.

For the first time, I worried they had brought me back simply to be Dr. G's research subject. It hadn't occurred to me they might no longer require my services as an agent.

I stumbled but didn't fall. They caught me too quickly. Rather than allowing me to gain my footing, the two men dragged me until I got my feet back under me. This did not bode well.

*Shit. Fuck. Shitfuck.*

After three lefts, a right, a left, and some hallway—or maybe the other way around?—I was completely lost and pretty much done with this crap. Finally, they stopped. The man on my left held me up to keep me from falling when I tripped over the sudden halt.

"Bring him in."

I knew that voice. My handlers pushed me sideways, dragged me a little farther, and plopped me in a chair. It swiveled. I tried a slight rocking back and forth.

The blow came out of the darkness, catching me across the cheek. I fell to the side. Helping hands pulled me back into the chair.

"Knock it off, asshole."

Yeah, definitely knew him.

One of the men untied the hood and pulled it off, leaving me blinking in the sudden harsh fluorescent glare.

"Agent Keller." Ramirez, the closest thing to the top of the chain of command I'd met at MONIKER, still wore his lumberjack flannel and loud ties.

He sat at the head of a long, polished wood table flanked by rows of mostly empty chairs. My comfy swivel chair stood at the foot. Karen and Calix sat across from each other at the middle of the table. I didn't see Dr. Gratusczak. Perhaps he hadn't been invited.

"Retired." All I got was a noncommittal gaze. I tried again. "Retired Not-Agent Go-Fuck-Yourself Keller."

"Manners, Rick. That kind of talk…*es geht nicht.*"

The urbane, cultured tone, brushed with hints of a Russian accent, froze my blood. I worked my jaw but couldn't get anything to come out.

No matter.

A slight man, face lined with too many years, walked around my side. He rested a hand on my shoulder as he passed, squeezing almost imperceptibly before letting go and taking a seat at the table a few chairs down from me.

Dmitri Pietrovitch Nicolaiov. The kindly Russian Grandpapa demeanor belied a sociopath of the highest order. If I hadn't been eating MRE cheese for three days, I probably would have crapped my pants at his touch.

"Rick, Dmitri tells me you go way back?" Karen watched me closely. I didn't know what she knew or what she suspected, but even with her head not completely in the game, she was intelligent and perceptive. I'd be watching my step.

"We met." Dmitri had me on his table, too, once upon a time. Not only had he wrung some of the deepest, darkest secrets from my psyche with not more than a few rudimentary tools, he'd... No. Thinking of that time opened doors in my memory I didn't want to go through. The notebook he'd kept had somehow made it into Gratusczak's hands. How the hell did he get here?

"All right, we've all met." Ramirez took charge of the meeting. "Rick, last time you were here, we needed an Agent." He sat back in his chair, arm outstretched, drumming his fingers on the table.

In all the walk here, I'd never escaped the presence of silver. It embedded everything. Every single foot of this building had some concentration of the metal coating or covering something, or just plain out in the open. In this room, thin lines of silver lay embedded into the tabletop in a tree of life pattern. It clouded my senses, put me off my game.

"This time, you have a choice," Ramirez continued. "I have two men who require your services."

He nodded at Karen. She pulled out a small, polished box and placed it on the table.

"Doctor Gratusczak is closing in on the final stages of a project for which, he assures me, you are a mandatory attendee." Ramirez rolled his eyes. "I really don't give a shit. He can get a couple vials of blood, cut a little hair clipping, maybe some toenails. It'll tide him over."

So...did I get any say in whether or not the good doctor got to take souvenirs?

"It's either that or you get to hang out in his lab with him full time," Ramirez added, reading my mind. "Permanently." He quit with the finger tapping and folded his arms across his chest. "Or there's option B."

If Option B involved Dmitri, Option A sounded fine to me.

"The other option you have is to come back to work for us." Ramirez stared me down across the length of the table. "Reinstated to full agent status. You'll get a paycheck and everything."

"Corner office, too?" Sign me right up!

"Don't push it, Rick." Ramirez pushed back from the table. He nodded at Karen.

Karen stood and opened the box in front of her, extracting a syringe. She walked toward me. I tried to push myself back, out of reach, but the men behind me held my chair. I whipsawed my gaze between her and Dmitri. He hadn't said another word since he sat down, just gazed at me with his piercing shark stare.

"Rick." Karen's touch was gentle, but it burned my skin like ice. "Don't move."

Quickly, expertly, she rolled my forearm over, inserted the syringe, and sent home the plunger. I felt a pinch and a quick burn, and then it dissipated.

"I've got the change under control." The last time Karen had injected me with something, it turned out to be a compound that had destabilized me from the inside out, forcing me to ride out the change, re-learn how to control it.

"It's a tracker." Karen withdrew the needle and pressed a button, retracting the sharp tip into the syringe. "It's coated in a decaying compound. The inner compound is something you don't want to face without the antidote."

"This is some real *Escape from New York* shit right here," I retorted.

She caught my eye for a moment, and I caught a flicker of the old Karen.

"Can my code name be Snake?"

"Rick." Dmitri raised an eyebrow. It had an immediate and chilling effect. I shut up.

"Agent Keller," Ramirez started, then stopped himself. "It is Agent Keller, isn't it? And not Subject Charlie?"

I didn't answer. But I would totally be Subject Alpha.

"Mr. Smith here helped us track you down," Ramirez said. It took me a second to realize he was referring to Dmitri. "In return, he asked the favor of our assistance. And yours."

Well, that explained how they found me. Figured they hadn't just relied on the chance I might check my voicemail. He'd probably been the one to have Karen call me on her friend's behalf. Speaking of which.

"You got anything to say?" I asked Calix. "Everyone else seems to have an opinion."

She shrugged. "You helped me with my sister. We're square."

By my accounting, that meant she owed me one.

"Director Ramirez, may I have a moment to speak with Rick?" Dmitri didn't raise his voice or even use much inflection. Somehow, the question came out like a statement. Nobody argued.

"Do you need—?" Ramirez nodded at the two men flanking me.

"No, no." Dmitri waved his hand almost languidly. "Rick and I are old friends."

I'm pretty sure I didn't actually whimper. Pretty sure. I held my shit together while everyone filed out of the room. Calix was the last one out. She turned and winked at me before leaving. I didn't get the joke.

Dmitri waited until the door closed firmly behind her. Then he turned.

"They seem..." He left me hanging while he chose his words carefully. "They carry themselves very specifically."

I didn't know what to say, so I kept my mouth shut.

"It is very interesting being here with these agents." Dmitri caught my gaze. "And this doctor they have working for them." He steepled his fingers, gazing at me over his fingertips. "He reminds me of certain men."

"Dmitri, you—" I broke off. Tried again. "You're not exactly seeing me at my best."

His gaze flickered down to the silver-encased metal restraining my wrists and ankles.

"I am sorry your agency has proven itself so...short-sighted." He brushed at a piece of lint on his slacks. "And I am also sorry that I must call in your debt. I have a great need for your assistance."

8

I did owe Dmitri a debt. And I'd known he would come calling to collect. I just always thought it would be later. Like, maybe I'd be long dead before he came looking for me to help him with something he couldn't handle. Because whatever he couldn't handle scared the shit out of me.

"Rick, I have a daughter."

Didn't see that one coming.

"She's involved with something, and I don't like it."

If Dmitri needed me to track down an errant boyfriend, I was all for it. Get me out of the office.

"It's not that simple." Dmitri frowned at me like he had actually read my mind. After the time we had spent together, he could read me well enough that he didn't need telepathy. "The organization she's involved with…it would be as difficult to extract her from them as it would be to do the same with you. From here."

"Dmitri," I said, as respectfully as possible, just in case he was hinting at an offer. "I'm paying off a debt here. Not incurring another one?"

He smiled, as reassuring as a wolf smiling at a lamb. And I would know.

"My friend, I simply need your help." He shrugged. "This task must be done...the right way. And you seem to have useful friends."

"Friends." I lifted my hands to demonstrate the shackles. "They're just the very best kind."

Dmitri turned to face me, placing his hands on the table palms down, slowly and deliberately.

"I am about to tell you something that nobody else knows." He looked at me and slowly tapped each finger on the table. "You find yourself embedded in this organization?"

"That's a good word for it."

"I, too, have found myself unable to extract myself from a situation. And an organization to which I once owed allegiance. But which sank and disintegrated under the weight of its own corruption."

"And your daughter?"

"Russia is a new country," Dmitri answered. "But some parts of it stay the same. Just polished over and painted with new slogans."

The realization hit me. I had more in common with my old enemy than these new friends. It chilled me to the bone.

"If you cannot help me, my friend..."

"I repay my debts." I held Dmitri's gaze. "Let's do this."

<hr>

MONIKER was satisfied to think I'd again agreed to stand in as their resident cannibalistic biomorph. Dmitri—well, who knew what Dmitri thought? He'd let me know eventually. Hopefully, I'd be alive to appreciate it.

At the end of the day, I would have done anything to get the silver off my body and out of my lungs and to figure out how to escape the Las Vegas facility. But before I did, I decided there would be some caveats on this deal. First, no matter what I did, MONIKER would never learn about the Change. I didn't care what I had to do, but under no circumstances would I be anywhere near them on a full moon.

Second, I would pay my debt to Dmitri and never see him again, and definitely never, ever again ask him for a favor. Unless I really had to.

And last but not least, it would not be enough to just get Karen and Calix out and head off into the sunset. The organization was infected, and the rot spread through and through. If I ever wanted to be free of the machinations and scheming of the agency, I'd have to burn it to the ground.

I wasn't sure how I'd accomplish all of these noble goals, but I'm not above making things up as I go along. It works most of the time. This might even turn out to be one of those times.

Like most of my plans, this one started off by failing. After agreeing to come back on the payroll and help Dmitri and the gang, I expected them to take off the cuffs, issue me a shiny badge, and we'd get started again.

No such luck. Instead, they fitted me with a bracelet that locked around my left wrist, made of a thin band of silver—enough to keep me from changing—surrounded by a thin steel coating that made it just about bearable. Some joker had engraved little Scottish terriers around the band. It looked like someone's grandma's costume jewelry. Oh yeah, this place was going down.

The two men who'd marched me to the conference room also escorted me to the intake where all this fitting took place. I'd expected Karen to take care of all of this. The nameless men made me realize that even though I'd been invited back as an agent, MONIKER still didn't entirely view me as such.

After everyone satisfied themselves that my collar fit nice and snug, the two men escorted me back into the hall.

"What's next?" I looked from one to the other. "Can I get an outfit like yours? Maybe a TASER? I always wanted one of those."

The first man ignored me. The second one prodded me out the door.

Two more MONIKER staff met us in the hall, a man and a woman. The two of them flanked a familiar face.

"Doctor." I nodded. "Hope you die and rot in hell."

He laughed in response. The sound reminded me of a cat scratching on a post. His team prodded him forward.

Mine nudged me into step behind him. Did not like this one at all. I slowed my steps, but the guy behind me just kicked the soles of my feet. Stumbling, I regained my footing and glared at him.

He didn't glare back. If anything, his saggy face looked bored. "Cut the crap, asshole."

Damn. The insult slid off my back, but lack of reaction tensed my gut worse than if I'd eaten an entire bar of chocolate. Their assuredness of the fact of my submission didn't smell like overconfidence, and that jarred me on a deep, subconscious level. I was used to minions being at least a tiny bit nervous around me.

For one split second, I thought about cutting and running. Or at least doing something other than walking where they wanted me to without even putting up a fight. Then I thought of Dmitri and Karen, and how I appeared to be in some sort of labyrinthine maze. Even if I ran, I'd be completely lost, and a facility MONIKER designed to keep me in would likely do just that.

I settled down like an obedient hound—*not* a damn toy terrier—and followed where they led.

When we hit the basement corridor, the lights started to do something funky. They were on some kind of motion sensor. As we walked, they clicked on overhead, clicking back off as we passed by. It was disorienting. Couldn't see where we were going. Couldn't tell where we'd been.

It shouldn't have been so bad. The tracks we made, scent paths, and the other sense I relied on should have shone clear behind us even in the darkness. But even down here in the concrete, embedded shards of silver kept me confused, burning my sinuses.

We came up on the double metal doors before I even realized it. They were painted in a color I guessed was red from the dark gray I saw, windowless, and accessible only with an eight-digit code. One of the men escorting the good doctor punched numbers into a keypad. As the doors opened, I tried to ignore the giant biohazard symbols painted in black, one for each door.

The man and woman escorting Dr. G. peeled off. Looked like they were detailed to stand guard—possibly to make sure nothing got in. More likely to make sure none of us went for an unauthorized wander around the property.

"Rick, in here." Calix stood by a table near the center of the room. Karen sat next to her, swinging her legs. Was she drinking a…beer?

I wanted one.

Seeing me, Karen hopped down. She smiled at me and patted the table next to her. "Climb on up."

No, thank you. The table had straps. I don't get on tables with straps. It's basically my philosophy in life.

"Rick, don't be an asshole. Get on the table, or I'll make you get on the table."

"What are you going to do? Beat me with a beer can?"

"Mr. Keller, MONIKER has sanctioned this action." Gratusczak's voice, like his laugh, scratched my nerves like a cat. "Please get on the table. If we make this as pleasant as possible, it will be over quickly."

Inside, the change perked its head, baring its teeth. I rolled my head, cracking my neck. The minute this cuff came off, I would finish where we left off with the agency's resident mad scientist.

I couldn't help myself. I snapped at Gratusczak as I passed him. Calix stepped to the side as I hefted myself up on the table.

"Lay down." Gratusczak didn't bother turning around as he gave me the instruction. He busied himself at a long table covered in various pieces of equipment. His desk stood a few feet away. Everything was meticulously placed, and scrupulously clean. Not one paper dared slip out of place.

Then I saw it. Carefully squared up on the desk next to the computer keyboard. Dmitri's notebook. Fuck.

"Why?" I didn't care why. I needed to stall, so I could think about the notebook and what it might contain.

"We need several vials of your blood," Karen said. "This could take a minute, so it's easier if you're reclining."

"I thought I was back here to rejoin the team," I said, trying to catch her eye.

She lifted her head and looked me straight in the face. "You spent seventy years as a science experiment. We're revisiting that portion of your service. Lay down."

I followed orders. Every once in a while, I caught a glimpse of the Karen I knew. But down here, this new person had completely taken over. I found it profoundly unsettling, like meeting Mr. Hyde after falling in love with Dr. Jekyll.

Karen strapped me down at the hands and feet. Didn't know why until Gratusczak turned back around. He handed a tray with a syringe and several vials to Karen, who came to the other side. With quick, efficient movements, she tied a tourniquet, coaxed a vein, and inserted a syringe. Removing the tourniquet, she began drawing vial after vial.

It shouldn't have been freaking me out for them to draw maybe half a pint of blood. No big deal. But the way Gratusczak just stood there and waited told me he planned something worse.

I tried to catch Karen's eye again, but she actively avoided me. I didn't want to look at Gratusczak, so I settled for scanning the room. It was big, and dark around the edges. My forte was sudden and brutal violence, not biochemistry. Still, to my admittedly inexperienced eye, this place looked like MONIKER had spared no expense in getting this guy back up and running as soon as possible. It looked almost exactly like the place we'd raided in Germany. I wondered if Gratusczak had even had time to fart before MONIKER put him back in business.

Gratusczak ran his thumb around my forearm. Oh, hey, creepy. It got even more freaky when he paused and massaged an area close to my elbow.

"Good," he said, almost absentmindedly. "It stayed put."

The touch of his skin on mine had the change howling and scratching inside me, going crazy at not being let out.

"This is a new device," he continued. I thought he was talking to me, but he looked up at Karen. "I wasn't sure if it would stay where it was supposed to."

Oh, great. Nutballs here gave Karen experimental tech to shoot me up with, and he wasn't sure if it would even work. Jesus.

"I'm finished." Karen capped the last vial. She extracted the syringe from my arm, retracted the needle, and took the tray to the long table. Grabbing a rack to hold the vials, she began labeling and placing them in a specific order.

Calix hadn't said a word the entire time, just hovered around.

"You have anything to contribute?"

She didn't answer, just smiled at me. Sharp white points in the darkness.

"Dr. Willet, the cart, if you will." Gratusczak kept rolling the pad of his thumb over and over my forearm. The strap kept me from flinching. I flexed my fingers, willing the claws to grow from them, but the silver cuff did its job.

Karen rolled over a cart with two levels. On the bottom, several piles of gauze, sterile bandages, anything you might need to staunch a flow of blood. On the top tray, all the tools a crazy horror-movie doctor might need to start the blood flowing.

By now, I'd already started sweating. I hoped, just once, to catch a flicker of a nod or wink to clue me in that the old Karen rattled around in there, or maybe the new Karen had just the slightest bit of hesitation about what she was doing. But all I got was a blank stare and the smell of more than one beer on her breath.

"What…um…what are you doing?" I finally asked. "What is all this for?"

Gratusczak smiled like I was his favorite pupil in a class full of people smarter than me.

"This agency has all manner of intriguing research," he said. "They have been studying you for many years, and just to have access to their data…" For a moment, I thought I'd lost him as he stared off into the distance. His jaw hung slightly agape, and his tongue flicked out, caressing his top left canine. "It was all very fascinating. Of course,

John Tell provided me with most of what I required. But the archives here…most helpful. Most helpful."

He came back to himself and sniffed, then pored over the tools on the cart, hovering his hand over each of them like a chef selecting the perfect knife.

"Ah." The scalpel he selected was basic, but very, very sharp. "And yet, the samples they collected were minimal. Most were so old as to be completely useless."

The scalpel was so sharp that I didn't feel it slicing into my skin at first. The numbness lasted a few seconds before the pain made itself known. I screamed, arching my back up, straining against the straps that held me securely. I couldn't move, and I couldn't escape the pain.

Gratusczak moved slowly and deliberately as he made another cut, then took two clamps, opening up the flesh on my arm to the bone. I screamed again and couldn't seem to stop. I've felt some pain in my life, but Gratusczak took it to another level. To add insult to injury, these were the people I'd just agreed to work for. I'd better get some fucking hazard pay.

The doctor paused in his surgery, and I panted hard, trying to get beyond the pain. I couldn't even formulate a wiseass crack, just sat there and hoped it would be over soon.

Carefully, deliberately, he cut thin slice after thin slice of flesh, affixing them to slides and passing them to Karen to be labeled and cataloged. By the time he finished, I couldn't scream anymore. Instead, a continuous keening whimper echoed around the room. Apparently, it came from me.

When he finished, he took the tray from Karen and returned to the table. She took over, cleaning the wound, stitching flesh, placing the sterile pads, and winding them into place with gauze.

By this time, I wasn't sure if my face was wet from sweating or because I was crying from the pain. It didn't stop after she finished, either. Just kept going on and on. I wouldn't have minded if there had been even a shadow of regret I could scent somewhere in there, but the old Karen was gone.

## 9

I t took three days for my damn arm to reach the point where I could move without snarling or whining at the pain. Not only did the cuff hold me back from the change, but it also slowed the healing process I usually relied on. All my carefully laid plans and sworn goals had faded into one simple one. Get this silver abomination *off*.

At least I had the run of the facility. The architects had built into the side of a mountain with large, south-facing glass windows to take advantage of the desert sun. If you don't think I wouldn't try to launch myself through those windows the first chance I got...let me just tell you, MONIKER thought of everything and coated them with a thin film that incorporated silver as a base element. I bounced off of it, dislocating my arm in the process.

When I first came back to MONIKER, they'd prepped a room in the training facility meant to keep me in one place long enough for them to continue their research. It mostly consisted of re-asserting my control over the change and acclimating me to a new chemical they claimed they'd discovered another agency formulating. Back then, I should have been entirely more suspicious about their claims. Now, walking through an entire building designed to function as that small basement had, I couldn't keep the chills from crawling over all my skin.

More than ever, I found myself reaching for the change—either, both, any—no matter how many times it ended in frustration.

After a day of aimless running, getting the lay of the land, I ended up mostly just sitting in the large solarium. It was a circular room, surrounded on three sides and three-quarters of the ceiling by glass. I had a view of the Spring Mountains and not much to do. A layer of snow covered the ground, and the pine trees clustered thickly in clumps all around. I wasn't going to get much closer to home for a long time. Or so I thought.

Dmitri would stop by when I hid there, reading a book, mostly to shoot the breeze. At first, I remained deeply suspicious of any information he shared freely.

A day later, listening to him talk about what sounded like old history, I suddenly realized he was briefing me on mission background. Instead of PowerPoint, he chose to do it over coffee and a danish. Much preferable to other techniques, and it kept my mind off the pain in my arm.

At this moment, he was telling me about his time in Germany. Home. He sat on a long, low white couch, legs crossed, sipping an espresso. I lay under a palm tree—real, not fake—and tossed a stale pastry in the air, catching it and tossing it again with my good arm.

"There was a little place on the corner of the street where I lived, had the most amazing sandwiches." Dmitri spoke softly, but I heard every word. When we were together, he spoke in Russian, and I answered in German, sometimes switching it up. Felt good.

"I miss real bread." I caught the pastry and sniffed it. "Not this American *Scheisse.*"

Dmitri raised an eyebrow. "Much superior to the Soviet *xleb.*" He sipped his espresso. "I don't know if you were aware of this, but I was stationed there not as a spy but as a propagandist."

"No shit?" I tossed the pastry back into the air.

"Indeed." His eyes went dark, and in the middle of all the sunshine,

I felt a chill. "That was, of course, the excitement generated over finding a creature such as you."

That was a new one. MONIKER was so used to thinking of me as a supernatural nuke that I hadn't gotten out of the habit of thinking of myself as a weapon. "How so?"

"Well, can you imagine?" The look on Dmitri's face reflected less nostalgia between two old soldiers and more regret at missed opportunities. "The new Soviet superman, half-man, half-beast, capable of great feats in honor of the Motherland. The great Russian wolf against the corrupt American eagle. Oh yes...it could have been amazing."

"I'm not Russian," I said, for lack of anything better to say. "It would have been the German wolf. You guys needed to find a bear or something." I tossed the pastry in the air again, this time with some extra added emphasis.

Dmitri shrugged. "Eventually." He finished his espresso and set it to the side. "Without our test subject, the research stalled and was lost. Sold, I imagine, sometime in the nineties when everyone got rich selling old Russian weapons and tech to the highest bidder."

"And you?" The pastry came down faster than I expected and nailed me in the face. So much for wolf-like reflexes.

"When the wall collapsed, I was on assignment in Germany," Dmitri replied. "Bavaria." He switched to German with a perfect Southern accent. "I assumed the role of a middle-class university intellectual and influenced students to reject the capitalism of their parents."

"Seems a waste of your talents."

"There are always opportunities for talented men." Again, the shark smile. "I was married, had a daughter. When the wall fell, the Russian government...forgot about me."

"That's it?" I asked skeptically. "They lost some paperwork or something?"

"They might have had some assistance."

I believed him. Dmitri had the connections and the wherewithal to fade away, out of the reach of his former organization. Perhaps I should ask him for a few tips.

And yet, there was something else that was bugging me—something just on the edge of thought that kept escaping me. Dread whispered through my bones and, beneath the silver, the change rolled over in the darkness. What was it that scraped against my bones like winter's ice?

A shadow of a doubt that said if Dmitri could erase his own name from the Soviet rolodex, why did he need me now, to do basically the same thing for his daughter? More questions I didn't have the answers for and wasn't sure I wanted him to give me.

"This is the daughter we're tracking?"

"Yes." He leaned back on the sofa, draping one arm alongside the back. "We named her Sofiya. But she doesn't use that name anymore."

"Well, if they don't let me out of here, I'm not going to have much of a chance to help you with your mission."

Dmitri raised an eyebrow. "All organizations are the same. They can't see beyond what they want. We have the advantage here because we know they are no longer working for their best interests."

I sat up, brushing crumbs from my shirt. "What are you talking about?"

"Surely you don't think Director Ramirez is the one calling the shots here?"

"Seemed like the one in charge to me."

Now Dmitri frowned at me like a professor whose pupil had once again proven to not be paying attention. "You've seen the research facility downstairs?"

"Intimately."

"Do you think a man like Doctor Gratusczak obeys the petty commands of a man who wears red flannel?"

"You think G is calling the shots?"

"I wouldn't put it quite that way, but I will tell you this." He coughed and cleared his throat. "In the late nineties, as the gangsters and former KGB were consolidating their hold on the Russian Feder-ation, a group of men—opportunists, soldiers of fortune, former security services—started an organization called *Chernaya Gora*. Black Mountain."

Pretty sure I growled at the mention of their name. The change roiled inside me. I couldn't seem to stop calling it, and every time the silver blocked it from responding, I got a little crazier.

"I see you've heard of them."

"Same outfit killed my pack up in the north," I told him.

He raised an eyebrow.

"Two helicopters full of fat men with rifles and a couple security escorts. They're dead."

"I assumed that would be the case." Dmitri nodded. "When I learned that MONIKER sought your existence, I saw...an opportunity. They needed you; you were already being tracked by the Black Mountain corporation. There was an opportunity to work together."

"How so?" I still didn't quite get it.

"My daughter is extremely smart," he said. "I say that as both a proud father but also as someone who grew up in a place where knowledge and intellect, coupled with a certain crafty nature, could guarantee political success."

I rolled over and got up, stretching.

"She graduated uni with very high marks, speaks several languages, and took to tradecraft like a fish to water," Dmitri said. "Black Mountain recruited her almost as soon as she walked off the graduating stage."

"Your daughter works for the Russians?"

"Against my hopes and my wife's wishes, yes, my daughter worked for the Russians." Dmitri's face hardened. "We were very close. She grew up with stories of what her father did, had no illusions about the man I am. Although she went to work for the new Russians, she never went more than a few weeks without meeting to talk shop with her father."

"How long has it been since you heard from her?" I asked.

"More than six months," he answered. "After two months had passed, I began my own inquiries."

He paused, but I didn't interrupt. We had skirted around this topic probably about a dozen times in the past two days. He would approach it and then back off, telling me another story about the old days, mostly about the interrogation work they'd done or what they'd been attempting before I fell into their hands. On one level, I recognized Dmitri as a master manipulator, and the fact he'd made me feel so at ease with him was a sign I should be running for the hills screaming.

On the other hand, we were already in the hills, and I wasn't running anywhere, so unless I wanted to hide in my room and scream until they strapped me to another kind of table, I might as well enjoy the camaraderie. I certainly wasn't getting it anywhere else.

Dmitri cleared his throat, and I realized I had zoned out. "Sorry, got lost in my own thoughts. You started an inquiry? It go anywhere?"

"At first. Then, I hit a wall." His upper lip curled slightly. "It's madness how quickly the Russian people forgot their history and elected another preening strongman. It…complicated…old loyalties."

Man, did I know *that* feeling.

"I eventually found a former handler of Sof—Maria's, and applied some persuasive techniques," Dmitri continued. "He told me that she had been assigned to a special project. Retrieval of a research scientist who had been working on a project so secret it wasn't even named on her orders. One day she was there; the next, she was gone. But, he said, you can't stop rumors, and for a while, they had been talking about a project called *Byeli Volk.*"

"That sounds familiar." It was Russian for "White Wolf." Although, to be honest, I'm more of a tan and grey fellow, being of central European descent and not one of the far northern packs.

"So you see, the sins of the Father come full circle." Dmitri dug in his pocket and pulled out an old cell phone. By the dings and scratches on the abused device, I recognized it as mine.

"Your country retrieves you, shapes you. My country, or rather, the businessmen running it, attempt to steal you back." He tossed me the phone. "And my daughter is sent to seek you back out."

"Wait." I started pacing, tapping the phone against my thigh, too caught up in thought to wonder how he got his hands on the device.

"Is Doctor Gratusczak—was he working for this Black Mountain outfit when Tell sold me out?"

The people he'd been working with had introduced themselves to me as "The Collective," but names were interchangeable labels, and Black Mountain Holdings struck me as the sort of organization to have very many subsidiaries.

"I would assume so." Dmitri cocked his head. "But I do not think he was loyal to the company. He is a man of science and persistent vision."

"He's an asshole."

"They are not mutually exclusive. But you may want to check your messages. We're about to have company, and I do not expect they will let you keep that if they see it."

Weird. But all right. I flipped the phone open. One whole voice-mail message. It was a new record. I would have deleted it if I hadn't recognized the number, but the tiny letters informed me Randall had tried to get in touch. I pressed "Play."

*Hey buddy, it's me. Listen, I got some news, could be good, could be bad. That skinny blond dude I was telling you about, took your shift, John Pell or whatever, they found him dead up past the ridge we were working. Said it was some kinda animal attack. I don't know. That could be bullshit. I remembered you knew him or something, so I wanted to let you know. If you're coming back, I can get you back on the team, Lara says hi, by the way, so if you come back up, let me know, we'll get—BEEP.*

The machine cut him off. Man did not know how to stop talking.

"They're here," Dmitri said.

Quickly closing the phone, I slipped it into my pocket.

"Calix and your friend Karen," he added.

I looked around. No one else in the room. After a short moment, Karen walked in, followed by the other woman. Not for the first time, I wondered if Dmitri was completely human.

"We have some new information," Karen began.

"You've found John Tell's remains, and you think they might somehow be connected to this other organization that is also pursuing the fabrication of the beast-change," Dmitri said, face completely unreadable. "So, you are going to tell us that this might be a lead for us to follow up in the search for my daughter."

Karen stared.

"I'm not so naïve as to think you agreed to help me in exchange for the simple favor of tracking Rick down," Dmitri told her. "You also hope to learn as much from me as you can in order to control Gratusczak and his research."

Karen didn't react, although Calix raised an eyebrow. The faintest hint of a grin played around her mouth.

"What I'm here for is to offer Rick a chance to get out of his kennel." Karen didn't even look at me. "But if you two want to stay here and trade ancient war stories, be my guest."

Oh, hell, no. If someone wanted to give me a chance to get out of this glass and silver prison, you didn't have to ask me twice.

"When do we leave?"

## 10

The answer to my question was: immediately. I barely had time to grab a couple extra shirts and a muffin I had stashed away from the room they assigned me and report to stairs that led to the roof. Dmitri beat me there. The others showed up about ten minutes later.

I had tried multiple times to enter this stairway but hadn't been successful. It was blocked by a heavy metal door, and you could only get access through a keypad. My skills were more of the tearing the bad guys to pieces variety, and not the hacking my way out of prison sort. Maybe I needed to learn new skills.

Karen punched a code into the keypad, and the door opened. I stepped forward, but she stopped me with an outstretched arm. "Wait."

She drew what looked like a key fob out of her cargo pocket and depressed one of the buttons with her thumb. Something in my cuff clicked and beeped.

"Now, walk through."

Apparently, some of the security measures were not as obvious as a lock and key. I didn't want to know what would have happened if I had tried to walk through without her deactivating whatever had just clicked and beeped. Probably something painful and debilitating.

"Let's go. Our ride's waiting for us at the top."

We headed up the stairs, a motley cast of characters looking nothing like a team of MONIKER professionals on a mission. First, Dmitri in his khakis, button-down shirt, loafers, and a cardigan sweater with leather patches on the elbows. Calix followed, dressed in cargo pants, combat boots, and Rancid T-shirt, sporting a black trench coat that covered her back where she carried her ancient sword.

Then me. Jeans and a T-shirt.

Finally, behind me, Karen. In spite of everything, I couldn't help but feel a frisson of excitement tinged with nostalgia with her at my back in her combat gear. Something had changed, but I would still rather have had her watch my six with the arsenal she carried than anyone else.

About halfway up the stairs, the cold, sweet air began seeping down. I gulped at it, finally freed of the suffocating, burning silver.

We emerged onto a rooftop helipad; a medium-sized aircraft with no markings awaited us. The pilots signaled across the concrete, and Karen gave them the thumbs-up sign.

"All right, let's go," she said. "Keep your heads down. Except you, Rick, you're short enough; you'll be all right."

Was that…a joke at my expense? I grinned like a fool. Karen didn't acknowledge it, just led the way forward.

The pilot had already prepped the aircraft for flight, blades spinning, engine thrumming steadily. We each hopped into the bird, and the copilot met us inside.

"Welcome aboard today's flight on this Boeing Vertol 234," she shouted over the engine noise, showing us the seat straps. "We'll be in the air for less than an hour. Don't touch anything, and if you're looking for in-flight service, you're on the wrong flight. Sit tight, and we'll have you at your desert destination in no time."

We barely had time to settle in before the pilot took off. The helicopter lifted vertically, then swooped forward, banking as we traveled just above the treetops. We flew out of the mountains, coming out over the Red Rock Desert, the rock formations undulating below us, glowing in the afternoon sun.

To the east, the flickering neon lights of Las Vegas beckoned. We turned our back on them, heading west out over the desert.

In the rush of escaping from the facility, the adrenaline started pumping, and the old pre-mission excitement washed over me again. We were rolling out, on the way, and if this team wasn't actually a team—or even close to one—the soldier in me didn't care.

But the change—even before we lifted off, I sensed it, butting against my senses. For one brief moment, as we sped over the snow and pines, I tried to call it, hoping somehow that free of the facility, it would come.

The cuff not only threw up its familiar wall, but it zapped me good, too. When I flinched, I caught Karen's knowing stare. *Shit.* Did Calix know? I had no idea. Woman had her nose pressed up against the glass, watching out the window as we flew on our way.

The high desert eventually gave way to flat, boring desert, and a short time after, signs of civilization began to dot the ground. A long, winding road intersected the plain, heading straight to a larger, built-up area.

The pilot started chatting on the radio, and I figured we must be getting close. Sure enough, about ten minutes later, the copilot popped her head back around.

"We're about five minutes from Twenty-Nine Palms," she shouted. "Make sure you're strapped in for the landing."

Worst in-flight entertainment ever.

On the ground, the heat slapped us in the face. The dry, hot air strangled me, and I wondered if anyone had packed an extra water bowl. With any luck, we wouldn't be on the ground long.

---

My luck stayed about the same as it always does—completely shitty. We were supposed to connect with a military flight that would drop us up north. Instead, an airman with a couple of stripes on his sleeve who couldn't have been much older than my pants approached us, apologizing. Apparently, the plane we were supposed to take to Alaska had broken down in Hawaii and was delayed waiting on repairs. Would we be so kind as to wait in the hangar?

Broken down in Hawaii. I snorted. To my surprise, Karen twitched a lip.

"Lead the way, Staff Sergeant," she told the kid.

Staff Sergeant? They were promoting them young these days. Or maybe I was really too old for this shit.

He led us to the hangar, then to a room made up of four temporary walls thrown up inside the larger space to approximate a waiting room. The accommodations boasted a few rows of plastic chairs, a refrigerator full to the door with generic bottled water, a couple of boxes of muffins, and, against one wall, a stack of boxes of MREs. Yum.

Dmitri sat in one of the chairs, crossed his arms, and immediately fell asleep sitting straight up. Karen disappeared somewhere, probably to go see about the details of our flight. I liked having someone else in charge of logistics.

I grabbed a bottle of water, about to follow Dmitri's example. Until Calix strode up, plopped herself in the seat next to me, picked up my muffin, and unwrapped it.

"Oh. Do you mind?"

"They're free," I told her. "Also, there are about five more boxes over there."

Either she misunderstood, or she didn't give a shit because she started eating it. Whatever. I lay down across several of the chairs, tucked the water bottle under my head, and closed my eyes.

"Rick." Calix kicked the bottom of my foot.

"Jesus, what?"

"Karen says you dated her grandmother."

"I did not." Fine. I guess we were having a conversation. Without opening my eyes, I said, "Karen's grandmother was a woman of discerning taste and intelligence and would have nothing to do with me. Also, she was married."

"Is it true you were a Nazi?"

At this, I opened my eyes. "No."

Ignoring the look I gave her, she added, "And a werewolf?"

"Jesus Christ." Giving up, I sat up, rubbing my eyes. "That's cannibalistic biomorph. Get it right."

"Huh." She polished off my muffin, brushing the crumbs off her pants onto the floor. "The bit in the penthouse and then at the house. I'm still not sure if I can believe what I saw. Is werewolf even the correct name?"

"What?"

"A lot of the knowledge has been lost, but I come from two families who believe in preserving tradition." As if to accentuate it, the familiar old blood and leather smell teased my senses.

"Two families?" Trying to follow this conversation was like walking up a down escalator. I didn't know which way to focus.

"Chumash on my mother's side. Okinawan on my father's," she said. "Although Okinawan by way of California by way of my grandfather joining the Marines to escape the internment camps in World War II, and my father continuing the family tradition."

"That's how you came to work here? Military?"

"Sort of." Throughout the conversation, she kept her voice lowered, as if suspecting Dmitri was not truly asleep. I'd bet on him following the conversation anyway. Man put the word "spook" in spooky.

"I met Karen when we attended a joint military school," she told me. "We hit it off, but after the class ended, we kind of fell out of touch. Few months ago, I broke up with a long-term girlfriend and decided to look her up. I needed a job, too, and the agency was hiring. It worked out."

Seemed plausible enough. So why did I get the feeling I'd missed something? Either that, or she'd deliberately not filled me in on everything.

At that moment, Karen interrupted the conversation, walking up to where we were hanging out.

"Grab your shit. We've got another plane on the tarmac. It's going to take us up to Wainwright. We'll grab some transportation from there."

The woman was a miracle worker. Now if only we could shake her out of whatever state of mind Doctor G had imprisoned her in. Hopefully, once we were out in the woods, I would be able to help her remember herself.

Although I'd planned to talk to Karen once we got on the plane, I fell asleep almost before we took off. The omnipresent silver of the Vegas facility had made for restless nights as the constant pain and mental disruption took their toll. Although the cuff on my wrist blocked the change, at least it didn't gift me with chronic insomnia. Speaking of which, the damn thing refused to respond to any of my attempts to figure out how to pry it off, and more than once, it rewarded me for my efforts with a sharp electrical shock. Unpleasant.

It did move a little, though. It wasn't welded to the skin. I might be able to dislocate my thumb joint. Possibly slip it off. If I got desperate enough or far enough away from the others to do so without getting detected.

I woke up as the plane's landing gear hit the tarmac. Karen had arranged everything, including renting a four-wheel-drive truck to drive to the town. We transferred under the light of a thin, waxing crescent moon. I stood for a moment under the sky, basking in the sweet, crisp cold. Past the rank diesel miasma of jet exhaust, I caught the promise of the north country snow and pines under the starry night sky.

The inability to change, to run, to feel the cold under my paws ripped me apart, especially after so many months wearing that form.

Calix also paused, ignoring Karen's impatience and the hint she sent, turning the key in the ignition. The woman stood, mouth agape, staring at the lights streaming across the sky. Without the benefit of the *Überwechsel*, they were rendered to me in shades of white and gray. But I could wait. The full moon was on its way.

"I've always wanted to see the northern lights," Calix murmured, more to herself than any of us.

"Hey, join MONIKER, see the world, especially all the cold, shitty parts of it," Karen told her, leaning out her window. "Now get in the truck. We need to make time."

Dmitri got into the front passenger's seat without even calling shotgun. Typical. Calix grabbed the seat behind Karen, and so I sat behind Dmitri.

"Rick." Karen glared at me in the rearview mirror.

"What?"

"Roll up your window. Everyone else is freezing."

Grumbling, I obeyed.

"Good boy."

I shared my thoughts with her in the form of my middle finger, where she could see it in the mirror. She ignored me and put the truck in gear.

Maybe I wasn't the only one who found the Vegas facility crazy-making. Maybe all she needed, too, was to get far away from the presence of the evil they were keeping in the basement.

Again, I wanted to talk to her, even with the others there. Since we were all in on each other's secrets. Or at least they were all in on mine.

But again, I fell asleep, not waking up until the sun rose and we were rolling past the airstrip.

***

"Man, you still look like shit."

Randall Tso greeted me outside the diner where Lara worked. She wasn't on duty, but he had agreed to meet us for breakfast, and tell us what he knew about what was going on in town. It never hurt to have as much intel as possible. Dmitri demurred and stayed with the vehicle.

"Eat me," I told him. Randall, that is. Not Dmitri.

"Eat shit?"

"Look who learned to take a hint."

He laughed out loud. "Who are these lovely ladies?"

I winced. I don't know anyone but Randall who would look at two pissed-off Amazons armed to the teeth and refer to them as "lovely ladies." *Please, please,* please, *do not let him make a lesbian joke. I do not need to be picking up pieces of my friend off the street.*

"Randall, this is Dr. Karen Willet, a friend of mine who works investigations for Homeland. And Agent Calix..." I realized I didn't know her last name.

"Just Calix is fine. Nice to meet you, Randall." She extended her hand.

"Thanks, likewise." As they shook hands, I recognized the half-stricken look on his face. It was probably a good thing Lara didn't come with him to meet us. Not that she had anything to worry about. Randall might lose his voice in the presence of a commanding woman, but everything about him screamed loyalty to his new family.

"Shall we go in?" It was my stomach talking. After sleeping as long as I did, I needed food in a bad way.

Randall held the door for the women, who accepted his chivalry. I attempted to follow them, but he went in front of me, leaving me to dodge the door as it closed behind him.

After we'd settled ourselves at the table and placed our order, Karen turned to Randall.

"Rick tells me you worked with one of our former agents, John Tell?"

That's all the encouragement the man needed.

"Yeah, he showed up—oh man, must have been two or three months after this guy disappeared on us." He jerked a thumb at me. "We had an open spot on the shift, and the guy needed a job. He seemed okay, knew his way around the work, didn't bitch and moan like a lot of the new kids, come up from whatever middle-class life they're trying to escape and don't like it that their dream of being an outdoorsman actually requires them to work outdoors, you know?"

I tried and failed to keep the snarky grin off my face. Karen and Calix just stared. It can take a bit of getting used to Randall's stream-of-consciousness blather. He paused for a quick breath and kept going.

"He worked out pretty well, too, but kept to himself, you know? I didn't even know his last name, I kept having to ask Lara—she knew him, came into the diner all the time, she said he said he hated eating alone, so he liked to come in here, order, be around people even though no one ever saw him actually talk to anyone."

At this point, our food arrived, forcing Randall to take a tactical pause to get the orders to the right people. Even before the waitress set the last plate in front of us, he was off and running again.

"Except for a couple of times, those Black Mountain guys were in here. Then I saw him talking to them. Or actually, Lara saw him. She's not nosy or anything, but she really pays attention to her customers. Says it gets her better tips. I think she knows everyone in town by their first and last names—she's the one who told me his last name. Did I tell you that?"

"We're getting a bit off topic here," Karen suggested. I grinned around a mouthful of bacon. She had no idea.

"Oh yeah, sorry." Randall shoved a heaping forkful of eggs into his mouth, and started talking while chewing and swallowing. Lovely. "Anyway, Lara told me that she saw John Tell talking to the Black Mountain guys, which she noticed because, like I said, guy never talked to anyone, but the most interesting thing—" He broke off, coughing. He pounded himself on the chest with his fist, took a sip of coffee, then dug his fork in for more.

"The most interesting thing?" Karen's tone was suspiciously even.

I buried my face in my plate. No way would I let her catch me grinning at her. Then I made the mistake of looking up at Calix. She caught my eye. The corners of her mouth quirked up, and then the two of us were dying of silent laughter, shaking with it.

"What is it with you two?" Karen glared at us, which made us even more hysterical.

Randall swallowed his eggs and continued without showing a sign he had noticed our little exchange.

"The most interesting thing was that Lara said they spoke Russian."

Well. Talk about your anticlimax.

"And Lara, she actually speaks Russian, account of her folks moved here in the eighties, and they talked Russian at home, so she can't really speak it *per se*, except for the cuss words, but she understands it really well, and she said that the Black Mountain guys were really reaming him out, threatening him, asking him for information, telling him he better have something soon. Or else."

"Or else?" Karen asked.

"Yeah," Randall said. "They weren't real specific on that one. But I guess, with what happened, we found out what that meant." He looked over at me. "That's what I meant by I thought that was some bullshit. Because of that conversation."

We ate in silence for a bit after he stopped talking, processing the information.

"Hey, listen," Randall said, finally. Silence was not his style. "I got a friend, works in the Sheriff's department. Which means they also work for the fire chief, the coroner, and the dogcatcher. You want me to call 'em up? Ask to see the body?"

It was a weird kind of macabre offer. But we didn't turn it down.

R ick, hey, this is Agnes. Agnes, this is my friend, Rick." Randall waved his hand around. "And Rick's friends. How ya doin'?"

Agnes stared at Randall over the top of her reading glasses. She manned the desk at the sole entry point to the municipal building. I estimated her age at about fifty years old. Her blond hair was cut in almost a buzz cut, accentuated with a streak of some shading, and she wore a women's suit jacket with a small pin attached to the lapel. Looked like a fist grabbing something.

"What the fuck you want, asshole?"

Some friend. Randall smiled his goofy smile. The one he pasted on when he wanted to ask you to take his shift for him so he could go hunting. "These friends of mine knew the man who was found deceased in a terrible fashion just yesterday. I thought perhaps they could assist the local authorities in their quest to identify the body and possibly bring closure to his poor family."

"Man, you are so full of shit. And don't call me Agnes." The woman, who was apparently *not* called Agnes, stuck a cigarette in her mouth and lit it.

Karen coughed and looked pointedly at the "No Smoking" sign.

"Can it, sweetheart, I work here. You wanna complain? Go talk to the mayor."

"Where can I find the mayor?" Karen retorted, not one to be intimidated by another hardass with a punk attitude.

"*I'm* the mayor, sweetie." The woman stood up from behind the desk, revealing the rest of her outfit: long jeans and hiking boots. She extended her hand. Karen took it, and they did the firm 'I respect you' handshake. "Call me Rose."

"Rose, nice to meet you." Karen indicated the mayor's lapel pin. "What unit is that?"

Rose gave her an approving look. "Good eye. 720th Military Police Battalion, out of Fort Hood. Fort Cavazos, they're calling it now. Did ten years, four deployments, and then got out and moved up here." She tapped her smoke, dropping ash on the already-stained floor. "You serve?"

"Not in the military."

"OGA?" Rose snorted. "Oh wait, you could tell me but...alright, enough bullshit. You wanna go see this guy, we're going to have to make it quick. This one's a little sticky."

"Sticky? Sticky how?" Karen asked. Behind her, Calix paid only cursory attention to the conversation. Instead, she looked around unobtrusively, observing everything—the placement of exits, the number of cars in the parking lot. She caught me watching and shrugged.

"Let me put it this way. I've had a shit ton of bullshit coming down the pike, requesting cooperation with this Black Mountain outfit." Rose spat on the floor, indicating her opinion of what people could do with that request. "Then these federal assholes show up yesterday, kick me and my people out of my office, and decide they're going to take over the place."

"Can they do that?" Why did I ask? I would have preferred to stay comfortably off her radar.

"Of course they can, asshole." I assumed Rose used these epithets as terms of endearment. "Who's going to stop them? There's me and the Sheriff and one whole deputy. If we add the dogcatcher, we'd have a whole army to take them on." She rolled her eyes.

A noise came from around the corner. Rose stubbed out her smoke. "Come on, let's go before someone asks me why the circus is in town."

She led the way outside and around the back of the building. The medical examiner's office was accessible via a separate entrance. As we waited for her to unlock the door, Calix finally spoke up.

"What assholes?"

Rose paused from jiggling the key in the lock. "Could you be a little more specific, honey?"

"You said, 'these federal assholes,'" Calix said. "Who are they?"

"I did say that." Rose gave up trying to fiddle with the lock. "Stand back." We moved out of her way. She stepped back, then forward again. As she did so, she landed a solid kick in the middle of the lock plate. The door popped open. "Come on in. That door sometimes sticks, so you gotta help it along."

"I'd like to have had her on my breaching team back in Tal Afar," Calix muttered to me as she passed me to file inside with Karen.

"You coming?" I paused inside the door. Randall had made no move to follow.

"No way, man," he said. "I don't need to see that when I'm trying to go to sleep at night."

Fair enough. I followed the women inside, closing the door in time to hear Rose answer Calix's question.

"They said they were FBI," she said, flipping on a series of light switches. Fluorescents flickered on, humming overhead as they started to get brighter. "I called this morning once I got in, tried to find out what the hell was going on, but all I got was some puke in a suit telling me they can't comment on an ongoing investigation." She disappeared inside a small closet, then came back out holding a box of face masks. "So much for professional fucking courtesy, right? Assholes. I put in a request for more info, but I'm still waiting for them to call me back. Whatever, I'm not holding my breath. You want one of these?"

Karen and Calix each took one. I turned her down. That's not how my nose works.

"All right. We're going to go in there, you're going to take a look, tell me if it's your friend, and then you're going to piss off out of here, got it?"

We nodded all around.

"Why did you get out after ten years?" Calix's question stopped Rose momentarily. "You were halfway to retirement. Why not just finish it out and get your money?"

Rose brushed her chin with her fingers as if unconsciously groping for a smoke. "Army?"

The look of horror on Calix's face. Heh. "Marines." I swear she sniffed.

"Huh." Rose shrugged. "I left on my own terms with no regrets." She cast an eye around the three of us. "Can you say the same?"

Didn't realize my head was that easy to get into, but somehow her words lodged in my brain like an earworm, winding around and around as we followed her into the back room.

***

John Tell and I had a complicated past. He'd sold me out, but before he did, he'd been a teammate and someone I'd trusted with my life. Hell, we'd even shared drinks after beating the shit out of each other. Which is as close to a bro moment as I'd come in a long time before meeting Randall.

There had been an unexplained bitterness underlying his laser focus on the mission. Glimpses of something he'd only ever let out one time at the bottom of a Pilsner glass and then shut down.

He'd died a hard death. A death someone who had once been a soldier didn't deserve. The first time we'd met, he'd grinned at me through the bars of the cage. Whatever had caught up with him had left a mockery of the same grin, twisted in a rictus across a face that displayed unimaginable pain.

"I'll be outside." I couldn't stay inside. Karen didn't answer. She bent over Tell's body, observing. Calix's expression remained neutral, but she nodded.

Rose followed me outside into the snow, patted my back as I lost every bit of my breakfast against the side of the building, and held me so I wouldn't sink to my knees in the middle of the mess.

She pulled me to the other side of the building, away from the door. It didn't help. I could still smell the decay even from outside the morgue.

"Good buddy of yours?" She pulled her pack of smokes out of her suit jacket, tapped two out, and handed me one.

At first, I waved it off. I hadn't had a smoke since the Cold War.

"Are you sure?" She left it out in front of me.

"Yeah, you know what? Thanks." I accepted the cigarette. She used her lips to pull the other one out of the pack, then took a lighter out of her pocket.

She lit my smoke, then hers. The first drag made me cough, but I took another one and then another, and like that I was back in the habit. It didn't make me want to run right out and buy a pack of my own, but for a moment it gave me something to do. And it deadened the smell somewhat.

"No, no, he wasn't."

"Sorry?" She raised an eyebrow.

"He wasn't a real good buddy." The memory of his betrayal stung deep, the attack in Germany that had left Karen and me at the mercy of Gratusczak and his mad science.

But there was also the time we'd shared drinks—and the experience of being O.C. sprayed by Karen. And training together. Karen had told me he'd been a cop in New York. I'm sure that came with its own special set of demons.

The cigarette was in danger of going out. I took another drag. What lay in the morgue told a story of someone who had made some wrong decisions but had received something far beyond justice for his sins.

"There was a kid in my platoon, real asshole," Rose began. "Didn't do shit unless you were standing right over him, telling him exactly what to do, making sure he did it." She stubbed out her cigarette and fished for her pack. "That kid...you know the saying, ten percent of your troops are gonna take up ninety percent of your time?"

I'd never heard the saying. But the concept was familiar. Before MONIKER had gotten its hands on me, I'd worn a uniform in the service of my country. Different country. Different uniform. But soldiers have more in common with each other than many civilians would like to think, no matter what side they were on.

"Anyway," Rose continued. Not sure if she was talking for my benefit or hers. "One day, we're heading out to patrol a village. Just a little cordon and knock, say hi, do some community liaison shit." She coughed and spit. "No, wait, it was a well opening. Or something like that. Whatever, doesn't matter. We were out, on our way, and we got hit."

She said it simply, without a lot of drama. But I knew what she meant.

"Bad?"

"Yeah. Real bad." Rose let the cigarette burn for a little while. "This kid...didn't make it. I mean, he got hit right off the bat. No chance for redeeming heroics, no chance for anyone to get to him. Just boom. Dead."

A car passed out on the road, sporting the Black Mountain logo. She watched it as it sped away. After it had left, she took another drag.

"Well, the rest of us got it together, suppressed the attack, withdrew, did all the right things. I mean, by this time, we were about six months in. We knew what we were doing, had all the right reactions; if there were a fucking textbook, you'd see our damn platoon was in it."

Rose shook her head. "His death messed more people up than any other soldier we lost. Why was that?" She answered her own question. "People didn't know how to mourn. I mean, I wanted to cry. I'd lost a fucking troop." She swiped at her eyes with the palm of her hand. "But I felt like a fucking hypocrite, too, right? Like, I'm an asshole because I'm fucking sad and pissed, and I never fucking liked that guy when he was alive." She cracked her neck, blinking, then stubbed out her cigarette. "Shit."

"Yeah." There wasn't much to add.

Randall came around the corner of the building. "Hey, you guys—where's the others? Still inside?"

In answer, Karen and Calix emerged from the building, looking around for us.

"Over here!" Randall called.

I let the cigarette fall to the ground and stubbed it out. The temperature had dropped about fifteen degrees, enough to become really uncomfortable, even for me. As Karen shook hands with Rose, thanking her for her help, I tucked my hands under my armpits to keep them warm.

The change drifted across my mind. *Zap.* I jumped. Stupid cuff. I was just thinking about it, for crying out loud.

*Zap.*

Jesus Christ.

"Calix, why don't you run Randall back to his car?" Karen spoke, interrupting my private game of Operation. "Rick and I will meet you at the place. I'll text you the reservation info. Get Dmitri. We're going to need to game plan this out."

Calix raised her eyebrow again, glared at me, then gathered up Randall and started heading back. He was talking her ear off before they made it more than ten yards.

"I'd better be heading back to my desk," Rose said. "The good people of this shithole don't pay me to sit around showing tourists the sights."

"Thank you very much for your assistance, Mayor," Karen said.

"Any time," Rose responded. "You need anything else, stop on by."

"Really?" I asked.

"I'm being polite," she said. "Actually, fuck off."

I laughed and shook her hand. "Thanks for the smoke."

"Good luck," she replied, holding her other hand over mine for a split second before relaxing her hold. "I mean that."

Karen was silent until we were out earshot, then: "Seems like you made a friend."

"She was enabling my smoking habit."

She side-eyed me. "You don't have a smoking habit."

"That you know about." That earned me a slight quirk at the side of her mouth. It might have been trying to be a smile.

"Hit you, too." Karen's face remained stoic. No sign except her words that she'd felt anything outside clinical detachment standing over Tell's mangled remains.

"Yeah." If it helped her for me to admit it. "Yeah. He was an asshole, but he was a partner for a short time, and no one deserves a death like that."

"Yeah." She blew out her breath, swinging her arms, shaking out the tension. "So, what did you find out?"

"The mayor likes to smoke and tell war stories."

"Not that, dick." Karen didn't smile, but it felt good for her to call me a dick. Meant she still maintained part of herself somewhere in there. "What did you learn from his body?"

I shivered. The cold reached under my skin with its long, bony fingers.

"He died scared," I said. "They worked him over for a while." The scent of dried urine had been overpowering; she had probably noticed it. What she wouldn't have realized, discerned, were the subtle differences that told the story of losing control of his bladder, drying, then again, and again. Someone had tortured him and not let him go for a long time before he died.

"And?" Karen's voice was cold and tight.

"Someone was treating him between sessions—I could smell the antiseptic and the bandages. Not sure if it was the guy questioning him or whatever killed him."

"You couldn't tell?"

I shook my head. "It's weird. I can get all this...pain. Blood." The change nudged up against me. I searched for the right words to explain how I knew what I knew. It wasn't just the smells I could pull up—I'm not a fucking basset hound. It came from more than that. It stemmed from the same energy that powered the change and guided my senses.

And what Tell's body told me was much more than the fact that he'd pissed his pants.

A sense void hovered over Gratusczak. The man not only didn't have a scent, he was surrounded by a sense vacuum.

Standing near John had plunged me into the weirdest sense of déjà vu, as if some of Gratusczak's void had drifted over me. I didn't know what it meant, but it made sense, I guess. He'd dealt with the doctor before, but that had been almost a year ago.

"Anything else?"

"Whatever did that wasn't an animal," I told her. "Not sure if it was human."

"That's less than helpful."

A horn honked two short blasts somewhere in front of us. Our vehicle headed toward us, Calix behind the wheel. She pulled up next to us and popped up the locks.

The windows were up, thanks to the cold. Karen moved to get in the car, and I placed my hand on her arm. She recoiled, and I stepped back. Quickly.

"There was one other thing, don't know how helpful it'll be."

"Yeah?"

"Whoever he was hanging out with smelled of shitty cognac."

"Could he have been drinking it?"

"Nah, it wasn't that; it was…more like someone who drank it regularly rubbed up against him. Like, carrying him or escorting him."

Karen nodded. "Intel is intel." She went to open the door again.

"Karen—"

She stopped.

"What?"

"What's going to happen with his…remains?" I touched my St. Jude medal. They'd given it back to me with my belongings. Everything except my damn notebook.

For just a moment, her face softened. "I think he had family in New York. MONIKER will reclaim the body. We'll find some polite fiction to give them with his remains."

At that moment, Calix rolled down a window. "Will you two get in the car? I'm getting a crick in my neck trying to eavesdrop."

That was the last time Karen and I spoke of our old partner. I'd like to say I never see his savaged face when I close my eyes, but if I did, it would be a lie.

## 12

From the way Karen had said it, I'd thought she'd either rented someplace or gotten us a hotel room. It turned out to be somewhere in between. She'd found the place Tell had rented in town and the fact he'd paid up in rent until the end of the month, and so Calix had gone over there, pretended to be Tell's girlfriend here in town after hearing about the awful tragedy that had befallen her true love, and presto! We had a key and a place to stay, and nobody knew we were there.

"Surprised they didn't lock this place down," I said, stepping over the raised threshold. "Crime scene and all."

"Not really," Karen said. "His body was found miles from here. They probably gave it a quick search, removed anything incriminating, and forgot about it."

It felt beyond weird to be there in the place Tell had been living. And yet, almost nothing in there indicated he had ever stepped foot in the place.

The apartment was a room with a bath that had been part of a larger house. Someone had walled off the connecting door, so we had a modicum of privacy. I couldn't find a stove, but a counter ran along part of one of the walls, and he'd set up a hot plate and electric kettle.

A mini-fridge underneath completed the kitchen set-up. I wondered how everyone would react if I checked it for a beer. Hm.

Aside from the bed, there was a table with two chairs set up around it, and a desk with another chair. We gathered around the table, leaving one of us the odd man out.

Normally I would have had no problem stretching out on the bed and letting them plan our tactical approach, especially since Karen usually did the planning. Her plans were always smart and practical; all I needed was for her to point me in the right direction.

As tired as I was, I'd rather hop back on Gratusczak's lab table than John Tell's empty bed. And also, while I still trusted Karen, her instincts were shot. Something told me I should stay awake and keep an eye on what they were up to.

"All right, let's figure this out." Karen pulled a tablet out of her bag and laid it on the table where everyone could see. She placed a wireless mouse and keyboard in front of her.

Dmitri took the second chair. Calix pulled up the third, flipped it around, and straddled it, resting her folded hands on the table. "What have we got?"

Guess that left me odd man out. I wasn't about to stand, hovering over someone's shoulder. I decided to sit down and rest against the wall. With any luck, they'd forget I was there, and I could catch a nap. Or keep trying to get this damned cuff off my wrist.

"Our primary mission is to find Maria," Karen said. "As Mr. Nicolaiov has shared with us, the latest intel points to a branch or some other kind of subsidiary of this firm, Black Mountain."

"All they've got up here is some kind of dinky operation ferrying sport hunters out over the mountains," Calix said. "This can't be the main effort. It's too small."

"That may be so, but we know they were connected to John Tell, who is connected to Rick, and so it's likely that this operation is a front for their continued pursuit of our biomorph." The way she explained it seemed pretty logical. And cold. Karen continued. "I'd like to start here, with some initial surveillance."

"I don't know, it seems like we have limited resources and time,"

Calix returned. "We may make better use of those resources by starting with one of the larger branches. Maybe even the head-quarters."

"Good point, but we'll have to make a trade-off." Karen clicked through a few screens until she came to a PowerPoint slide. I stifled a moment of panic that we were going to have to sit through another briefing, but this one simply displayed a wire diagram. "Black Mountain hosts hundreds of smaller organizations under its umbrella. Some, official stamped, aboveboard, legal, all that. Some, we only have a few hints at their existence."

"Some, they allow you to see so that you will not look any harder," Dmitri interjected.

His interruption threw Karen off for a moment. If she were on her game, she would have rolled with it, but instead, she took a moment to re-gather her thoughts.

"And…uh…yes. Sorry. That is why we'll start with basic surveillance of their operation here." She turned to Calix. "You and Dmitri will approach them, posing as vacationing father and daughter. Dmitri—is there any way that they might recognize you? Know you?"

"Is always a danger," Dmitri said. "But the people running these disgusting bullshit tours? No. They will not."

"Dmitri, this language—*es geht nicht.*"

He chuckled, drily. *"Danke, Herr Wolf."*

"All right, while you're doing that, check out as much of the grounds as possible. Ask questions, see where the areas are where you're not allowed—"

"Karen, it's not my first op," Calix reminded her.

"Understood," Karen acknowledged with a nod. "Sorry. While you're doing that, I'll work the phones and the web, see what information can be found on Black Mountain. From MONIKER and whoever else."

"And then I'll go back in at night, find out what's in all the areas we're not allowed in?" Seemed a pretty safe guess. After all, the ability to change was what endeared me to the agency in the first place.

"No," Karen said, surprising me. "You'll stay here. Wait. We'll—"

"Like hell I will." Off her game or no, friend or no, I'd just about had it with this bullshit. "Look, we've worked together before. Covert is what I'm good at. Give me a good reason why I won't be following up with a furry visit to our Black Mountain comrades."

"MONIKER has not given you authorization to change," Karen said. "There's no reason, either, for me to take that cuff off you."

Oh, the cuff. That made it all clear.

"Dr. Willet," I began, formal and unpleasant, biting at each word. "I do not give a shit what you think you will allow me to do. I gave my word I would come to help Dmitri. I didn't think you would need more than my word to believe I would do what you need me to do."

The change inside me growled along, fueling the bitterness that poured out of me. "This—" lifting my hand to show the cuff, "—is pure, utter crap. You don't need it to control me. You have the tracker. And my word, which I may have mentioned." Calix and Dmitri stared at me intensely. Karen stared at the tablet screen.

Hoping my poker face was good to go, I spread all my cards on the table in a giant bluff. Hey, they'd just taken me on a vacation to the strip. Viva Las Vegas, baby.

"Here's the deal." I stood up and stepped to the table, leaning on it, forcing Karen to look at me. "I will not work for MONIKER while this cuff remains on my wrist. And if you leave me behind on this mission, I will go find Randall and have him remove my hand with his chainsaw, and then I will change into myself right in front of him to see if my body will cleanse me of this tracker."

"Will your body heal itself from that?" Calix asked.

"I have no idea." I really didn't. I've had body parts mangled beyond recognition but never completely removed. Thus, the bluff.

My words dropped a curtain of silence over the room. A minute passed. Then another. Someone in another part of the house flushed a toilet. Finally, Karen nodded.

"I will take the cuff off. On one condition."

"And that is?"

"The first time you disappear on me, I will track you back down, ship you back to the Las Vegas facility, strap you down to the table in Gratusczak's lab, and leave you there."

Close enough. "Deal."

Karen ignored my extended hand, leaving it hanging awkwardly in the air. She fished in her bag and pulled out a small plastic and metal box with a square touchpad on one end. Depressing the pad with her thumb, Karen waited until something inside beeped, and a hidden drawer clicked open.

She withdrew a thin, circular piece of metal with raised ridges engraved in a wavy pattern all over one side.

"Give me your wrist."

Karen slid the piece of metal into a slot on the cuff. The device beeped and whirred, and then the pieces separated. She slid the cuff off my wrist and shoved it in her bag.

The full force of freedom hit me with a gale of longing for the change.

"Rick." Karen gave me a warning glare. "Stay with us."

"I'm staying. Woof." I stuffed both hands into the pockets of my jeans and sat back down.

I meant every word of the condition she extracted from me. I wasn't going anywhere. But with the cuff off, I could move ahead with not just Dmitri's mission, but my unspoken plan. That, and the promise of a chance to sneak around in someone else's highly secure facility, had me almost bouncing with anticipation.

Also, it hadn't escaped my attention that Karen—not MONIKER—had made the decision to set me free. Perhaps, out here, away from Gratusczak's shadow, she could become herself again. Perhaps, between Calix and myself, we could get her out of there. Things were looking up.

---

We decided the risk outweighed the rewards if we sent Dmitri and Calix in wearing any kind of digital tracking or recording devices.

And by "we decided," I mean Dmitri suggested casually something along the lines of Black Mountain likely being the paranoid type of outfit that would screen even the most innocent-seeming of visitors, and it didn't make sense to jeopardize the mission when you had two people who were trained in observation and surveillance. Everyone just nodded along and found it impossible to disagree with such logic presented so reasonably. And that is why I find Dmitri so damn scary.

Calix and Dmitri jaunted off to see about going on a helicopter ride. Karen and I were left hanging out in a dead man's apartment, staring at the walls in an effort to avoid staring at each other.

"I need one of those tennis balls Steve McQueen had in *The Great Escape.*"

Karen sat hunched in her chair, arms folded, head down. I wasn't sure if she was napping or not until she looked up at me. "Huh?"

"Steve McQueen? *Great Escape?*" No recognition. "Only one of the greatest movies of all time."

"I've heard of it." Karen sat up, stretching her back. "Never saw it."

I feigned shock. "Your education in the classics is sadly lacking."

"Now you sound like my mom," she retorted.

"She sounds like a smart woman." I hid a smile, not wanting to jeopardize this tentative repartee we had going on.

"She was," Karen answered thoughtfully. "She was highly intelligent. Disappeared into the ivory tower after I was born, was suitably horrified when I chose the military for a profession." She shrugged. "I somewhat redeemed myself when I took—"

I waited, but that was all she had. With an unreadable expression, she ignored the awkwardness of the hanging conversation and went to dig her weapons out of one of the bags. She set her M4 on the table, along with two pistols, a few knives, and assorted cleaning equipment.

"Want some help?"

Wordlessly, she handed me the knives, a cloth, and a sharpening set.

"Excellent!" I stared straight at her, calling just enough of the change to me to pop a handful of claws. Picking up one of the sharpening stones, I ran the claws up and down. "But really, are you sure you don't just have a nail file I could us?"

"You are…" Karen paused in disassembling the M4 to show me how she was not laughing. "…such an ass."

She had much too strong a poker face to let on, but deep under her words, I heard a ghost of her old self stir to life.

An alert sounded on her tablet, breaking up any chances of the moment going anywhere.

"Finally." Karen pushed her hair back from her face, tying it back with an elastic from around her wrist.

"Your eHarmony profile went live?"

"Rick, you keep disappearing into the woods and coming back out ten years later in cyber years." She didn't spare me a look as she started using both the keyboard and touchscreen to manipulate whatever commanded her attention.

I scooted my chair around to see what she was doing, then immediately scooted back. The program she worked with, CRIMAN, was a criminal analysis software that networked research from various sources into a wire diagram. The last time I'd watched her work her magic with the data, I'd almost gotten sick from the motion.

This time, she browsed through the data much more slowly, clicking, reading for a moment, manipulating something on screen, clicking again.

"There's not much here," she muttered.

"Are you talking to me?"

Karen looked up from the screen. "Sorry. Talking to myself."

"And what are you saying?"

"That this corporation is really good at making themselves look… good." She clicked again, scanning through, her eyes twitching back and forth. "I've got some of the cyber whizzes back at the New York agency connecting dots all over the globe, crawling all over the dark web, trying to make sure we get as complete a picture as possible. Every single little…"

She dove back into the screen. This whole trailing off midsentence and leaving me hanging was getting annoying.

"And what does the picture look like?"

"Like a fucking Thomas Kinkade English cottage. All pretty and sparkling, and I know it's fucking fake." She sat back, grabbed her M4, and started to clean its innards, brushing away at what appeared to be an already-pristine bolt carrier assembly. "I just can't figure out..."

"How? Why?" I prompted.

Karen stared into space, her hands falling at rest on the pieces of the weapon.

"Karen, what the fuck is going on with you?"

As soon as I said it, I wanted to punch myself in the face. Dumbass. She wasn't the only one off her game.

She didn't answer right away. Instead, she carefully put the M4 back together. With practiced movements, she performed a functions check, locked the bolt back, and laid it on the table. Then, she looked up at me, gazing straight at me.

"Rick. Back off."

Without another word, she got up, shrugged on her jacket, and headed out the door, letting it slam behind her.

***

Karen walked back in about ten minutes before Dmitri and Calix returned. She carried a cardboard box full of take-out from the diner and completely ignored me and everything that had passed between us. Instead, she plopped the box of food down on the table, pulled out her tablet, and started back again reviewing intel.

Not one to wait for an invitation, and starving once again, I helped myself to a couple of burgers and a plate of fries.

"Hey, you two, shame you missed the adventure." Calix stamped her feet as she came in the door. Dmitri, holding it for her, did the same. It had started snowing, and the fresh powder clung to their boots and the bottoms of their pants.

Karen mumbled something and sat back down in front of her tablet, diving deep into her data. I didn't miss the look Calix threw her before meeting my eyes. Her eyes tightened in an imperceptible shrug before sitting down with Dmitri and me to make a dent in the food.

Not that I needed any help. In fact, I was considering helping myself to pieces of them if they got too greedy with the fries.

"The facility is much as expected," Dmitri began. He smoothed his napkin on his lap, brushing away an imaginary crumb. "Very comfortable, with beautiful women to bring us fresh coffee and convince us to spend all our money to remain in their presence."

"Damn," I said. "Sounds like my kind of place."

"Mine, too," Calix responded without missing a beat.

I snorted. Dmitri kept going without acknowledging either of us.

"There was very nice presentation," he said. "Not much information, but lots of pretty pictures."

"Did they show their fucking hunting parties?" The words came out spitting. "The blood and fur in the snow? Nice white and red for the perfect contrast."

"As a matter of fact," Dmitri said, "they mentioned they are having quite the season. Talked lots about all the rich people they fly out on their special tours."

"Didn't mention the ones who didn't come back," Calix said, again without missing a beat.

"Did you get any useful information?" Karen looked up from her tablet. The uncharacteristically harsh note and impatience in her voice grated up and down my spine.

Calix threw her another look, but she ignored it.

"Time is finite, and we need to go in. Tonight." Karen turned the tablet off and adjusted her chair to face us. "Let's cut the shit and get to business. You," she pointed to Calix. "I want you two to run ops. Rick and I will go in."

That didn't make tactical sense. Why would we not bring Calix, who had the benefit of having laid eyes on the facility? I thought it; Calix said it.

"I've just spent the day wandering around their facility, trying not to stab people who kept staring at my ass, and you want me to stay here instead of running point?"

"Do you want to argue with me some more? Or get this mission going?" Karen stared at her.

I kept eating. Everything was awkward, but I had hunger. Dmitri also ignored the interplay between the two. He meticulously finished his dinner, wiping imaginary crumbs away from the corner of his mouth with the precision of old-school European table manners.

Finally, Calix rolled her eyes. "Fine. We'll run ops. You two go have fun getting lost."

The rest of the time before we left was filled with an uncomfortable silence. No one wanted to talk about their feelings in a big group hug, so we just prepped as best we could and avoided saying anything to each other outside of the few words necessary to do our mission prep.

Mission prep, for us, involved Karen strapping on a variety of weapons of different shapes and calibers. We typically moved unencumbered, except for what we carried on our bodies, and this mission was no exception. Of course, for me, that meant an ear bud. Usually.

Except now, Karen handed me a vest and a pistol.

"What the hell is this?" I stared at her. Wolves don't have opposable thumbs.

"You're not going in furry," she told me. "Ramirez's orders. You're supposed to be still wearing the cuff, remember?"

I did remember. I'd hoped she didn't. Maintaining eye contact, I took off my shirt, then my pants. Dmitri and Calix both pretended they weren't looking.

Karen's face didn't show me anything. I swear, if we got back to Vegas in one piece, I was taking her to play the tables.

Waiting for her to shoot me or spray me or tase me or whatever, I called the change, nice and slow. It came this time in a wave that was so slow as to be wiseass enough for me. Fun effect, slow motion, even as the usual pain of the change ripped through my body. I sweated, trying not to whimper until the last bone had rearranged itself, and I stared at her with teeth bared.

"I hope it was worth it." Karen didn't smile or acknowledge the joke, but the ghost of a chuckle whispered in her deadpan tone. She rolled her eyes and checked to ensure her earbud wasn't going anywhere. "Let's go."

13

We drove to a secluded road not too far from the compound but out of sight of prying eyes. With little delay and no conversation, we left the vehicle, ghosting out past the outskirts of the town and cutting a broad swathe through the woods to come up on the secluded back entrance to the facility.

The waxing moon threw half shadows over our paths as Karen and I made our approach. The soft powder under our feet left me incredibly glad I had taken wolf form, able to run without sinking too far in. Karen, on the other hand, cussed and swore—tactically, of course—as she slogged through the damp flakes, every once in a while breaking through the snow's crust. Luckily, the snowfall kept up, blanketing our tracks and deadening any noise we made.

Karen had foregone her usual black in favor of cargo pants and a long-sleeve tactical shirt in mottled grays and whites. I mean, I assumed that was the camo scheme she was going with, as true grays show up a little more intensely in my monochrome sight.

It took us a little more than an hour to get situated. Karen scanned the facility with a night vision optical device, a mono lens that sat on her helmet and came down over one eye. I scanned the facility the usual way, cataloging scents and their intensities, letting the energy waft over me and whisper the secrets they thought they were keeping.

"Ops, we're in position." Karen's whisper barely carried to the radio mic at her lips. "I'm detecting no movement." She looked over at me from where she lay in the prone position. "Rick hasn't alerted on anything."

What the hell was I—a drug-sniffing dog?

Thinking uncharitable thoughts, I raised my head, prowling back and forth, careful to stay out of her line of fire. We had circled so far around we were now surveilling a loading dock. From the aroma of rotting vegetables and sour milk, they used this primarily to stock their cafeteria. The wind picked up, and another scent snuck by. Hm. Caviar. Been a while since I'd found myself in the vicinity of that delicacy.

And vodka. Oh hey. I dropped to my belly. A man dressed to ward off the weather approached. I'm not going to say he was drunk at work, but he had certainly taken a slug to ward off the cold. Maybe two slugs.

As he neared our position, he shivered and stomped his feet. Although he carried a rifle, he dangled it loosely in one hand while he blew on the other, trying to keep warm, and then switched off. Clearly, the man was more concerned about the warmth at the end of the shift than keeping watch. I didn't blame him. The snow had picked up, swirling around us with a vengeance.

As the man passed, I gathered my legs under me and leapt. My momentum caught him in the middle of switching hands, and I bore him to the ground with little resistance. A snap of my jaws at his throat, and his blood spilled in a dark spray across the snow.

I panted and glanced back at Karen. She nodded and got up. I led the way across the short expanse to the loading dock, sparing a moment of regret for the salty heat rapidly cooling behind us. But I'd already eaten, so I wasn't that upset. Besides, steak is better with fries, and we'd scarfed those all back in the room.

There's something particularly satisfying about sneaking around places where you're not supposed to be, especially when the people who inhabit them go to great lengths to keep you out. The loading dock was deserted. Two standard doors flanked three giant metal sliding doors, the kind that could roll up to accommodate the fast load and unload of food and alcohol deliveries. The smaller doors were secured with keypads and double bolts. The sliding doors were padlocked at the bottom, one lock per door.

Maybe they weren't worried. Maybe they were relying on someone to be watching the security feed religiously. Maybe they didn't give a shit because this was a little dinky outpost in the middle of nowhere, and people got bored looking at snow and ferrying rich assholes around.

And maybe you should pay more attention to your security manager.

Karen popped one of the locks in fifteen seconds, rolled the door up about a foot and vanished inside. I followed suit. With the vanishing inside, I mean. It's hard to pick locks when your opposable thumbs have turned into dewclaws.

I barely had time to whisk my tail from under the door before it slammed closed, and we were inside.

The building immediately reminded me of the casino we'd walked through in Vegas—the same smell of perfume and sweat, the warren-like floor plan designed to get people lost and prevent them from leaving too quickly or easily. Once again, my mind flashed back to Calix and wished she were here to give us the benefit of her recon.

As if on cue, her voice sounded in our earbuds.

"You're going to head down the first hall, then make your first right and..." We lost the rest to static.

Karen paused, fiddling with the wire that attached her earbud to the radio ALICE-clipped to her vest. "Say again?"

"First right. Second left." Pause. Calix left the button depressed on her end, so we heard a quick staticky back and forth. "That's it. First right, second left and you'll see a door marked 'Private'."

By now, we'd passed the first right and had to turn and retrace our steps. The turn led to a short corridor, along which branched several more halls. The sense I got from what I could glean from the stale air was that the hallway we were in bisected the building. To our right, smells of comfort—leather, electronics, food. To the left, I caught scent-shots of canvas, grease, and a pervasive cold, as well as tobacco.

"This way." Karen took the lead at the second left, and ta-da, we'd completed our quest. The first door in the short throughway was the one we were looking for. "Anyone around?"

I chuffed and pawed the door. I don't know if she expected me to answer. In my other form I could, but for now I was just your garden variety *canis lupus.* So to speak. Or not.

With a callous disregard for Karen's eyesight, I called the change, and suddenly the hallway got much colder. Luckily, we were both in deep shadows, because some things were not meant to be exposed to those temperatures.

"What's up?" Karen pulled a small box from a pocket on her pants and placed it on the door's digital entry key. On the surface, an LED display began circling through numbers. I thought that shit only existed in spy movies.

"There's a bank of servers behind this door," I told her. "Motor pool is through the door at the end of the hall—I can smell the metal and gas."

"What's through there?" Karen nodded at the third and last door in the short hallway. She didn't actually sound interested, but I told her anyway.

"Bathroom."

"Good to know."

"With a supply closet. Lots of bleach. Drain cleaners. Fun stuff."

"Also good to know."

The numbers on the LED stopped cycling. Karen popped the door open and slipped inside. For both our sakes, I called the change back.

Also, I'd detected a very interesting scent and thus needed my nose to be in proper working order.

While Karen did whatever she needed to do with the computer, I padded back the way we came and headed toward the comfortable part of the building. We'd had some good luck so far, but since I don't believe in good luck, I wanted to find out what was making my nose twitch.

As soon as we'd entered, I'd picked up small rustles, the sorts of noises that came from far away but were loud and urgent at the source. I followed the trail around the corner, staying to the side of the corridor as much as possible. Most security cameras were set in the middle of the ceiling, aimed at picking up the movements of persons as tall as the average male.

Not only am I short, but as a wolf, I'm pretty much a ghost on a shitty surveillance system. Amateurs.

A quick burst of Russian came from an open door about twenty meters ahead of me, answered by a chuckle and a friendly insult. The men in the room were more interested in watching whatever was causing both of their erections rather than keeping an eye on the screen where they might have spotted us wandering around. Oh well.

I crouched low to the ground in the shadows outside the open door, muscles tensed, ready to spring at my prey.

"Rick, come in," crackled in my ear. "Where the fuck are you?"

Karen needed to work on her timing. I shook my head, then scraped it along the ground for good measure, dislodging my earbud. Free of Jiminy Cricket whispering in my ear, I crouched again. Saliva dripped from my jowls.

I ignored the familiar scent of rosemary behind me until—

"Jesus Christ, Shaggy, what the hell?" This time, the urgent whisper came not through my ear but from a very pissed-off Dr. Karen Willet, who had come up whisper-silent behind me. "We're not leaving any bodies on this one."

Killjoy. I whined and slunk back, leaving the Young Pioneers to their vodka and pornography.

All this effort to go sneaking around and breaking in, and we didn't even get to set a bomb or anything. Karen had just used the bleach to wipe down the surfaces where she'd touched the door and the computer out of necessity. Boring.

Head hanging, grumbling to myself, I followed her down the

hallway and back to the loading dock, where once again, we prepared to slip unnoticed through the door and head on our way.

"*Stoi! Chto vi dyelaesh?*"

So much for slipping away unnoticed. The light flipped on over-head, blowing out Karen's night vision and burning my eyes.

An alarm started up, blaring with an ear-piercing harsh electronic tone. Lights placed along the corridor flashed and strobed in time with the siren.

There were four of them—two approaching from each side, at least one of them still buttoning his pants. They each carried an AK-47 at the ready, with an additional pistol on a drop holster at their legs.

"*Ne dvigaitesh.*"

"Shit." Karen dropped to the floor into a prone position. The hallway was long and free of anything that could conceivably be used for cover—except for me.

The first bullet tore into my side, stitching a fiery seam across my thigh. *Scheisse!* Forgot how much getting shot sucks.

Time slowed. Behind me, Karen depressed the trigger of her weapon, returning fire with fire. One of the teams pulled back, their aim stymied by their friends who, by shooting at us, lined them up for some fratricide.

Ignoring the first shocking burst of pain, I scrambled back to my feet. I sprinted toward the two men firing at us.

They were semi-disciplined, taking turns. The first man fired three to six rounds, covering his buddy's approach. Then, he'd take a knee, and commence to fire. If they'd had any sort of talent at aiming whatsoever—and silver bullets—I'd probably be bleeding out in some oligarch's private freak collection right about now.

Instead, I darted left, then right, then straight ahead. In the space of a muttered Slavic curse, I leapt on the first man's throat. He screamed. The sound lasted a half second before he choked on his own blood.

The second man's rifle clicked. The bolt chamber opened on an empty magazine. Rather than trying to reload, he dropped his rifle and fumbled for his pistol.

Where the dim light cast shadows on the wall, the gloom was now joined by darker sprays that glistened as they dripped, leaving mottled streaks against the paint.

Behind me, Karen's excellent marksmanship removed the threat to our rear. Vaguely, I registered her return, not a hair or piece of equipment out of place. Quite the contrast to my gore-streaked haunches.

She halted a few meters from me, giving me a look I had seen more than once. Or twice. Or heck, every time we worked together. But I was hungry, and the rapidly-healing holes in my side needed some fuel.

"Come on, Rick, that alarm's going to bring a lot more guys than we can handle."

Karen was right. As per usual. And the wounds from the last couple of bullet holes were quickly closing.

I gave the corpse one last shake, licked my lips, and followed her out of the facility.

Snow had begun to fall in earnest, increasing until almost whiteout conditions. We took off on a trot in the general direction from whence we came.

"Fuck, I can't see where we're going." Karen had her GPS out. "This piece of shit refuses to connect."

I whined and nudged her with my shoulder, thinking of several wasted one-liners about relying on technology. She tucked the device back into one of her many pockets and pulled her fleece cap further down her ears.

She pulled on a pair of gloves, not pausing as she kept up with my pace. Then, one hand steadied her rifle on its sling while the other rested on the scruff where my neck and shoulders joined. Taking her hint, I assumed the lead.

Unerringly—okay, so maybe I might have gotten slightly mixed up and taken us in a small-ish circle at one point—but mostly unerringly, I got us back out to the side road where we'd left our vehicle.

Driving in the snow was no fun, but we made it back to the house with only a few minor heart attacks (on my part.) You know, fur is great and all, but modern heat is a wonderful invention.

We pulled up to the outside of John Tell's old apartment. Karen killed the engine. I waited for her to open the door; the snow hadn't let up, and I lazed in the car's heat, too comfortable to want to blast the more fragile parts of myself with the blizzard.

Instead, she opened the glove box. The minute she did so, I smelled it, faint but recognizable. That stupid cuff.

"Rick, I'm going to need to put this on you."

Nope. No way.

"Rick. We need to go back. There's no way we can stay here and get this data analyzed in time, and every minute we don't leave, we're tempting fate that these Black Mountain operatives put two and two together and come find us."

I growled.

"Suit yourself."

Damn it. The cuff had captured my attention, which pulled my gaze away from Karen. She took advantage of my distraction to stick a syringe in my side and depress the plunger.

"Don't worry," she said as I drifted off into a very pleasant slumber. "There's no silver. Just a heavy dose of large-animal tranqs."

Man. *Wonder if I could get MONIKER to give me some for recreational—*

# 14

My system usually metabolizes anything I throw at it within a matter of minutes, which makes it a son of a bitch trying to go on a bender. MONIKER, however, had access to some good stuff—better than I could find on a regular basis. It knocked me out long enough for the team to pack everything, head back to what passed for civilization, and shovel me on a plane.

Somewhere after takeoff, the drugs wore off just enough for me to be aware I'd been drugged, but not so much as to shake me out of the dream—or maybe hallucination?—that had overtaken me.

Aleksy and I sat on a fallen limb in the snow, watching a convoy of trucks pass below us. A familiar scene, with just enough difference to be uncanny. For instance, Shin, my Korean buddy, sat on my other side, smoking a cigarette. One of them shouldn't have been there.

*"Wie geht's, Herr Wurst?"* Aleksy leaned behind me to tap Shin on the shoulder. The soldier handed him his pack of cigarettes. He grabbed one and started smoking without lighting it. Dreams are weird.

"Are you haunting me?" I grabbed for the pack, but somewhere in there, it vanished.

"Maybe." Aleksy's skin was pale blue, with dark bruises around the mouth I didn't remember him ever having. His round Polish face should have been tanned, and rough from exposure to the outdoors. This dream Aleksy had a death's-head pallor.

"Well, then, make yourself useful, ghost of Christmas past." I reached for his cigarette. "Tell me what's in store for my future."

I took a drag. The smoke filled my lungs, cool on the inhale. At the back of my throat, the taste of candy lingered, almost too sweet.

Aleksy shrugged. Shin said something in Korean, and he nodded. I don't know what he said. I don't know how Aleksy suddenly knew Korean.

I didn't know why the snow-covered forest scene around us began to fade into a gray and tan color scheme and then slowly disintegrate.

"My friend says you need to cut the leeches out of your life."

"What leeches? MONIKER?"

The last of the trees disappeared. The two other men remained—the soldier and the partisan. Aleksy tilted his head, but Shin spoke, the same heavily accented English with perfect syntax I remembered.

"Why are you still serving a cause that has begun to rot from the inside?"

Somehow, in the mix of hallucination and lucidity, I found myself seated upright on the webbed seat of a small cargo plane, flanked by my imaginary friends. The cuff was back on my arm. I tried to move, but every attempt met some sort of sleep paralysis. Nobody else seemed to recognize I was awake—but maybe I wasn't.

"I'm just doing a favor for a friend," I finally grumbled. I felt like I was saying it out loud, heard the sound of my voice—but nobody else acknowledged the statement. Nobody who hadn't been dead over fifty years that is.

"And your friend, their services? They don't mind their hands with dirt? Maybe they touching blood?" Aleksy, for all his gift of gab, sucked at making English do his bidding.

"Karen is a good person, doing the best she can." The words came out more defensively than I meant. Across the plane, Calix had fallen asleep, her head in Karen's lap. The subject of our conversation was reading, playing with Calix's hair as she turned the pages.

"We're all good guys when we look in the mirror," Shin said, not objecting or arguing with me. "How long did your uniform make you a good guy?"

Well, fuck. He had a point. Hindsight was a bitch. I'd been loyal to the German flag for longer than I should have—longer than I cared to admit; even after my country had lost its mind, I had hung on until that night. I'd watched the flames consume the pages of the books ripped from the Institute—flickering shadows on the faces of young men I'd once shared a uniform with. The waning gibbous moon had been blotted by the smoke rising from those flames, a shadow of rot that had already changed too much about my country to ever see it the same again. I'd spent the nights between the raid and the burning furry, far away from the friends who had become family. From the friend who'd become closer than blood. I'd meant to protect them, but instead left them on the night they needed my teeth and claws the most.

MONIKER. They had offered me redemption and a chance to cleanse the rot from my country. In the process, I'd adopted a new flag, language, and place in the new world order. I never stopped to think what it meant that, even when I'd changed sides, the rules and the game had remained strikingly familiar.

"Politicians are always making promises," Shin said. "It's when those politicians wear uniforms and spout words like 'patriot' and 'justice' and 'honor'—it's then that you must be doubly suspicious."

He wasn't wrong.

"So, you head back to MONIKER, become pet werewolf again?" Aleksy asked.

"Just until I figure out how to get Karen out of there."

He laughed, and Shin joined him.

"You can't even get yourself out of there," Shin said. "You need help, brother."

He was right about that, too.

"Where am I going to get that?"

Aleksy nodded toward Dmitri, who sat alone at the other end of the plane. I snorted in dismissal.

"Pay attention, wolf." Aleksy's voice contained an uncharacteristic heat. And he never called me wolf.

I took another look at our Russian partner. The old man appeared to have nodded off, lulled to sleep by the plane's vibration.

Until I realized his eyes were only half closed. I stared at him, and after a few seconds, I could have sworn I detected a sly wink before he went back to feigning sleep. I swiveled my glance at Karen; she had put her book down and was also staring at me, but although she stared straight at me, she wasn't making eye contact. Somehow, only Dmitri had sensed where my little trip took me.

"Look again," Shin chimed in.

I did. Dmitri hadn't moved. Hadn't changed position. So how had the sun suddenly pooled light around him? In less than three seconds, the sunlight had coalesced and deepened into a rich amber color. The effect outlined him in a glowing, living aura I'd never seen before.

Maybe I wasn't seeing it now.

"You're seeing it," Aleksy told me.

Across from me, Calix yawned and sat up. "Where are we?"

"About twenty minutes from starting our descent into Barstow," Karen replied.

Calix stretched and cracked her neck, and when she finished, she glanced over at me. "He still out?"

"Yep," Karen said.

"Hmm." And now she, too, stared at me as if she could tell I wasn't completely in one place or the other. But I had to be dreaming. First, Dmitri's aura. Now, Calix's eyes. Instead of their normal dark color, they glowed a brilliant crimson. She licked her lips, and I broke the gaze.

Shin took one last drag of his cigarette and threw it on the ground, stubbing it out. "Good luck, brother."

The next moment, he was gone. One hallucination down.

The crew chief poked her head into the cargo space to let us know we were about ten minutes out and we should buckle up to get ready for the descent. Karen nodded. Calix was the only one who'd unbuckled herself during the flight.

I waited for Dmitri's aura to diminish or Calix's eyes to return to normal, but they didn't. I turned to face Aleksy. "What the hell is going on?"

My old friend shrugged. "You know, you are not the only extraordinary creature to ever volunteer in service of their country."

That made sense. Him suddenly speaking perfect English did not. But maybe I was still dreaming.

"Once you started working for MONIKER, it was inevitable word would leak out." Aleksy grinned. "Your cooperation with the agency made a lot of very old, very powerful lineages very nervous."

"Dmitri and Calix…they're not—"

"Human?" Aleksy's grin faded as he shook his head. "No. But I think you sensed that."

Well, Dmitri scared me shitless. I felt a little better knowing he was more than human. Calix—well, she was interesting.

"So, what are you?" I asked Aleksy. "My former Jedi Master come to give me life coaching advice?"

"No." Aleksy smiled, wider than before. "I'm the ghost of your good deeds, come back to haunt you."

And then I swear on the Gods of the North, he did that creepy Cheshire cat thing where he faded out until all you could see left of him was his giant, cheesy ass grin. Smart ass.

"I see you've rejoined reality." Dmitiri raised an eyebrow.

I wondered if he knew everything I had seen while on my long, strange, MONIKER-induced trip. If he had been treated to a picture of me talking to my hallucinations, or if he'd seen Aleksy and Shin sitting next to me.

For that matter, was I awake? Just as a test, I tried calling the change to me.

Fuck! Ow. Yep. Awake. And the damn cuff hadn't lost any of its effectiveness.

The wheels dropping shook the plane with a clunk, and a fast descent later, the cargo plane waddled down the runway and braked to a halt.

Groggily, I unlatched my harness and staggered to my feet. Karen was already stepping down the narrow ladder on the tarmac, Calix close behind. Dmitri followed after, but not before giving me one of his soul-scraping glances. Still had the power to empty my bowels, no matter how sunny his aura appeared.

I stood in the aisle for just a moment, pondering my life choices. Aleksy's words came back to me. The ones about everyone being a good guy when they looked in the mirror.

MONIKER tangled people in webs of their own making—their feelings of honor, loyalty, family. I'd sworn never to wear their leash again, yet look at me. Standing there with this cuff on my arm, telling myself I was helping Karen and paying off Dmitri's debt.

Calix poked her head back in the door hatch. "You get lost or something?"

Her eyes had faded back to normal. I shook my head. "Spaced out. Coming."

She grinned. "Was wondering if you had decided to cut and run."

"Not yet," I answered, following her down the ladder. The jet wash rolled over us, the heat sickening after the time we'd spent in the cleansing cold of the north. I needed a good, long, wild run. "Still not a fan of where we're going."

I fell into step next to her as we headed for a car across the flight line. Or rather, I trotted in a general fashion to keep up with her long strides. I thought again, longingly, of running. A sharp stab in the temple reminded me to keep my thoughts away from the change.

"You don't trust many people, do you?" Calix inquired idly.

"Not if they have anything to do with MONIKER," I answered. "Present company not excluded."

"I know what they've done to Karen, but what's your story?"

By this time, we'd reached the car. She opened the door to let me slide in.

"They cut off my balls once when I was in wolf form."

She rewarded me with a slack jaw and an uncertain expression as she tried to figure out if I was joking.

"He's joking," Karen told her. "Get in the car. I want to get on this data as soon as possible."

No appreciation for my jokes. Calix rolled her eyes and closed the door. The car started, and I had to swallow back a tremor. I hate enclosed spaces, and until now, I'd been distracted, not thinking too much about where we were headed. I'd sworn to end the agency, and not only had I not come up with a plan, but I hadn't even managed to get the cuff permanently off my arm.

My last-ditch bet hovered in my consciousness. Modern technology was powerful, even when corrupt, but the *Überwechsel* wasn't more than a week away, and we'd see then how science stacked up against ancient magic.

---

The data Karen had downloaded from Black Mountain's server made it back to MONIKER before we did. By the time we walked into the facility, travel-worn, hungry, and in dire need of a shower—it wasn't just me this time—the agency's analysts had dived in deep and showed no signs of coming out any time soon.

Karen went straight to where the analysts were working in a large, bull-pen-style office area, sat down, and we lost her, too. I hoped they were finding something good in there. For a brief moment, I considered following her but decided against it. Wherever Karen was, Gratuszcak was not far behind, and I preferred not to run into that basement troll if I could avoid it. I liked all my body parts where they belonged.

Dmitri went off and did whatever old Russian spies do for fun when they're alone. Probably read a book. Or devised new methods of psychological torture. Calix stated her intention to hit the showers, and that sounded good to me, although I refrained from saying so out loud for fear of being mistaken for making an innuendo. I keep a healthy respect for people who carry large swords.

The hot water was fabulous, the MONIKER-issued razor was dull, and the jeans and T-shirt somebody had left for me fit. Some joker left me a Duran Duran concert tee, and let me tell you, if I had known that song was going to be such a hit, I would have eaten the band in the eighties.

And if you don't get that reference, I'm not going to spell it out for you. I don't need it stuck in my head for another two decades.

I was in the kitchen raiding the fridge—and somebody's case of Yuengling—when a sudden draft caught my attention. It came from across the building, and before you roll your eyes, I assure you, given the giant silver prison that was the Vegas MONIKER facility, my senses were attuned to any hint of the outside.

Beer in hand, I plodded casually along, doing my best to feign a desultory wander. There wasn't much acting involved. Up north, with my leash off, I'd once again tasted snow and freedom. Being crammed back into captivity scratched under my skin. The beer tasted fine, but it didn't come anywhere near taking off the edge.

Now that the adrenaline started to wear off and the reality of silver walls and shackles settled around me again, my mind kept showing me pictures of John Tell. He stared at me through silver bars —my first glimpse of the man. The closed-off smile when we'd shared a drink together at a bar in Germany, the day before he sold me to the Collective. The broken man sprawled lifeless across the table in Rose's northern morgue. With every picture that flashed, the smell of blood hit me again, the scent memory washing out the visual.

A faint trace of something sweet as blood—but not as cloying— interrupted my downward spiral into the past. Just as well. The beer was not half-bad, but nowhere near strong enough to help me forget anything. I sniffed again, this time with more focus and interest.

Cinnamon. Dark chocolate. Just the faintest aroma of old dust and blood. Calix?

I sneezed, and the memories clouding over me dissipated, although they hung around the back of my throat in a bitter aftertaste. The heavy silver tang that the building's walls exuded still lay predominantly over everything, but now I could almost see the tall woman with the long, black hair and the dangerous sword, stalking her way down the corridor.

Even as I opened my senses to the image, it began to fade. I hurried after the scent before it became too faint to follow.

My path led me to a heavy metal door. The unmarked slab was painted industrial gray. Standing beside it, I could sense the silver shooting through it and emanating off the handle. To touch it would be to risk a severe burn on my skin.

But the path stood open, and I couldn't resist the temptation of an open door. I didn't even try.

Wrapping the bottom of my T-shirt around my hand, I grasped the handle and pulled until the door opened just enough to get my hand in the crack and open it the rest of the way. I spared a quick glance around. Any minute now, I thought, the alarms would blare, and MONIKER would come chasing after their favorite science experiment.

Nothing. Hm. Suspicious.

The cold air washed across my face, and I couldn't help but lean forward, the change demanding to be heard. Ow. Fuck. The cuff still worked.

Behind the open door, a set of concrete stairs went up, flanked by a metal railing. Interestingly, nothing in the corridor carried more than a hint of silver. Straining my senses, I tried to detect anything else, but all that came to me were hints of moisture and metal.

There are a few things I can ignore, but an open door and the chance for escape don't fall into that category. I stepped forward, my foot edging over the threshold.

A soft beeping started, just a short series of quick sounds. I stepped back. Listened.

The hallway remained silent as the beeping faded with my retreat. Hm.

Open door. Obligations. Promises. Open door.

I shrugged. Fuck it.

The beeping started up as I stepped forward again. This time, I ignored its insistent whine. One foot made it over the threshold. The beeping intensified. I stepped forward again.

An electric shock tossed me off my feet. Sparks erupted. My body flew back into the hallway, and I slammed into the wall. The bottle I had been carrying shattered into a thousand sharp brown shards of glass.

Crumpled, I curled in on myself. The smell of burnt hair filled the air around me as I quivered uncontrollably in the aftershock, trying not to shit myself.

Fuckers put up an invisible electric fence.

## 15

After what seemed like hours, I finally managed to stagger to my feet. My ear twitched, keeping time with my left hand, which spasmed every so often. The area around the cuff was raw, the flesh burnt and charred. After silver, the next thing I hate with a passion is taking an electric shock to the body.

Stretching my arms out, I extended the middle finger on each hand and waved them around. If anyone watched on the security feed, I hoped they got a good laugh at my expense. My arm jerked, ruining the effect, and I bent over, shaking again.

I waited for an agency response, but nothing. Likely, the agency once again relied on technology to keep me where they wanted me. It worked. I really didn't want to get electrocuted.

And here's the thing—I owed Dmitri a certain loyalty, and Karen even moreso. I'd made a vow to bring this place down around their ears, so I owed myself that. But the open door yawned before me, and if I could get out, then maybe I could get this cuff off, and afterward, I'd be able to fulfill my promises.

I'm able to rationalize pretty much anything. It's a talent.

I stepped forward again, close enough to set off the infernal soft beeping, but not close enough to singe my fur. Hair. Whatever.

The rhythmic sound set an accompaniment to my thoughts as I debated my next move. There had to be a way out this door. I would figure it out, even if it killed me.

A stray aftershock caught me unawares, and I twitched again, a full-body spasm.

Which was why I didn't notice it at first. An almost imperceptible weakening of the signal.

And now, I really did expect the MONIKER shock troops to come pounding down the corridor. Because I'd found a weakness in their tech. Whatever powered the signal that kept me from leaving, whether in the cuff or the door itself, slowly died, beep by beep, as I stood there.

The signal diminished by half as I waited. The skin around the cuff repaired itself, leaving bright pink streaks where the flesh would take a few more hours to completely heal. I fought a battle to stand there and remain calm.

My nerves stayed on edge. With luck—and I rarely had any of that—MONIKER wouldn't notice what I was doing. Or they would notice too late. The beeping softened again, and I decided to make my move.

Gritting my teeth against the possibility of another fun ride on the lightning, I stuck my hand through the door.

This time, the electric shock stabbed every part of my body on its way through, but it didn't slam me against the wall, and my feet stayed on the floor. Closing my eyes, I pushed through the pain until I stumbled onto the stairs.

Panting, I huddled over long enough for the shakes to subside to the point I could start climbing the stairs.

More by force of will rather than any physical capability, I reached the top of the concrete landing. At the top of the stairs, another door opened to the outside. I forced myself to crawl toward it before I could think about whether or not the agency had designed a double failsafe.

No beeping greeted my ears as I half crawled-half rolled over the threshold and out the door to sprawl on my back in the cold, clean snow.

I took a moment to just breathe and let my body return to normal. The fresh air in my lungs both rejuvenated me and made breathing difficult until I got used to the cold again.

Assuming whatever I had done had run down all the batteries, I called for the change.

*Zap.* Ow. Fuck. Nope. Apparently whatever mechanism in the cuff prevented the change didn't rely on shitty battery power.

Okay. There were strains under the change. The *Überwechsel* lurked beneath the ordinary impulse of the change, stronger now. The moon was coming. The snow melting under me poked at my consciousness. It wasn't comfortable, but the transformation drew closer.

Tentatively, I tried ignoring the change and instead called for the *Überwechsel.* It was pure desperation. The more ancient Change never responded to my call, only the beckoning of the full moon. I'd only ever managed to Change outside the moon once—when Gratusczak had pumped his mystery drug into me that had spurred it in the first place.

But now...*now* I called for it, and although I once again had no luck, the strains of the higher, larger Change stirred just beyond my reach. I grasped for it, expecting any moment for the cuff to deliver its stinging rebuke, but for once, it stayed silent, inert. Hm.

The decision remained. Stay there in the snow and try to reach for the *Überwechsel*? Or follow the trail Calix had left—a trail that was very quickly becoming cold?

In the end, the taste of cinnamon and blood beckoned too urgently to ignore. The need to run in my other form, the call of the moon— those were things that would envelop me shortly. Feeling more confident, I scrambled to my feet and started jogging away from the facility. But if I was going to do the things I had promised, I needed to trust my teammates, and the mystery Calix presented couldn't be ignored.

Calix left a trail both unmistakable and completely weird. For one thing, as I slipped through the facility perimeter, down through the mountains, and finally came out nearer the city, the scent never wavered—in front of me. Behind me, the trail quickly faded, as if it were waiting for me to follow but didn't want anyone else chancing upon it. Like I said, weird. Trails don't act like this one did—at least not in my experience.

We were closer to civilization than I expected, and the little hike cleared my mind. The farther away from the facility, the better I felt, leaving behind the silver permeating the atmosphere and scarring the air I breathed.

Once I hit the highway, I slowed to a fast walk. Traveling long distances on foot didn't bother me. Or rather, four feet. This hoofing it on two was just plain annoying.

A car pulled up beside me, and I flinched, expecting MONIKER to have found me. Instead, the red Volvo lowered its window. One sober driver and two very drunk passengers, all men, all young, all crackling with the energy of humans on their way to a night of legal illicit pleasures, greeted me.

"Hey, man, need a ride?" One of the drunk ones pounded on the door with his hand. "My friend's totally sober, I promise."

I shrugged. "Thanks."

Upon getting into the car, the backseat passenger offered me a hit of their joint. I felt bad taking it—pot never had an effect on me unless MONIKER had laced it with one of their special cocktails—remind me to tell you more later about the sixties and a large portion of the seventies and early eighties—but I wanted to be polite. I took a quick puff, ignored how the scent burned my nostrils and scorched my throat, and passed it along.

"Man, what were you even doing out here?" the driver asked. While he'd appeared sober, now that we were in a confined space, hurtling in an enclosed metal heap toward the bright lights of Old Vegas, I could detect the tell-tale signs of a contact high.

"Had a fight with my girlfriend, and she ditched me."

As expected, my tale was met with sympathetic groans and the offer of another hit. I declined, and they spent the rest of the drive regaling me with the tales of the women who had done them wrong. They were what, twenty? Twenty-five? Once I hit the century mark, I found it hard to tell how old people were anymore.

They dropped me off outside the Old Vegas strip, then drove off in a cloud of pot smoke and testosterone, heading over to the shinier new casinos and clubs. Guess no one ever told them about Glitter Gulch.

To a certain extent, the cuff had cut me off from some more important aspects of the change. But it couldn't completely block *me*. I could still sense the coming moon, keep the trail and scent in my nose. And now that my feet were back on the ground, that trail burned through my senses.

I'd had a feeling Calix would head back here. Why, though, I had no idea. She didn't strike me as someone who could be tempted by the shiny pleasures of the city. Or the other, darker things it had to offer. And yet, the smell of cinnamon drew me right through the crowds thronging the sidewalk, past the open doors of the casinos through which could be glimpsed the people who, glazed and confused, sat in front of the machines.

Chocolate gives me serious indigestion, so I avoid it at all costs, but now the taste of it lay thickly on my tongue, spiced with the old copper tang of blood. What the hell was going on?

Then I spied her.

She was tall, and the energy emanating from her took on a red tinge that swirled around, highlighting and, at the same time, obscuring her path. I shouldn't have been able to see that. The color, I mean. Maybe the Change, the *Überwechsel*, lingered close enough to the surface that my eyes were giving me a freebie.

Her movements across the casino floor reminded me of a large cat stalking its prey, all sleek motion and silent lethality. And she had found her target.

The small woman sat alone at the end of a row of machines. Slightly plump, dressed in jeans and a T-shirt, she didn't feed any coins into the machine, simply stared down at her phone. Even from across the room, I could see the faint trails of tears drying on her cheeks.

Calix didn't even glance in my direction, but I couldn't shake the feeling she knew I was there. Draping herself across the machine, she sat down next to the other woman, her darker hair soft against the woman's light blonde aura.

Slowly, the blonde woman responded to her friendly overtures, putting the phone back in her purse, wiping her cheeks.

Within moments, Calix had her laughing at some small joke.

And something else. I'm not immune to the energy that builds up in people that can only be released through violence or sex, and these two were building up some serious vibes.

With a rapidity that had me biting back jealousy, Calix stood and offered the woman her hand. She took it and followed Calix toward the back of the casino floor. Ignoring the cussing from the people I bumped into, I hurried to follow after them.

I wasn't sure what I expected to find when I came out the back of the building. The casino had the usual squirrelly layout, coupled with some security. Calix seemed to simply drift through, the other woman protected by her casual trespassing. I got dirty looks and an attempt to stop me that only failed because I'm good at sprinting.

To the back of the building, I found an empty alley. The night sky had clouded over, but the lights from Old Vegas reflected back a glow that settled over the area like fog from a brooding weather giant.

There were a few dumpsters and some puddles of unidentifiable origin on the ground, but no place where I could see Calix bringing a —date? Paramour? Inside, the curiosity driving my steps was getting the shit pounded out of it by a growing rage that this person could talk a big game about wanting to protect Karen and yet could so easily betray my friend. A friend who, I knew from personal experience, did not casually divulge or dedicate her affections.

A soft breeze brought their scent back. This time, the trail didn't blaze in front of me. Instead, it had gone back to normal. Perhaps I'd seen all Calix meant me to see. Perhaps I'd been given enough of a head start.

Whatever. Pissed off to be still stuck on two legs and trying as hard as I could *not* to think of the change—ow! Fuck—I headed down the alley toward a parking garage structure.

The garage was about five stories high, filled with vehicles smelling of booze and Happy Meals. I slipped into the garage, the shadows covering my approach, following the scent of sex and chocolate and cinnamon—and blood.

Up the stairs, past the landing, I came out at the top of the parking garage. The structure was open at the top, with a shallow ledge around it to prevent people from driving off. Not sure how effectively it stopped people from jumping off. I wondered if it had ever been tested.

A soft sound came from around the corner of the enclosed stairwell. Clothing rustled, and flesh caressed flesh. Now that I was there, I wasn't sure if I wanted to see what was happening. But of course, I couldn't stop now.

All pretense at subterfuge aside, I turned the corner and stopped.

About ten yards away, Calix and the woman from the casino sat on the parking garage ledge, wrapped so deeply in each other that a wave of embarrassment at my voyeurism rolled me over, and I almost sprinted back the way I came.

More confused than ever, I stepped back, trying to melt into the shadows. I'm better at it when I'm furry.

I'd caught them mid-kiss. Or maybe at the beginning of the kiss. At the five-minute mark, I started getting concerned if they were going to breathe any time soon. Anything to keep my mind off the pheromones that wrapped me up and squeezed. It had been a long time since I'd shared that sort of embrace with anyone, as my body reminded me. Insistently.

The woman slumped slightly, her kisses straying from Calix's lips to her ear, neck. Lower. Calix held her, wrapped in her legs and arms. I had a quick vision of the taller woman as a praying mantis, all long limbs and predatory hunger.

Even as I blinked the vision back, the scene shifted. At first, I thought the movement to be a simple caress of a momentary lover.

Calix brushed the other woman's hair back over her shoulder, her two hands moving along the woman's back and arms in what could have been an embrace or a bracing gesture.

With the woman steadied in her hands, neck bare, Calix looked up. Her eyes met mine, and this time I could not mistake the dull red glow emanating from within. Again, the thought flashed through my mind, how did this color penetrate the monochrome sight I was cursed with twenty-eight days out of twenty-nine? She held my glance deliberately, not mocking, but as if to say, look and learn.

And then the light caught just the barest hint of a flash off a mouth full of sharp teeth as she bent to her lover's jugular.

I felt like the world's dumbest supernatural nuke. And also, kind of hungry.

My stomach growled for the third time as I waited outside the parking garage. After witnessing the little show, I'd decided to head back downstairs and give the ladies their privacy. I hadn't really eaten, save for that half a bottle of Yuengling, and I needed to put something solid in my stomach, but I had too many questions to concentrate on figuring out how to get food. Inconveniently, I had no wallet, no car, and no way of knowing if the woman Calix had seduced would wake up groggy somewhere with her memory wiped, come flying off the top of the garage, or be disposed of some other way.

"She'll be fine."

I nearly fell off the curb. Calix had managed to walk up behind me without me noticing, definitely not something that should have been possible. I scrambled to my feet.

"So…do vampires mind-read as well?"

Calix shrugged. "For a secret agent, wolf, you're surprisingly easy to read, my friend."

Oh, we were friends now. Excellent. Maybe she would answer some questions.

She held up a set of keys and jingled them to get my attention.

"Come on. We're going to borrow my friend's car. MONIKER is probably freaking out right about now, and I don't want to get fired."

There wasn't much to say to that, so I nodded and followed her around the corner and into the garage. The keys belonged to a Subaru station wagon of an indiscriminate grayish color. Typical soccer mom vehicle. Maybe the blonde woman actually was a soccer mom. A kid's sweatshirt and various food wrappers littered the back seat, and I spotted a seat that sort of looked like a car seat, kind of a raised platform with arms.

We got in the car, Calix driving, me rolling down the window to bask in the fresh air. The seatbelt prevented me from hanging my head out. This form has all sorts of disadvantages.

She started the car and pulled around to the exit gate. We both shrank into the shadows of the car as she paid. The gate lifted, and we headed back out.

Calix drove carefully yet aggressively. She knew her way around, too, swinging us through the maze of streets until we were headed out of town. As we drove, I thought of and discarded the questions that welled up. I mean, where do you start?

Once we pulled out on the highway, Calix seemed to settle back, as if a tension had left her suddenly.

"It's always the worst with the ones in the closet." She spoke more to herself than me. "You get stuck in their headspace and can't get away."

"You actually get in their heads?"

"In a manner of speaking," she replied, never taking her eyes from the road ahead. "It's part of the process."

"You want to fill me in on the rest?"

"Sure don't." She drove with one hand on the wheel, the other resting on the window, fingertips drumming a rhythmic pattern that kept time with the car's pace.

"Does Karen know?"

"No, she doesn't." The fingertips stilled. "And if you tell her, I will cut you into ten pieces and feed from your remains."

That was a curiously specific threat, but I had no doubt she meant it.

"You want to share with the rest of the class what all that was about?" I asked. Because I hadn't been wrong—she had meant me to follow her. She had known that I was there and waited until I arrived to feed in front of me. I'm not a fan of theatrics. Unless, of course, they're mine. "Inquiring minds want to know."

## 16

There are a lot of people pissed off at you right now," Calix began. "There've been rumors for the past, I don't know, fifty or sixty years, that the mundanes had gotten ahold of proof of things—people, creatures—that exist outside the scope of explainable science."

Oops.

"We've been getting complacent, I know," she continued. "We were comfortable with the fact that modern science didn't seem to have a place for us anymore—and that was fine. I mean, I'm pretty much over getting accused of witchcraft and being burned at the stake."

"When you say 'we,' you mean…vampires?" Even saying the word out loud made me feel ridiculous. I get it; I'm a werewolf. I grew up in a pack, but we still lived with and among humans who wrote off the supernatural as a freak accident. Forgive me if I was still getting used to the idea that we weren't the only thing that would go crunch in the night.

Calix rolled her eyes, gave me the finger, and continued driving. "It took us a while, but eventually, we learned about MONIKER. And then Black Mountain. I was sent to infiltrate your agency."

"And Black Mountain?"

"We still haven't heard back from the agents we sent there."

"Was your sister…was she part of it? Was she a—whatever you are?"

Calix's face turned to stone. "Let me explain this to you, Rick, and then I'd like to never talk about it again."

"Fair enough."

"We—vampires, yes, is the popular term—we call ourselves Family." She left off the fingertip drumming, grasping the steering wheel with both hands, knuckles white. "We are most often born in sets of twins unless there is a complication in the womb." She shook her head. "I was born a twin. My sister—well, it's usual that one twin will be born like me. And the other twin—Arista—she's… She was-" She broke off, taking a moment to regain control over the emotions that seethed under the outwardly dispassionate surface. When she spoke again, her preternatural calm had reasserted itself. "Arista was as human in nature as anyone else in that room."

"What were you both doing here?"

"I followed Karen; Arista followed me." Calix relaxed her grip on the wheel. "We were collecting as much information as we could. I was doing it within the organization. She was working as a waitress with a temp agency. It was supposed to be so she could get placed around many different places and see if she could make any additional inroads. Find lower-level geeks sneaking out on the town, make friends, get some intel. It wasn't the first time we'd been in the field together."

So many still unanswered questions. Were vampires—sorry, *Family* —as long-lived as our pack? What about the human twin? Did they heal or rejuvenate? Where did they come from? Did MONIKER know about them? Why didn't we have supernatural meetups so we could get to know each other?

"Did you kill the little girl?" Not the question I'd meant to ask, but one that had been preying on my mind since the last time we'd painted the town red.

"No." She took a quick glance at me, eyebrow raised. "I did take some of her blood—it's how we glaze."

At my blank look, she continued. "Sorry, Family slang. We kind of massage people's memories when we feed. Glaze them over. It's hard to explain."

Inside me, the change rolled and pressed against the walls of my consciousness. I tamped it firmly back down, quite well aware, thank you very much, that the waxing moon was rising higher over the desert. I didn't need to get zapped as a reminder.

"She remembers a night when bad men came for her, but her daddy was the hero who saved her life by giving his," Calix said. "It's not going to make her life any easier. But no, I didn't kill her."

She turned to me again, and this time, the red lurked in the back of her eyes. I don't know how she kept it hidden. Maybe it was the sort of thing that once it had been seen, you couldn't ignore it.

"But her father is very, very dead." She put her eyes back on the road, slowing and flicking on the turn signal. "And I enjoyed sharing his last few moments with him." Again, glints in the moonlight of teeth that formed and re-formed to very sharp points.

She pulled to a stop. Ahead of us, the narrow mountain road stretched up to the facility.

"Rick. I want to take down this agency. I want to remove all traces from human awareness that we exist. And I want Karen to come with us because I do not want to see her destroyed with the rest of them."

A thought occurred to me. Did Dmitri know who or what she was? Did she include him in her calculations? And Dr. Gratusczak… I realized she was waiting for me to say something.

"I promised Dmitri I would help him find his daughter." I peered at her face to see if she reacted to the mention of the old Russian. Nothing. "You may be a pointy-toothed creature of the night, but he's something else entirely."

"Yes, he is." Calix put the car in drive. "Fair enough. You pay your debt. Then we take them down."

Sounded like a good plan to me. Or good enough.

———

Talk is cheap. When we pulled up to the front of the facility, I forgot all the fancy words about debts and honor, about to suggest we just head back down the mountain and drive away. MONIKER had sent a party to meet us. They looked pissed. And carried weapons. Including a net with which I was very familiar and didn't need a refresher.

What were we doing? Karen didn't need our help. She was no damsel. And if there was distress, she was probably the one causing it.

I caught the slightest signs of tension returning to Calix. A tightening around the eyes and corners of her mouth. The smell of cinnamon intensified.

Calix killed the engine. At this point, I really had no choice. Get out of the car or get dragged back. I'd much prefer to walk in under my own power if I got the choice. As if on cue, my stomach growled. If there were a chance of food, I'd sign up for another four-year tour.

We covered the short stretch of turf between the mom-mobile and the group of MONIKER soldiers in a few seconds. They surrounded us and began ushering us to the yawning door of the facility. It wasn't quite frog-marching. But it came close.

Karen caught my eye but didn't otherwise acknowledge me. A curious absence surrounded her—her usual scent of soft rosemary was buried deep under the sharp tang of silver. To my senses, it left a scar like something had been excised.

Once inside, the troops closed the door behind us. A few feet in front of us, another door opened. As we went through that, it closed and locked as well. My cuff twinged. With the full moon so close, every part of me strained for the change—no, the *Change*—without even thinking about it.

"Rick." Karen nodded at the MONIKER troops to dismiss them. "Calix. Had fun?"

Calix shrugged. I grinned.

"Viva Las Vegas." Now, to important business. "What's for midnight chow?"

Karen rolled her eyes. The two women fell into step together, and I followed them down the hall. There was no sign of anyone else—

perhaps Dmitri was actually human and slept at night. As for Dr. G., with any luck, they'd locked him in a cage, too.

---

The cafeteria had been shut down for the night, but someone named Jared had left a chicken sandwich in the fridge. I knew this because it said: JARED'S SANDWICH. Now it was "Rick's Sandwich." And it was delicious.

There were a few other, more anonymous, leftovers in there, some of which were dubious indeed, but I still ate them. When I'm caught in a pre-Change appetite, I'll eat pretty much anything. And if I hadn't been wearing the cuff, I would have eaten Jared, too.

Both women turned down offers to share in the spoils, choosing instead to nurse identical cups of hot, black coffee. The smell of it crept into my senses and threatened indigestion, but my insides don't give up food easily.

I polished off the last of someone's tapioca pudding they had left, half-eaten, in the back of the fridge. By this time, the morning sun had risen high enough up the mountainside to drag its way across the room where we sat. A tall man who smelled of curry dropped in briefly to stow his lunch in the refrigerator and grab a mug of hot water. I almost waited until he was out the door before I stole his lunch and sat down happily.

"Very ballsy, my furry friend," Calix noted.

"If I were furry, I wouldn't have to settle for stealing his lunch."

"Rick would probably just eat him." Karen rolled her eyes, an old, familiar gesture that clashed with the strain on her face. We'd only been gone five or six hours. What the hell...

Calix moved right past that one. I thought it showed great restraint on her part. Also on mine, for not pointing out I wasn't the only cannibalistic biomorph in the room. "Find anything while we were gone?"

Karen sipped her still-steaming coffee. "We're still crunching data. Probably will be for a while." Her usually alert eyes deadened for just a moment. I paused from eating to see what would happen, but in the next second, she came back to us. "We do have a lead. It looks like Black Mountain is flowing a lot of money through a certain currency exchange bureau in Germany."

Road trip? Please, please, please, let us go on another road trip.

"It came to our attention, mostly because MONIKER uses the same bureau for essentially the same thing." Karen shrugged. "Money —and people—flow in. Nothing flows out, not that you can tell. Whatever pops up is clean as a whistle and mostly used to fund our research and development arm."

"So that's where you guys get the money for Dr. G's delightful playroom."

Karen ignored me. "We could stand to do more surveillance, but it looks like our target for all the right reasons."

"Any sign of the woman?" Calix asked.

"Potentially." Karen finished her coffee in one long gulp. "Your little field trip got everyone worked up, but now that you're back, we'll have Dmitri confirm it. We've got a couple of blurry photos and possibly a conversation, and that's about it."

"You said MONIKER uses the same bureau for its operations," I said. "That's a hell of a coincidence."

"I doubt it was," Karen replied.

I thought of Tell, Gratusczak, MONIKER, and Germany, and how everywhere I went, I seemed to be caught in a sticky web of my own making. "When do we leave?"

"Leave?" Karen's eyes deadened again, blank and absent.

"To pursue the lead," I prompted.

"We're not pursuing." Her voice was as flat as her eyes. "There's a team in Germany that will take over."

Calix and I exchanged glances. First, this was our mission, as reluctant as I had been to take it on. But now, I felt a sense of owner-ship. And claustrophobia. If we weren't going to Germany, I didn't foresee many options for getting the hell out of the facility.

I tamped down on my natural reflex to call for the change. Once again, a strange movement stirred, as if the *Überwechsel* reached out for me instead of the other way around. I needed to find someplace with some privacy and see if I could answer back, call it to me outside of the full moon.

"Rick?" Calix kicked me in the shin under the table. "You still with us?"

I scraped the last bits of curry out of the container, put the fork down, and licked the inside. With a satisfying belch, I nodded. "Does Dmitri know he's getting sidelined?"

Karen didn't answer. Calix looked at her, trying to catch her eye. Karen ignored us and stood, pushing her seat away from the table. The old Karen always pushed her chair in and never left a dirty dish on the table for someone else to clean up, but the old Karen wasn't entirely here anymore.

"Come on." She turned, expecting me to follow.

Calix and I stood. I asked the question. "Where are we going?"

"Dr. Gratusczak has requested your presence." There wasn't even a flicker of remorse or reaction in her eyes. "Do you want to walk there, or should we explore another option?"

"Yes, I'd like the option where I get a beer, and a steak sandwich, and a nap." My outer wiseass concealed an inner tremor at the thought of returning to the lab. Calix gave me a look to let me know I concealed nothing.

"Rick, come with me and get it over with, or I'll have you dragged down there."

"I'll take him." Calix laid her hand on my forearm. The sudden touch startled me, but a sense of calm immediately washed through me. Even the change settled down a bit.

"Fine." Karen was halfway out the door. "I have to get back to..." She trailed off as she walked away.

Even under Calix's weird touch, I trembled.

"Rick."

"Calix."

"The full moon is in what, five days? Six?"

"Four."

"Bide your time." The glow in her eyes deepened, intensified, then vanished. "Bide your time."

---

Pain has a way of warping time. The moments in between the pain play with your mind. At once both an eternity and an eye blink, they suspend any sense of normality.

When the pain begins again, the long moments stretch out even longer until all you feel for eternity is the scream your throat is too raw to release.

Years ago, after I'd defected and come to MONIKER, I'd at least been part of my pain. The experiments I'd actually volunteered for. Their scientists had kept me in the loop. This chemical compound destabilized, then restabilized, the change. This disrupts your healing; this one controls the transformation; this one makes you taller, this one makes you fall, and this one was a placebo, doesn't do anything at all.

Just kidding. Nothing made me taller.

Even after I'd come out of retirement, albeit unwillingly, Karen had still told me everything they were putting into me and why. Some of it had been the lies John Tell fed her. But they still afforded me the dignity of some amount of agency in my own demise.

This time, they didn't give a shit. Gratusczak had free rein, and I was sure he would come close to killing me. Maybe that was the point all along.

No lab table for me this time. Instead, I swung from two manacles attached to the ceiling by chains. Très sadism chic. I half expected some trashy billionaire to present me with a contract and a ball gag.

A final wave of pain passed over me. I waited, and my head cleared enough to get my feet back under me. There was just enough play in the chains for me to stand on my own. Once I finished twitching.

"Is there a point to this?" My throat was sore, and I don't know if all the words quite made it out.

Gratusczak shrugged. He busied himself at his table, recording the last few notes on his pad. A series of vials stood lined up before him like obedient little soldiers. Each one held a different carnival of pain. At this point, he had made his way about halfway down the line, treating me to the agony inside each one.

"You're not a very efficient weapon, *Herr* Keller." The good doctor chose the next vial and drew a fair portion of the liquid into a new syringe. At least I wasn't sharing needles with myself. I shivered. Not from the cold.

I flinched away from him as he reached for my arm. No use. He grasped my arm firmly, the skin of his hand cold under the latex glove. Even in my wrecked state, I could still detect the curious lack of presence burning my sinuses.

"You are not the fastest, not the strongest," he continued as he jammed the syringe into my arm and depressed the plunger.

I waited. Nothing happened.

He shrugged and capped the syringe. "You're just another loose nuke rattling around some forgotten Cold War arsenal."

Unlike the other vials, whatever this one contained didn't immediately send me spiraling into myself. In fact, nothing much at all happened. At first.

"So, we're taking you apart; see how you work." He dropped the syringe into a biohazard waste box fastened to the edge of his work table. "See if there are any parts worth pulling out and saving for something else."

Okay, now it was happening, less of a physical reaction to the pain than I'd undergone with the previous compounds. Instead, all the shadows in the room were brightening, taking on a glow like the screen of an ancient television when you first turned it on.

Nausea rolled in my belly, threatening to spill over my gums. The light show intensified, the glow increasing and then decreasing, until everything in the room settled into a sort of stasis, outlined with the light.

Except Gratusczak. Him, the glow obscured, shifting and shadowing his body with an effect that reminded me of temperature gradients on a weather map. Huh. Maybe I was seeing temperatures? In black and white?

My brain couldn't focus. I felt light-headed, dizzy, still nauseous. The chemical worked through my bloodstream, and I broke out in a cold sweat.

The manacles around my wrists dug into my skin, more so as I sagged against them, unable to support my weight. A burning started again in my shoulders as the tendons holding my joints together protested. The panic at being left alone with Gratuszczak faded into a dull resentment at Karen and Calix for dragging me back and leaving me here. Even trying to summon up enough energy for actual hatred turned out to be too far beyond me.

My eyelids drooped as my senses drifted. Once again, the Change —the big Change—pawed at the wolf inside me, who seemed to have curled up and fallen asleep. Twice shy, I recoiled from it. Patiently, it reached out again, wafting like smoke toward my center. Hesitantly, I uncurled the wolf, making a half-movement toward the *Überwechsel* that teased at me. Unlike before, no shock or pain swatted me away.

I wasn't sure what was happening. Hell, I couldn't even figure out what was real, what was not, if an actual wolf stood before me, the moon was affecting me, or it was all a figment of this bizarre trip, courtesy of MONIKER pharmaceuticals.

On my periphery, another glow came around the corner, not imaginary wolf or Dr. Gratuszcak. The light took a human shape but without the gradients; instead, it shone white-hot, with a sharp, thick dark line around the outline.

"Doctor." The figure was a glow stick, but the voice was Dmitri. I wasn't sure if this made me happy to see him or not. "*Herr* Keller."

Okay, he acknowledged me. Awesome. So was this drug. So shiny. And glow-y.

"How may I be of assistance?" Gratuscak's glow momentarily darkened and sparked, then returned to normal.

"I require *Herr* Keller's presence," Dmitri's voice explained mildly. His glow intensified. "You can release him. Now."

17

MONIKER had been content to let me spend the rest of my days rotting away in Dr. G's lab, but Dmitri had other ideas. And Dmitri's ideas usually translated into reality, which was why instead of hanging by my wrists, I sat strapped into the seat of yet another cargo plane, trundling our slow and steady way over the dark waters of the Atlantic.

The vibrations of the plane jarred my still-healing senses; the last of the drugs Gratuszcak pumped into me was still very much in my bloodstream. I massaged the skin around the cuff. By now, it should have been healing. The red marks remained, however, and showed no sign of decreasing. Annoying.

Annoying *and* dangerous. Ramirez had somehow learned I'd been allowed to change in our mission up north, and he'd made a big deal about the fact Karen no longer had any sort of key to release me from its imprisonment. Fucker.

We were heading to a suspected Black Mountain facility in the western Czech Republic, just over the border from eastern Bavaria. The trail Karen and the other analysts followed looked sketchy, and there were questions about the source's credibility. Still, enough stars had aligned to warrant sending in a team. After Dmitri had extricated

142

me from Gratuszcak's experiments, a couple of MONIKER strongmen dumped me at the table in the conference room. I'd tried to pay attention, but everything had still been glowing, and I'd seen lots of things that probably weren't there. Maybe.

The part of the conversation I'd been able to follow had been a discussion between Ramirez and Karen and some of the other analysts debating whether they had enough intelligence to go in.

The final straw hinged on a picture they'd found, fuzzy, grainy, and shot at a very long distance, but that showed some superficial resemblance to Dmitri's daughter.

In the end, Dmitri had spoken up in his always reasonable, always even-tempered tone, and somehow everyone around the table had agreed that, of course, they should dispatch a team to infiltrate and surveil, with the follow-on mission of extraction if possible. And said team should consist of Karen, Calix, and myself, with Dmitri observing. It all just made sense.

Creeped me out. But I wasn't going to argue.

The plane droned on.

---

We landed on some shrouded, anonymous airstrip shortly after midnight. The plane touched down just long enough for us to download all our gear. Then the pilot made a U-turn, headed back down the runway, and took off, leaving us standing there as the navigation lights faded into the dark sky.

The moon shone down, just a few more slivers away from being full. The light had me twitching out of my skin, relieved only when the clouds drifted back over the sky. I smelled rain on the way. Cold and wet. Just how I like it.

"Grab your shit; I've got a car waiting for us." Karen hoisted her two bags and picked up the handle to a giant hard-plastic case on wheels. At least two of the three containers were packed to the brim with an assortment of weapons. You never knew what the situation would call for.

Calix grabbed her own bag, a smaller backpack, and followed Karen. She held the sword she favored in her hand, scabbarded. I shook my head. Dmitri had a small rolling suitcase in brown houndstooth print. I wondered if he was making a joke at my expense.

Another wave of vertigo swayed me. To be of any use to the team, I needed to get this stuff out of my system.

"*Herr* Keller?" Dmitri regarded me with curiosity but offered no help. "Are you joining us?"

"Sure." Nodding was out of the question. I wasn't sure I could move my head without another bout of dizziness. "Wouldn't miss it."

Walking stiffly to avoid courting another round of glowing and blacking out, I started after the two women. Alone of the four of us, I carried no bag. I'd left Randall's duffel back at the compound. MONIKER hadn't scheduled any shopping expeditions, and I didn't have any stuff. Not even a change of underwear. Just the St. Jude medal around my neck and a positive attitude. Dmitri fell into step next to me.

"You are anxious, yes? For the..." Instead of completing his sentence, he glanced skyward where the almost-full moon waited behind the clouds. I don't know why he didn't just come out and say it.

"Full moon?" I prompted.

"Not that." Once again, he gazed at me steadily, like I was a student he was waiting on to quit joking around and give him the answer he sought.

"I am always waiting for that, Dmitri Pietrovitch," I answered, knowing full well he meant the *Überwechsel*.

"It is curious, is it not, that you can so easily call the smaller wolf to you? And yet, for him, you wait."

I held up my arm with the cuff. "I'm not calling any change right now."

Dmitri shrugged. Somewhere in the back of my memory, I heard the ghost of Aleksy's mocking laugh.

Karen and Calix waited for us next to a black Land Rover parked at the curb just outside the fence. As we walked up, Karen seated herself behind the wheel. Calix grabbed Dmitri's suitcase and tossed it —gently—in the back, then closed the hatch. Nobody argued with him when he took shotgun, even though it was, technically, my turn.

"Everyone got their seatbelts on?" Karen glanced back. Dmitri had already put his on. "Hold tight."

She didn't peel away from the curb, screeching to alert everyone in earshot. Instead, she calmly pulled away, accelerating steadily until we were speeding along through the Eastern European night, on our way to rescue a girl.

"That doesn't look like some super-secret R&D compound." Calix and I had settled in for some morning surveillance halfway up the mountains that bordered the Black Mountain facility. "It looks more like some expensive spa. I think that blotchy guy is getting his toenails clipped. Gross."

She offered me the binoculars, which I waved away. There are sights I'd like to never see, and some naked dude getting his toes done is one of them.

"Makes sense. Their facility up north looked like an upscale bullshit adventure tour place." I shifted, trying to get comfortable. We were both lying prone on our bellies, and there were rocks. This was stupid. The thought made sense, so I said it aloud. "This is the dumbest idea ever."

"Any particular part of it?"

"All of it." Especially the part where I sat in the snow, getting cold and wet. As a rule, I rarely hate on one form or the other. All the different forms of the change are me, so what's the point? But if they wanted to find some sucker to sit here in the snow and freeze his balls off, they didn't need me to do that.

Besides, I knew these woods. Maybe not this particular stretch of forest, but we were back on my hunting ground. My pack had run the paths of the tall pines and mottled, rocky earth, chasing the Green Man for centuries.

It didn't feel right to be here like this—not on two legs. If all were right with the world, I would be just one more wolf, slinking down from the north, unnoticed and unremarkable.

"We've got some kind of movement." Calix had gone back to the binos.

"Let me guess. Now some slick Russian is getting his balls shaved?"

"Close." She didn't bother to look up at my crude jest. "Take a look."

This time, she practically shoved the glasses over my eyeballs. Fine. Still grumpy about the fact that I wasn't furry, and generally pissed at everyone and life, I looked through the glasses.

"What luck." By luck, I mean a woman had just walked into the large, glass-enclosed sun room where several patrons reclined, basking in the rays while protected from the harsh weather outside. She stood as tall as the man who glowered over the room, hands clasped in front of him, bulge of a weapon under his suit jacket—a guard inside the door? Was he keeping people out or preventing them from leaving? Were super-rich people that paranoid?

The woman tugged the hem of her dark-colored dress; it didn't come down much more than halfway past mid-thigh, and she wore a pair of flat, knee-high boots. Her features were sharply defined, symmetrical, her hair cut short, and her lips darker than any natural coloring. Maria looked exactly like her picture.

Something stirred inside, and it wasn't hunger—although you've probably guessed I was starving. Full moon. Hunger. It's a thing.

Rather, this woman struck something inside me. A note of famil-iarity—a memory that rested just outside of remembering. The more I chased it, the faster it slipped away.

Maria walked over to another man within the room—not a patron. He sat ramrod straight, dressed in an expensive suit, perched on a stool at a low bar that looked like it ran the length of the back of the room, although the roof overhang obscured most of it from our view. As she bent to his ear, his face darkened.

Again, I wished in vain to be in a form that heightened my senses instead of crouched in the snow, relying on my eyes at this distance to tell me the story. The binoculars went out of focus. I'd been gripping them with a death grip and quickly loosened my grasp to bring the picture back.

I had missed something. Maria was in the process of standing back up, the man's hand raised. Had he hit her? Did he mark her?

"Rick." Calix tapped my shoulder, then offered me her hand, palm up, to return the binoculars. "You're growling."

With effort, I swallowed my impulse to head down there and tear the man in the suit to pieces and then eat them. Only two more days. Crap. Ow. Fuck. Forgot for a moment not to call the change.

"I almost felt that one." Calix grinned.

"If you want, I can ask them to make one of these for you when we get back."

She laughed, and even cold and wet, the sound chilled me further. "Just a few more days."

Were vampires—excuse me, the Family—telepathic?

"I told you. You're just very easy to read."

I extended my middle finger casually. Yes, my poker face needed work. But now she was just fucking with me.

The click and static of the radio crackled. "Base to team, you got anything for us?"

Calix depressed the button on the handset clipped to her vest. "Team, this is base. Target positively identified."

Click, click. "Got a bead on security?"

Click, click. "Pretty standard perimeter. Internal as well."

Click, click. "Roger. Base out."

For all that the facility resembled a high-end Eurotrash resort, the picture on the ground resolved into a building into which someone had poured a lot of expertise into making it as hard to break into as possible.

No chain link fence topped with barbed wire surrounded the place. However, the wall that did was made of two-feet-thick stone— at least—and topped with art deco lamps that would likely flood the well-maintained grounds, robbing any intruder of a convenient shadow in which to sneak.

Any and all trees had been cleared away from the wall at least ten feet on both sides, and most of the grounds were flat and covered with either grass or some sort of sports equipment. Here and there, a large, old tree had been left so as not to completely de-nude the place. But still. Any intruders, like us, would find it hard to move covertly. And that didn't account for things we couldn't see but assumed were there—motion sensors, alarms, roving patrols, *und so weiter.*

From the looks of the inside, they were prepared there as well—in addition to the interior guard, we caught a glimpse of a canine patrol. Likely, somewhere in there would be a second, hidden facility, much like the operation up north.

Whoever these Black Mountain assholes were, they were well-funded and knew what they were about.

"Does she look like she's being held under duress to you?" Calix mused aloud.

Until she said it, I hadn't thought it. Being so laser-focused on rescuing Dmitri's daughter, I hadn't actually stopped to think about what it might mean if she had maybe disappeared on purpose. After all, that's what Dmitri had as much as told me he'd done. What if she had taken a page from her father's book, and we were going to rescue a damsel who preferred to shack up with the dragon?

This is why I tried not to think too much and just get on with it.

"She looks like she knows what she's about," I finally answered.

"Good looking," Calix added, not reacting to my reply. "Even if she does kind of remind me of her dad."

Ew. On so many levels.

She stowed the binoculars. "Something is not right about this."

"You want to tell Dmitri we're backing out?" I grinned at her.

Calix frowned. Dmitri never really seemed to have the same effect on her he had on others, but that didn't mean she wasn't aware of his strange influence. "No. But I want to make sure we head in there with our eyes open."

"Fair enough."

Below us, the man on the stool caught Maria by the hand. From this distance, squinting, I could just make out his actions. He pushed the sleeve of her dress up to reveal something shiny that caught the glint of the sun and flashed it in our direction. I blinked away the sudden light flare.

My cuff itched. Without thinking, I scratched around it. My thumb brushed over the slight lump of the tracker they'd embedded under my skin. More problems with no solutions.

Yeah, something was weird. Story of my life.

"We gotta get back, figure out our approach." Calix turned to me. "Are you getting anything else I should know about?"

"Not much. This—" I held up my wrist, "—is pretty much damping everything I could find."

"Just do me a favor and try once," she said.

I shrugged. Sure thing. "I'm smelling pine trees, snow, dirt, and kimchi."

"You're a fucking asshole, Rick." She smiled and let the points of her teeth sharpen just enough to give me a hint. "Just do it."

"Okay, okay." I closed my eyes. I don't need to, but most of the time it helps to block out the most useless of my senses to concentrate on what vision can't show me.

As I expected, most of what immediately came to me was information from my immediate environment. The pain of the silver in my cuff laid a miasma over most of it. The change inside me lay coiled tightly, perking up for a moment, then subsiding with a jerk as the cuff zapped me. Maybe I'd gotten used to it; it didn't seem as painful this time. The other, deeper Change sat right below the surface, as if I could reach out and just, maybe...

I pulled myself back from my inner space and sent my sense back out. Like I said, snow and pines and dirt. Maybe a little kimchi. Minute vibrations under my hands alerted me to the small vermin that had grown used to our presence and returned to their slumbers. In the distance, a bird of prey called.

Careful not to try to call the actual change, I did my best to sink into the wolf, casting farther out with the sense that was neither sound nor light nor scent.

The silence droned on, the buzz of the silver disrupting the calm that settled in the morning over snow. In the distance, the rumble of engines alerted me to traffic passing.

What the hell? *No, no—*

I started to scramble to my feet. Calix reacted in a split second, pushing me back down and holding me there with the weight of her body. I struggled, panicking, against the pressure, but she didn't budge.

I ceased my efforts, stilled, reached out again. The silver mingled with Calix's scent, but this time there was no confusion and no denial.

There, in the Czech forest, I picked up a scent I hadn't dreamed of in years—the harsh, yet sweet, smell of woodsmoke and charcoal ash, mingled with hints of hickory and yew. All buried deep in earthy scents of fur and sweat.

The pack.

18

"We got lucky." Karen didn't look up from the laptop screen. "One of their guests just called to cancel their arrival plans, but we were able to intercept and slip into their reservation."

"Which one of us gets a poshy spa date?" Calix polished her sword, her kit spread across the bed in the Soviet-era hostel we were crashing.

"Elishka Beranek and her crotchety old grandpa, Jakub." Karen rubbed her eyes, still glued to the screen. I wondered if she'd gotten any sleep at all. "Plus, their two attendants—one nurse and one bodyguard."

Oh please, let me be the bodyguard.

"Rick, you get to push the wheelchair."

Of course, I did. "Once inside, what's our play?"

"My daughter carries a great deal of information we can use," Dmitri offered. "But she cannot be seen to leave the facility of her own choice."

"We're doing a smash and grab, in case she needs to 'escape' later and head back in?" Calix surmised.

"Yes." Now it was her turn to get the best-student approving smile.

"Our end game is not the total destruction of this organization—rather, the ability to know it, understand it, and observe and influence their activities."

Trust a simple rescue operation to reveal levels of complexity Dmitri had conveniently forgotten to mention.

"So…we aren't removing MONIKER's competition, just tagging their ears?"

"You're not as thick as you pretend, *Herr* Keller."

Hey, wait a minute…pretend? Also, did MONIKER know about this complicated scheme? I somehow thought Dmitri had failed to disabuse them of their assumption that Black Mountain, a potential rival, would be eliminated.

"The Beranek party is scheduled to land at the airport early tomorrow morning," Karen continued, ignoring all of us and giving no reaction to Dmitri's words. "They—we—will be met by an escort shuttle from the spa."

"Let me guess, the Beraneks land, and then we grab them and stash them away for a few days?" It's what we would normally do.

"The Beraneks will never even get on the plane." Karen's face was as blank as her tone. "They called to cancel due to Jakub's timely death."

I couldn't bite back the growl that escaped me. The tension in the room sharpened to a knife's edge.

"Don't be sanctimonious, Rick." Karen continued to stare at me with her dead eyes. "She and her grandfather are responsible for a laundry list of crimes, some of which would make *you* blush."

A bold claim. I sometimes eat people.

"Human trafficking. Weapons trafficking. Sex slaves. Drugs. Ethnic cleansing."

"I get the picture." Same old, same old. You would think Eastern European gangsters would mix it up a little. I still didn't have to like it.

On the bed, Calix finished the last bit of polishing with a flourish. She placed the sword back on the covers and carefully put away her kit. Without saying a word, she walked over to the table Karen worked at, picked up one side, and slid that side closer to the wall.

Karen adjusted her seat to the new angle, also without acknowledgment.

Calix then approached Dmitri, who stood and pushed his own chair back. "Please don't let me inconvenience you, *Fraülein* Solares."

Addressing her by her last name caught Calix off guard. In one swift motion, faster than even I could track, she had her sword in a two-handed grip, resting lightly at his throat. The impossibly sharp metal kissed his skin, too close to fit a piece of paper in between but so tightly controlled so as not to leave a mark.

Karen and I froze. For my part, I neither wanted to get involved or be around in the aftermath of a fight between Calix and whatever Dmitri was. The silence stretched out. In the hallway, a group of young men stumbled past the room, shouting at each other in a language I didn't recognize. Romanian? Then, their drunken merriment faded, and we were back to silence.

I began calculating the number of steps to the door. Perhaps I could make good my escape, and when I got back, they would have figured it out.

Karen turned her gaze back to her work. "Don't kill him, Calix. Unless you want to dress up like Grandpop Beranek and ride in the chair."

Dmitri smiled. It wasn't a mocking smile or even a smile of relief. Instead, his eyes twinkled in what looked to me like approval, as if Calix, in threatening him, had passed some sort of test we didn't even know we were taking.

Abruptly, she removed the sword from his neck, holding it at her side and bowing to Dmitri, who acknowledged her with a nod. He picked up his suit jacket that had been hung carefully on the back of his chair and shrugged it on. "Dr. Willet, Miss Solares."

As if the previous few moments had never happened, he nodded congenially and headed out the door.

The three of us looked at each other, then Karen went back to typing. I had no idea what she was doing. Maybe updating her LinkedIn profile. The old Karen would be checking her weapons and loading ammunition, preparing for the next day's mission. This new Karen seemed to enjoy pushing papers more than my buttons.

In the center of the room, Calix took a deep breath. She placed the sword on the floor next to her feet, closed her eyes, and reached up to the ceiling, arms spread in a meditative pose.

Moving slowly and deliberately, controlling her breathing, she brought her arms down and joined her hands, palm to palm, in front of her.

The next few minutes, the silence was broken only by the tapping of Karen's fingers on the keyboard and the controlled breathing and soft susurrations of Calix's clothing as she started moving her deliberate way through a series of martial arts forms. She was mid-sword-thrust when my stomach growled.

I shook my head, the hunger and frenetic energy of the impending change breaking through my calm. I headed to the door and opened it, pausing just a moment to return Karen's curious glance.

"Going to grab some chow before all this New Age woo-woo rubs off," I offered.

Calix paused and extended her arm slowly, giving me time to bask in the middle finger she waved in my general direction. "Not everyone functions best as furry little rage puppies."

I laughed and headed out to welcome the coming moon as best I could in this limited form.

Night had fallen, the nearly-full moon just visible over the row of buildings lining the cobblestone streets. I'd swiped a couple of Euros from Karen's bag while she'd been distracted, which was enough to stop by a local restaurant and eat beef, cabbage, and potatoes until I felt almost sated. I got a couple of curious looks from the locals, but I ordered in German, so they shrugged and ignored me after I paid.

After I finished eating, I still needed more food, looking for something to fill the rest of the corners of my stomach. When the Change is coming, I'm never full. I bought a couple of pastries and took them with me, ignoring custom and good manners by eating as I walked. Whatever. The weather was cold enough that most people were either indoors or hurrying on their way there.

All I had on was a sweatshirt over a T-shirt, and the cold worked its way under my skin, combining with the wild moon energy and the sickness of the silver that the cuff kept against my body. I kept walking. As long as I was moving, I would be fine.

My steps led me along the bank of a small stream, the stone path skirting the river before rising up in an ancient bridge over the ravine. It was my fault—I wasn't paying attention to anything except my hunger, and every time the clouds parted, my body reminded me how close the moon was to full. Then the cuff sent another warning shot.

The attack came out of nowhere. Something large and blurry tackled me, driving me to my knees. I tried to react, but my attacker rained down a series of well-aimed punches to my kidneys, knees, and other sensitive areas. He had the advantage of surprise, and every time I tried to escape, he met me with another flurry of blows.

I curled up on my side, going fetal, feigning submission.

The large blur started laughing and pushed himself up. As soon as he gave me the slightest room, I scrambled away, coming back up to my feet. The scent of loam and hops drowned out the other night smells, and I swiped at my upper lip with the back of my hand.

"*Der beruhmte* Rickard Keller, black wolf of the family." My attacker topped out at six feet, with thick, dark hair that covered his entire body, and an impressive beard. He spoke German with a heavy Bavarian accent. "It's good to meet you, cuz."

The cuff spasmed, shooting another jolt through me. By now, the spark had definitely weakened, and I clamped down on any external reaction. No way I could display any additional weakness in front of an unknown. Especially not one who smelled like pack.

My silence didn't seem to perturb him. He extended a hand. I stared at it until he let it fall.

"Who are you? What's your lineage?" There was a certain protocol to how things were done. However, I'd been cast out almost a century ago, so it's possible things had changed.

"Your mom."

Well, now he was just being insulting.

"Seriously." He grinned again. "Your mom is my aunt." He extended his hand again. "Gunther Markus Roderick Keller. At your service."

This time, I shook his hand. He gripped mine with a firm and solid grasp, none of the tight-grip shenanigans powerful men and wolves sometimes indulged in. That told me a lot, namely, he felt comfortable enough in his power to not have to play games.

"Rickard Jakob Keller." I retrieved my hand and stepped back out of arm's reach, still wary. Pack or not, he'd taken me down easily, and I didn't want to give him the opportunity to do so again.

"What the hell is that on your arm?"

Of course, he would have noticed the cuff. *"Mu'dir Wurst sein."*

He shrugged, not taking offense that I'd told him to mind his own business. The scent of woodsmoke, hops, and loam intensified.

At that moment, clouds parted, and the moon momentarily shone through. Both of us involuntarily glanced up, growling in unison.

Homesickness washed through me, a tangible discomfort. Longing. I'd made my choices and mostly didn't regret them, but here with a fellow pack member, the pain of remembering the past tightened my throat.

"We've been hearing rumors," Gunther broke the silence. "Things changed after you left."

Considering the continent had endured two world wars, fascism, authoritarianism, genocide, capitalism, communism and the Iron Curtain, reunification, the European Union, and currently seemed to be doing its best to start the cycle all over again—that was an understatement.

"We lost about half the pack." He spoke the words without accusation, but I still felt it as such.

"My…mother?" I wasn't sure if I wanted to know. She had exiled me and placed the threat of final death on my head and those of any pack member foolhardy enough to stay in contact.

Gunther shivered but gave no other sign. "She leads not only our pack but those of the Five Generations."

Interesting. "You mean the Four Generations?"

"Five." Gunther shrugged. "About ten years ago, we started receiving an influx of new pack, refugees from the south."

Each Generation contained packs of lineage from different geographical areas. Gunther and I were First Generation—wolves who came down from the north and settled in central and southern Germany. But there were other families, other packs, each of whom settled in other areas. I'd never had contact with any of them. We all kept to our specific territories. Only the Generation leaders, our pack grandsires—which apparently now included my mother—ever ventured into other territories.

At least, that's how it had been when I betrayed the pack and enlisted as a soldier in von Bismarck's forces, disowned completely and cut off from everyone I'd ever known because I had dreamed of this other pack called "nation."

"Gunther—"

He held up a hand. "I go by Markus."

"Markus, then." My stomach growled. Or maybe his. "Why are you talking to me?"

"Nobody was sure anymore if you were real or some cautionary tale." He shrugged. "No nations, including the pack, made it out of the last century alive and in one piece. We've had to make choices, and who knows? If you'd stuck around, you might have had your chance to wear your pretty uniform."

"Go fuck yourself." I stood up and stalked away, heading toward the bridge. Who the hell was this asshole, sitting here, smelling of pack, judging me?

The pack had been decimated; the pack had been adapting. Did this giant wolf come seeking me? Or was he sent? And fuck them all for finding me after all this time. And fuck me for wanting them to find me and for making the choices that led me to this meeting with a cuff on my arm.

"Rick."

Footsteps behind me. I stopped and whirled, stepping back on an angle to stave off another attack.

Gunther—Markus—hustled after me, drawing up next to me. The two of us faced each other across the bridge, the stone reflecting the moonlight, neither of us entirely human in its glow.

"Rick." He spread his huge hands in front of him, palms up. "Wait. I'm not here because someone sent me. I'm here because I was surveilling that building and looking for a good place to run the moon, and I found you."

"And what will you do now that you have found me?" All of my instincts screamed to leave Markus by himself on this bridge. But my mind and my heart—and my wolf—couldn't turn their back on the chance to have this conversation in my native tongue with a wolf who smelled of home.

I may have said this before, but while it's true I've been speaking English for almost a century now, I still dream in German.

"Don't worry, your secret is safe with me." Markus leaned his back against the stone railing and crossed his arms. "If I tell the pack I saw you and don't bring you home, I'll be the next one exiled."

I stepped back again, keeping some space between the two of us. I wasn't sure what I would do if he acted on that intention, but he was much larger than I. At least in this form. At that thought, the *Über-wechsel* stirred, reaching out to me as before.

This time, I reached back, grateful for its comfort, pulling away just before I touched it. *Scheisse!* I'd never come that close to achieving it outside the full moon before. And I didn't want to give Markus any more information to bring back to the pack—and my mother—than he already had.

Did he notice I couldn't stop twitching? Probably not. He, himself, wasn't the picture of a calm forest evening. He kept glancing up and around, his fingers drumming against his arms. Occasionally, he would push himself up off the railing, then sit back down. He waited for the moon as well, her energy wiring him up for the change.

Markus caught me staring and grinned. "Or, we could run this moon together, cousin. See what havoc we can cause among the villagers and their modern superstitions."

*Yes! Yes, we want to run!*

Biting my lip until I tasted blood, I shook my head. Markus still looked hopeful.

"I will not run with you, cousin." He opened his mouth to answer, but I cut him off. "I am no longer pack, and you don't want to pay the price that's on my head."

"You have a pretty high opinion of yourself, don't you?"

I ignored the bait, even if I didn't think it was true. "And that facility is ours. Anyone who finds themselves present there tomorrow will be ours as well."

Markus pushed himself up off the wall, throwing up two fingers in a British salute. "I don't know you, cousin Rick, and you don't know me. I will stay away, but the pack is pack, and someday you will need someone to negotiate your return."

I doubted that.

He turned and stalked a few steps away, then halted. Swiveling around on the balls of his feet, he gave me another grin. This time, I could glimpse the giant of a wolf he would inhabit in a few days under the moon.

"Family is family, cousin." He spread his arms and shrugged. "If you ever decide to reconcile with yours, come to this bridge."

"Just come here, hang out, chuck some rocks in the water?" I couldn't help the wiseass comment.

"Something like that. *Auf Wiedersehen, Bruder.*" With another wolf-y grin, he turned his back to me and headed away down the road. The shadows swallowed every trace of his passing.

19

The four of us made an interesting if motley cast of characters as we stepped out of the van at the entrance to the Schwarzberg International Resort and Spa. The front was all white stone and glass, although the sheen off the surface made me think the glass had been strengthened with some sort of reinforcing sheeting.

Two attendants hurried out to meet us, helping me get Dmitri's wheelchair ramp down, unlocking the chair from its security buckle in the van, and then wheeling him down. I took over from there, pushing the chair after them as they led us into the bowels of the resort.

Dmitri played the role of feeble, yet feisty, old Jakub to the hilt. If I didn't know better, I would have sworn he was at least three decades older and not at all scary. Calix strode in front of us, looking around at everything we passed, playing the role of the interested granddaughter, wanting to ensure they were getting the proper attention and care for a man of Jakub's wealth and position.

Karen fell into step beside me. I leaned over and pitched my voice so only she could hear. "I feel like I'm working with Charlie's Angels."

"Does that make you Farrah Fawcett?" she returned without cracking a smile.

Her deadpan delivery reminded me of the old Karen, and I grinned, then hastily reverted to a more severe gaze. I was a nurse, after all, and they never smile. Just glare menacingly and threaten to knock you out if you don't quit playing with your IV.

Ahem.

From what we understood from the brochures, the Schwarzberg billed itself as a high-end institution of care, with medical facilities available and the best physicians around. I'd never seen a hospital set up like this place; rather, it appeared to be precisely like the resort and spa its name advertised.

We passed through several large, open rooms, where patients lounged in the late morning sun, reading or playing games in Sudoku or crossword puzzle books. Not a single television blared; the only sound was the hush of pages turning. The scuff of my feet on the floor made me feel self-conscious.

Mission jitters aside, something was off about this place. In addition to the near silence, the halls and rooms gave off no scent: no perfumes, no subtle aromas of urine and bleach, no flowery indoor plants, no aromatherapy—nothing. Almost as if the entire place was one giant void of sensation.

Calix looked back at us as if checking to see we were still there, then turned around again.

"This place gives me the creeps," I muttered.

To my surprise, Karen answered. "You're not the only one."

The sterile nature of the facility asserted itself even more strongly as we headed down another corridor. I got the feeling we were leaving the resort area behind us. The halls of open, inviting rooms and lounge areas gave way to small, boxy offices, and closed, heavy doors with no windows or identifying plaques.

My senses started humming. Next to me, I could almost taste the adrenaline that began building under Karen's skin, a sweet liqueur underlying her normal scents of rosemary and, now, cinnamon. It gave a welcome contrast to the uncanny lack of anything around us.

The attendants led us around several more corners. I was pretty sure I knew how we had gotten there, but I didn't want to test that knowledge. Maybe the others had kept track.

The two men ushered us into a large room at the end of the final hallway, waiting at the door as we filed inside. I briefly wondered if the others would react—clearly, we had not arrived at the all-expenses therapeutic bath and massage they'd assured us awaited Grandpa Jakub when he arrived.

"Please wait here," one of the attendants instructed in lightly accented English. "The doctor will be here soon."

The two of them left the room and closed the door behind them. The faintest clicking sound informed us they had locked the door as they left.

"Looks like someone was expecting us," Calix offered, prowling down one side of the room and up the other. One long conference table, a few chairs, and a water dispenser stood in an unreasonably large space. Unlike at MONIKER, no windows or shitty motivational posters adorned the walls. Just the giant room and the table. Maybe they had a lot of standing-room-only meetings. Who knew.

"Well, shit," was all I had to say. "So much for all that sneaking around."

"Shut up, Rick," Karen said, leaning her ear against the door. She looked like Nancy Drew, and I snorted.

"Don't worry, they're coming back."

"We were expected." Dmitri stood, brushing imaginary wrinkles from his slacks and suit jacket.

"What do you know?" Calix examined the walls, trying to find some hidden weakness.

"I know that a good operative, faced with the unexpected appearance of unwanted allies, would immediately think this is a trap, and she must be the one to spring it." Dmitri's face didn't betray anything except possibly some minor annoyance. In fact, he checked his watch, looking for all the world like a commuter whose train was five minutes late.

The lock in the door clicked, and we all turned, except for Dmitri, who clasped his hands behind his back, facing the rest of us.

"Good morning, *Herr* Beranek."

The woman who spoke was at least three inches shorter than either Karen or Calix, although she still stood two or three inches taller than me. The presence she exuded dwarfed the three of us. In fact, the only thing in the room that matched her intense energy was her father's slight figure.

We barely paid attention to the squad of heavily armed men who entered with her, surrounding us, patting us down. I didn't have anything on me to find, but Calix grimaced at the foolish mortal who relieved her of her sword, the gleam in her eye promising a slow disembowelment.

"Maria." Dmitri acknowledged her, turning to face his daughter. "You look well."

I stared at her, trying to square what I thought of her father with the woman who stood at the vortex of all the activity, like a mountain in the eye of a storm. Her eyes shone a light grey, and I wondered if they were green.

"Pull yourself together, Rick," Calix muttered.

Dmitri spared me a quick, calm look, and I almost crapped my pants. Now was not the time to be musing if his daughter had green eyes. In fact, probably never would be a good time to think about his daughter's eyes.

One of the Black Mountain minions slung Calix's sword over his back, and then they ushered us out of the room at gunpoint, leaving Dmitri's wheelchair behind as they herded us down another maze-like set of corridors. This is where a few weeks of planning and rehearsal would have been useful. Or even one of those corporate icebreaker team building exercises. We hadn't planned for a trap to be sprung, and I didn't want to be the only one to start clawing my way out of it and then realize the others were going with a different plan.

The strange sense void lingered throughout the corridors. From the minions and Maria herself, I couldn't detect anything. It reminded me, unpleasantly, of Dr. Gratusczak.

The resemblance grew stronger as we approached a reinforced steel double door and stumbled to a halt. Maria swiped her hand over a small, black sensor. It beeped, and then someone unlocked the door from the inside with a key, a curious mix of technological and mechanical security.

Inside the room, the déjà vu that had begun with the sense of nothing returned in full force. We found ourselves in a laboratory not unlike the one MONIKER had built for Dr. Gratuszcak.

"Come on up to the lab," I muttered again.

Calix grinned. "And see what's on the…slab."

We thought we were hilarious. Everyone else regarded us like we had farted in front of the Pope.

The only difference—and it was a major one—was that instead of only one research subject—yours truly—this lab had apparently decided to head into the testing phase of whatever they were working on. Along one row stood a series of six hospital beds, three currently occupied by two men and a woman, all far past middle age.

"Are those…patients?" Why was I asking them? This wasn't the movies, where some evil villain was going to spill the beans.

Speaking of evil villains, this lab came complete with its own version of Dr. G. A short, gnomish man of indeterminate origin had met our arrival with dispassionate, clinical interest. He held a clipboard, referring to it as he looked us up and down, then over at the beds.

"*Herr Doktor* Mengele, I presume?"

"The women, Ms. Nicolaiova." The man ignored my quip, gesturing with his pen in the general direction of the beds, then regarded Dmitri and I, assessing us both against some unknown criteria. "And the younger one."

"The older?" Maria asked in as flat and sociopathic a voice as I'd ever heard.

"Discard." He turned away from us, clearly expecting the orders to be followed without needing follow-up or close supervision.

The minion standing next to Dmitri raised a gun to his head, the hammer already cocked, and depressed the trigger. The shot echoed in the small space.

The next few moments happened so quickly that even I had trouble keeping track of time and reality.

Maria froze, betraying no sign of reaction.

Beside me, Calix went full vampire, eyes brightening with their intense glow, teeth sharpened to points.

Karen stepped toward the gnome-like scientist. She had no chance to reach him. Chaos would overwhelm her path. But her instinct was to go for the biggest monster in the room.

My ears rang. In the aftermath of the shot, as time started moving again, the minions reacted to the attack, piling on each of us. Two of them reached for me, and my instincts reached for the change.

So not only did I get the shit kicked out of me by Hans and Franz, but I kept jerking like a squirrel caught in an electrical fence. Under the onslaught, I lost track of the others. I lost track of anything except the boot that caught me in the ribs, the rifle butt on the side of my face, the electric shock that splayed me back out when I tried to curl in on myself.

A body thudded to the floor next to me. Dmitri? One of the others? The gnome Mengele?

Adrenaline flooded through me. I screamed, back arching, reaching for the change. The cuff gripped me in its charged embrace. I no longer felt anything else except white-hot liquid pain as the device took me for one long ride on the lightning.

Within the howl echoing through my head, as my ears deafened with the discharge of weapons in an enclosed concrete space, I screamed until even my inner voice had hoarsened to a mute growl.

My wolf and I drew a long breath, ragged and splintered from the agony. And in that half second of silence, the *Überwechsel* reached out.

I grabbed for the older, larger Change like a drowning man for a lifeline.

Somewhere in my subconscious, I knew it wasn't time. The moon shone just shy of its full orb. And yet, this Change called to me, and I opened myself fully to the invitation.

My bones cracked, and the skin stretched and split with the now familiar agony, but with a different type of pain. This pain had me howling for joy and eager for the hunt.

Some force outside myself lifted me up. The final manifestations of the Change twitched through me. The last vestiges of pain faded into slavering pleasure.

In the back of my mind, a flash of dark green, and leaves, and urgent *geas*. Green Jack whispered to me, loosing me on his mission of cleansing chase. *"Los! Der Mond ruft dich an..."*

Reveling—perhaps indulging—in this freedom, I howled until at least one of the lights overhead shattered, and then I leapt into the maelstrom.

Claws flashing, teeth bared, ripping and mauling, I laughed at these little men who screamed and scrambled and aimed their little guns as if something as pathetic as bullets or silver could stop me.

The familiar, comfortable red painted the floor, the ceiling, and everywhere I could reach. I savored the coppery taste in my mouth and the satisfaction of flesh giving way in my jaws.

The only sadness was that there weren't enough bad guys for me to wreak havoc among, and too soon I stood in a pile of bodies, panting, scanning the room for a new threat.

A bloody tableau met my eyes. Karen stood off to the side, holding Mengele or whatever his name was in a chokehold in front of her. His face betrayed no reaction, but she had seen me do this before.

Calix stared. Somewhere in the chaos, she had reclaimed her sword, and held it away from her, at the ready. The bright blade glimmered, shiny with wet blood.

I whipped my head around. Dmitri and Maria stood beside each other on the other side of the room. The first thing I noticed was that Maria's eyes were indeed a brilliant green, the sort of shade that sees past every defense you erect, right into the soul you tried to forget you had.

The second thing I noticed was that Dmitri's hands were smoking, and Maria held a ball of fire in hers.

What the hell?

Nobody spoke for a full ten seconds. I worked my jaw, trying to rearrange my tongue around all these teeth.

Finally, I simply pointed and growled: "Door."

Calix's jaw actually dropped, vampire face and all, which made me laugh. Karen snapped back to reality and rolled her eyes.

"What's back there?" Karen gave Mengele a little shake to emphasize her question.

The little man just shrugged.

On one of the beds, one of the older patients moaned. We'd all forgotten they were there, judging by the startled looks on everyone's faces. Not mine. Benefits of one's face being completely furry.

Maria gestured, and the fire burning above her hands faded away. She walked over and punched in the code.

A giant metal sliding door that took up the entire wall slowly opened. It was as if the wall gently stepped to the side.

Calix and I took the lead. I stepped into the room, claws up, senses spreading out. I knew what I would find from the stench of death that met me even before I crossed the threshold, but I didn't want to see it all the same.

I've seen horrific sights in my life. I've been in places where men became monsters who led their fellow men to horrific deaths. I've dripped blood from my teeth and claws, and hunted prey that walked on two feet. I've been the shadow in the night that took it down and ripped apart and reveled in it.

But the contents of this room showed us something far beyond that. Bright fluorescents overhead illuminated the gaping concrete cavern, their green-tinged lights casting a harsh green glow that lit, unflinching, the slaughterhouse within.

## 20

Death had stained this slaughterhouse for decades, the discarded blood and carnage seeping into the pores of the concrete until even I couldn't tell where the building ended and the horror show began.

The charnel hit me so hard I almost missed the army that faced us.

Row upon row of…creatures…stood, lined up with military precision, preternaturally still, highlighted in sharp, uncanny relief under the garish fluorescent lights.

They might have been human at some point in the past. They still stood on two legs and reached out with two upper limbs. Their skin still glowed under the lights with the pallor of human death.

But that was where their humanity ended, and the monster began.

"What in the cold hell…?" Karen's voice trailed off. In her grasp, Mengele began to giggle. After a few seconds, he showed no signs of stopping. The sound ricocheted around the room, returning to unnerve us once again.

"Thus, once again, we all play God." Dmitri spoke in a flat, unastonished tone of voice. His words did not affect the little man, who regaled us with his hilarity.

I reached out with one fist full of claws and ripped out his throat.

No one broke the sudden silence. Karen didn't even give me a disapproving look. Instead, she simply let Mengele's body—whoever he'd been—drop to the floor, sending its red pool out over the many-times-stained floor.

A movement from somewhere in the ranks caught our attention. Karen raised her weapon. We waited, but nothing else happened. Not right away.

I had thought Dr. Gratuszcak's twisted experiments strange enough. And indeed, these beings exhibited some of the same characteristics. They threw no scent. None at all. They lacked even the scent void that marked other, similar experiments. For the first time, it occurred to me that I would find this enemy difficult to track, let alone overcome.

"What are they waiting for?" Calix muttered.

At her side, Karen scanned the room, weapon tracking and at the ready. From the rank sweat clogging her pores, I sensed she had less faith in the rifle than she usually carried. "Are they even alive?"

In answer, a hushed whisper slithered around the room. The creatures in the first rank shifted almost imperceptibly.

"Not alive." Maria stood and moved her arms in a complicated gesture. Balls of green fire sprang to life at her fingertips. "Not quite."

Beside me, Dmitri mirrored his daughter, although the light he conjured shone bright white and blinding. I blinked back against the glare and crouched. Speaking in this form was possible but not easy, and I forced the words past drool and sharp teeth.

"Flank 'em." Drool. "Don't let them conth— concthethrate their mash."

Karen rolled her eyes. "Thanks for the tactics lesson, Benji."

Jaw deformities aside, I tried thinking up a suitably witty reply. I didn't get the chance before, in the instant she turned to me, all hell broke loose.

A wave of sound erupted from the throats of the creatures, an eerie ululation that ran shivers down even my furry spine. The phalanx of monsters charged, sprinting toward our small group.

To Karen's credit, she didn't hesitate. Running to the left flank, she fired round after round into the packed ranks.

From my crouch, I tensed my muscles and sprang up and forward. The roof of the giant room was higher than expected but still low enough to impede my movement, and I didn't land as far in as I hoped.

The monsters failed to give way under my landing, and I slashed with teeth and claws to find some purchase so as not to be over-whelmed. I'd expected them to turn and face my attack, break off their forward movement, but they ignored me in their march toward the others.

"*Sprava, Papa!*" Maria's voice rang out over the din of Karen's weapon firing and the blood rushing in my ears.

Something grabbed my arm and almost yanked my shoulder out of the socket. Another grabbed my legs, hugging and tripping me. Immobilized, I fought to get free. Teeth found the tender parts of my body. Throwing my head back, I roared and snapped.

These monsters were stronger and faster than I'd expected. It had been a long time since I felt fear in battle, but its icy fingers reached for me now in every hand and finger these things laid on me.

Twisting, I managed to slice across one of the limbs holding my arms. At least their skin opened and bled like any other creature. One of them fell away, holding its severed arm. I expected it to scream. It didn't. Its departure gave me enough room to scratch, claw and bite at the others.

All the time I fought, the close formation of the monster troops pushed me forward, pinioning me amongst their advancing ranks. As we approached where the sliding door had opened, our momentum slowed.

Now I started to get glimpses above the chaos. Scents and sounds. The others had formed a vague horseshoe to catch the formation. Dmitri and Maria stood at the head to block it, the soft scent and the flashing lights alerting me to their position. Whatever they were doing, it seemed effective. Monsters were falling, thinning the herd.

On either side, Calix chewed through the flank, sword flashing, eyes glowing. I caught glimpses as I fought my way back up.

Once again, the surrounding creatures slowly overwhelmed me, gripping one by one until about half a dozen immobilized me. The ones to my rear pulled back. Their fellows pulled forward and out, and even in my *Überwechsel* state, I resisted in vain. The tendons along my elbow and knee joints stretched, popped, and began to give way.

*"Scheisse!"* Great. My last words would be a German swear word before a bunch of Frankensteins pulled me to pieces. It would be my luck that's how I'd go. And what the hell happened to Karen? Her weapon had gone silent.

Fearing the worst gave me an extra bite of adrenaline. I twisted my head, gnawing in random directions, twisting under the creatures' grasp. I freed myself just enough...

"Herr Keller!" Dmitri's voice rang out over the seething mass. Now that the rifle had stopped firing, I had no problem hearing him. My eardrums were almost healed, even if I was about to lose my arms and legs past the bendy parts. "You must get out of there."

Easier said than done, but I didn't want to stick around to find out what would happen if I didn't follow Dmitri's directions.

More and more creatures pressed against me. I cursed again. Death swept me with a tentative caress. And this stupid move had been my fault. Grunting and straining, I pulled and pushed and gnashed and slashed in vain. They pressed in so close they were smothering me. My lungs, empty, fought to expand. Dark spots danced in front of my vision.

Laughter echoed past me. I recognized Aleksy's chuckle. What the hell? He really was turning into my own personal Yoda. Except that was it. Just the laughter. Maybe he wasn't visiting me. Maybe I was going to visit him.

"Rick!" Karen's voice rang out. "Get your ass out of there. Now."

Her voice snapped me back to myself. No way would I die smothered to death by some weird mutated experiment. I drew a deep breath, tried to calm my racing heart, and released the Change. Just a bit.

My arms and legs collapsed in on themselves, narrowing and shortening. My brain considered all the reasons why this wouldn't work, even as the wolf inside me suggested my brain shut up before I froze and couldn't do it. I'd never changed from the overwolf to my mundane wolf, but now my life depended on it.

It barely worked.

With my smaller frame, I twisted from their grasps before they could re-adjust to grab me again. All the time, we were moving forward. As my four legs hit the ground, I darted away, twining myself through their legs, finding the smallest gap to squeeze through. My teeth gnarled and slashed as I went. I bit at their heels and tore streaming ribbons of flesh, the taste rancid on my tongue.

No time to assess if I had an effect. I finally squeezed and shouldered my way past the first rank, tearing past the monsters and skidding to a halt beyond where the others waited in a ragged line, weapons at the ready.

"Close your eyes, *Volk*."

Dmitri and Maria barely waited until I had cleared the mass of oncoming soldiers. As one, they raised their hands and joined them, combining their weird lights.

A crashing sound, not as loud as a sonic boom but close, thundered through the rooms. The percussive roar threw me to the ground, immediately nauseous. Karen fell to her knees. Calix raised her sword. Blood trickled from their ears.

The light expanded with the noise, washing the room in a bright wave. I did not close my eyes, and my vision whited out and blurred to a gray and white static.

Silence.

I staggered to my feet. Breathing. Heartbeats. I wasn't alone. Dmitri and Maria came to me the strongest. Dmitri's heart rate was slightly elevated, but the man barely broke a sweat. Karen and Calix were still somewhere off to the left. Calix had a weird hiccup in her heart I hadn't noticed before.

The creatures? Were they gone? Shit. More implications of an opponent that left barely any signature of their presence.

"We need to get out of—" Even as Karen spoke, an alarm sounded. Footsteps scrambled several corridors down.

Cloth polished steel and the smell of blood momentarily strengthened then diminished as Calix sheathed her blade. I blinked, my vision clearing to where I could make out blurry outlines.

Karen shrugged on a white lab coat. It didn't quite cover her weapon and tactical gear, but it might work in a pinch as an improvised disguise. She led the way to the door, taking a quick look before motioning the rest of us to follow.

Calix headed out next, and I padded after. Better than wandering around the facility naked. Maybe I'd get mistaken for a therapy dog. The thought made me grin and drool a little.

"I'm following after." Maria nodded to Dmitri. He and I paused outside the door to the first room, curious and impatient.

Maria pushed first one hospital bed, then another, our way. She paused by the third bed, felt for a pulse, and then waved us on. Dmitri wrangled the beds out of the room as she opened one of the cabinets and pulled out two large buckets.

The liquid in them burnt the inside of my nose and singed my newly-healing eyeballs, even from across the hallway. She cracked them open and carefully splashed the contents over the dead bodies, the electronics, more of the bodies, Mengele's notes, and so forth until the entire room reeked with the acrid stench.

Maria hurried to the door and pulled out a book of matches. Striking one, she folded it into the rest of the matchbook until it flared up, then tossed it into the room, slamming the door as she did so.

From behind the door, the *whoosh* of oxygen being sucked out of the room thundered, and the door metal heated several degrees. Whatever she had stoked the flames with had started an inferno.

"*Davai, Papa.*" Maria hurried past us, taking the lead down the hall. Karen and Calix, ahead of us, had disappeared.

Dmitri merely raised an eyebrow, catching my still half-blind gaze, and nodded. We followed obediently after.

The rest of the facility teemed and swarmed with chaos. Several times, heavy footsteps converged on our position, usually made by heavily armed and armored men, heading to the door of the room we so recently abandoned. At first, I wondered why they didn't stop us, but then remembered Maria still had her credentials. After everything that had happened, I momentarily forgot that tidbit.

That struck me as weird. She had, quite quickly and comfortably, become a member of a team that was still having trouble actually becoming a team. We were taking orders and not even thinking about it. Must run in her twisted family.

We finally neared the area that looked more like a health spa than a military research facility. Elderly patients shuffled along, helped by nurses in starched uniforms and burly men with pistols strapped under their armpits.

The front doors had been propped open. In the hallway, the alarm had coalesced into an intermittent, ear-piercing blare, reminding us over and over to leave. Leave now. No problem. I intended to.

As we headed out the front, one of the burly men who had positioned himself near the exit reached toward Maria. She flashed her identification badge in his general direction. Perhaps unfazed by the badge, or extra suspicious of my presence, he tried again.

"*Gaspazha—*" He grabbed her elbow. "*Dyevuchka.*"

Maria did not stiffen or threaten. Instead, she paused. Turned to him. Smiled. "*Darf ich Ihnen helfen?*"

Whatever he saw in her eyes convinced him to drop his grip and lower his glance. He mumbled something under his breath and returned to waving people through the exit.

The three of us passed the large crowd that gathered a few hundred meters down from the exit. They presented quite a sight— patients shivering in gowns and thin blankets, flanked by paramilitary soldiers. From some of the patients' reactions, the military presence came as a surprise.

Whatever Maria had coaxed the fire with, it burned impressively. Smoke flooded its way to the front of the building, and flames licked out of several windows.

"Wait, where's Karen and the other woman?" Maria looked around. "They were ahead of us."

Shit. They were. I thought my eyesight, still healing, had kept me from finding them, but no. I should have sensed them, even in the crowd and the cold air.

"They'll be here," Dmitri said mildly. "We should be ready to go before we draw more attention."

"*Chyort.*" Maria tucked her badge away and lowered her head, letting her hair fall around her face.

Uneasy, I crept closer to her. One or two of the uniformed personnel looked at us, pointing. *Don't do it, hero. Just stay with the old people.*

The smell of smoke grew stronger, woodsmoke mixed with other more astringent aromas. If my sinuses were to be trusted, we were almost immersed in it.

I growled.

"Calm yourself, *Herr Wolf.*" Dmitri patted me absently on the neck and turned away. Any other man would have been disemboweled for the casual touch, but Dmitri's touch froze me instead.

"Glad to see you guys made it out all right." Calix's voice sounded hoarse. She coughed wetly. "Why are you just standing around?"

I have never in my entire life seen Dmitri as discomfited as the women's appearance made him. He didn't show it much—just a widening of the eyes and quickening of the pulse, then he turned and started toward the back of the parking lot where we'd left the van. By now, a series of emergency vehicles was streaming onto the property. Few people were leaving, but I placed my faith in Maria's magic badge. Had to.

"Had to duck out a side door," Karen explained. "Got a little hot in there."

And now the crowd responded to the new arrivals, who were corralling people, sorting them, moving them. If we didn't get going, we were going to be corralled and sorted, too, which would kind of negate everything we'd done.

Calix and Karen edged back and away, heading after Dmitri. With a final look at the facility and the faintest of shrugs, Maria and I followed.

---

Crossing borders wasn't as easy as it had once been, with the spasms of nationalism the countries making up the European Union were feeling these days. I wondered how long it would take before more of the old country lines were drawn, re-drawn, and fought over again.

We didn't want to take a chance, nor did we feel like running into one of the random checkpoints that just happened to spring up here and there. None of us had any extra cash for a bribe. While most of us could easily slip alone across any artificial geographic marker, none of us felt like doing so.

Dmitri drove without asking for directions or offering an explanation. What the hell was on him mind? His words from earlier ran through my brain. *My daughter cannot be seen to leave the facility of her own choice...* Funny how that had worked out exactly not according to plan.

I had a million questions and four people with no desire to give me answers. Also, it appeared we were *not* headed back to the hotel we'd been at. It was probably a good thing I didn't have any luggage, the way we were bouncing from one knee-jerk reaction to the next.

Grumbling to myself, I curled up in a ball and dozed until Dmitri finally pulled the van to a halt in front of a large stone building resembling something Bram Stoker once declined to use in a book due to excess dreariness.

"We're here," Dmitri announced. "Get out."

# 21

The inside of the hostel turned out to be as depressing as the outside. At some point in the sixties, some Iron Curtain fashionista had gutted the ancient building and re-dressed the inside from the *Little Gray Book of Correct Interior Soviet Design*.

The rooms weren't any better. Small and narrow, I was willing to bet they had been split into two or three rooms from the original structure. Each contained a bed with a striped blanket, a chair, a folding stand, and a brittle paper taped to the back of the door showing where the stairs were in case of a fire.

At the front desk, the old woman manning the concierge had frowned and spat a couple of rounds of fast Czech at Dmitri when she caught a glimpse of me. She'd been mollified by a short stack of Euros and shrugged, handing over a couple of sets of keys.

Karen and Calix peeled off to their own closet-shaped room. Maria did the honors for me at the room across the hall. I'm good at several things, but opening a door without opposable thumbs is a trick I haven't learned yet.

To my surprise, she followed me into the room. I growled. Top ten on my list of things I didn't want in my life was for Dmitri to see his daughter follow me into a bedroom and close the door.

No luck.

She sat at the desk, pulled out a phone, and started talking in a language I didn't recognize.

I waited ten minutes, then gave up. I felt bone tired. My brain tried to race around in circles, reminding me of everything I should be thinking of, but my body decided to hop up on the bed, curl its furry self up, and rack out.

My life is the moon waxing and waning. It pulls on me with ever greater urgency as the full moon approaches, no matter what form I'm in.

I awoke as the moon set, two hours before sunrise. Had I been dreaming? I couldn't remember, but I thought I might have.

A wrong note tugged at my consciousness. Something definitely felt out of place.

Oh, crap. I was human. I had fallen asleep furry and woken up human. I hadn't changed in my sleep since I was a teenager. When we're younger, and the change is more fluid, sure, there were plenty of night changes.

But now? Never. Not in a century and a half.

Still, there I found myself, in the flesh, awake at four in the morning, and the only clothes I could find were a neatly folded small pile on the folding stand. Jeans, button-down shirt, shoes, and a belt.

Next to this mysteriously appearing wardrobe sat a laptop, a cell phone and charger, and several discarded articles of feminine clothing.

No. Oh no.

If I thought allowing Maria to let me into the room and come in after me looked bad, this took the impending odds of my demise into the outer stratosphere.

Not only did I find myself human and butt naked, but Maria lay, stretched out beside me, in the same condition. I froze.

"*Ti ne spish?*" She spoke, sleepy, languid. She turned over on her side, propping herself up on one elbow.

"Just woke up." My voice sounded unnaturally loud in the small room, although I could swear I wasn't speaking louder than a conversational tone.

Maria smiled, and my stupid body short-circuited most of the signals to my brain. The bed we shared wasn't that large, the space between us dangerously small.

She reached out to me, brushing the tips of her fingers over my stomach.

Her touch sent the electric shock I needed racing through my nerves. I scrambled to the side and ended up gracefully falling on my ass out of bed, thumping my head on the wooden frame and knocking myself dizzy.

"Rick?" The concern in Maria's voice almost brought me to tears at the slapstick nature of my love life.

"I'm fine." I willed the pounding in my head to fade away. "I'm fine. I'm just going to…get dressed. Maybe go find some coffee."

Maybe go run it off. For half a second, I reached for the change. Before the second half of the second, I pulled back from it. The expected electric shock never came. Of course. I wasn't wearing the cuff anymore. The larger Change had purged the tracker from my body. And yet, the Pavlovian response remained. Shit.

On the floor, I waited for Maria to go back to sleep so I could figure out what to do with my life. Instead, she looked over the side of the mattress, giving me a once over. At that moment, I felt sure she intended to say something sarcastic, but instead, she just started chuckling.

Shrugging, I decided if she saw me as an unthreatening joke, I might as well take advantage of the situation and get dressed without embarrassment.

"I'm not laughing at you." Maria leaned back in the bed, pulling the sheet over her. "You've been spending too much time around Americans. You're all shy and everything."

That actually did hurt my feelings. Also, was she an actual mind reader? Or was I once again that transparent? I gave up and pulled on the pants.

"Where did you find clothes in the middle of the night in the Czech Republic?" I desperately needed to change the subject. My body, pissed I wasn't taking Maria up on her invitation, kept letting me know it stood ready to go. *Down, boy.*

"Oh, please." She rolled her eyes. "It wasn't difficult enough to be impressed."

"What would be difficult enough for me to be impressed?" I shrugged on the shirt, tugging the waist low enough to hide some of the awkward situation going on in my pants. "Landmine? Suitcase nuke?"

"Pff." She sat up, pulling her hair back as she did. "Please. Eastern Europe. I said, 'difficult'."

"I see your point."

"Rick. Come here." Maria held out her hand to me. Deep breaths. I took it, and she pulled me back down beside her. This time, with some clothes on and her under the sheet, I felt more comfortable. Still wouldn't want her father walking in on us like this. Or the other women. "You're strung up like a wire. What are you so nervous about? The mission?"

"More like Dmitri," I admitted. "You know your father is in the other room?"

"So?" She shrugged. "Of course. He needs sleep like anyone."

"That's not what I meant."

Maria regarded me for a few moments, searching my face. I wasn't sure what she was looking for. Or if she found it. "You and my father are a lot alike."

"We are?" An unexpected comparison. I didn't know if I totally agreed.

"You're both very old school." She snuggled against me, finding her way into the space under my arm until I gave up and put my arm around her. "My father trained me. He knows there would be nothing you could force me to do if I didn't want to. Quit worrying."

"I'll try."

She chuckled again softly. We lay together, and as the moments passed, it felt less strange. Almost comforting.

Outside in the hall, a door opened, then closed. Footsteps headed down the corridor to the communal water closet. Calix. I wondered if she could sense Maria and I curled up with each other.

And then I heard nothing, falling into a sleep deeper than any slumber I'd had in years. I dreamed of falling snow and running wolves, and a jade-eyed woman who ran by my side.

---

A werewolf, a vampire, two magicians, and a badass walk into a café.

Of course, to get to this café, we had to cross two borders and hop a train. As I said, border crossings had gotten iffy in the past year. The guards peered at us with suspicion, deserved on our part since our papers were mostly created out of thin air and some hand waving from Dmitri and Maria.

Karen had informed us we would fly out of Frankfurt, back to Las Vegas. MONIKER had taken care of the reservations, as long as we could reach the airport without attracting undue attention.

I'm the part of the team that does the growling, the sneaking and the fighting, which is why I was glad the other team members were good at the forging paperwork stuff. Even with a few suspicious border guards, we were soon safely on our way, comfortably ensconced aboard a train to Frankfurt, enjoying quite a late breakfast spread in the dining car.

They had wurst, thick German pretzels, yogurt, more wurst, *Käse*, mineral water…

"Rick." Karen's voice brought me back to reality.

"Mmf?" I spared her the sight of my mouth filled with sausage and cheese.

"Just checking to make sure you're still with us."

I nodded. Of course. But seriously, German breakfast is a beautiful thing, and it had been a really, *really* long time since I'd had one.

"We managed to get most of the server cloned before everything went to hell," Calix continued. I hadn't realized she'd been explaining why they'd been late escaping the Black Mountain facility. "That info dump should keep the MONIKER data monkeys going for a few months."

Dmitri nodded. He sipped a cup of strong, black coffee.

"We have some friends who will also be interested in what I could glean from working with them," Maria added.

"Friends?" My mouth was still full, but I could enunciate. Mostly.

"We work with…others," Dmitri said. "Not so formal. But useful."

"Now that we've retrieved your daughter, I take it we're not so useful?" Calix, her plate piled impressively high, joined me in eating our way through the menu. I wouldn't have guessed.

Dmitri shrugged. Maria sipped her coffee. Unlike her father, she preferred a dollop of cream. Every time I looked over at her, I couldn't stop staring.

"Where are you heading after we get off in Frankfurt?"

Karen's question startled me, and I almost choked on the pretzel in my mouth. It hadn't occurred to me that Dmitri and Maria would leave us after the rescue. Although, as I thought about it, that course of action made the most sense. After all, why should I even head back to MONIKER?

"That's an excellent question, Doctor Willet." Dmitri set his coffee cup down and folded his hands on the table, leaning forward. "One that requires, perhaps, some explanation."

"It would be welcome, yes," Karen answered.

"My daughter and I—you may have realized we are in possession of skills that are, shall we say, unusual for these times?"

"That's one way of putting it." Calix snorted.

Maria and Dmitri exchanged glances.

"This will be faster if we continue without interruption." If I'd ever doubted Dmitri spent time as a German professor, the stern disapproval he managed to pack into that short sentence resolved any lingering reservations.

Karen nodded, and Calix simply chewed and shut up. I hadn't even been tempted to talk. Not when the menu included German sausage. Four different kinds. And did I mention the cheese?

"My family is old," Dmitri began. "Older even than yours, Herr Wolf."

That didn't surprise me. Dmitri hadn't aged since 1943.

"Like your family, we have kept our secrets, hidden our talents." He sipped some more coffee. "Unlike your family, we have spent lifetimes standing in the shadows of the powerful, the elite."

"How old?" Calix couldn't help but ask.

"I am the eldest of my family line," Dmitri answered, "and I first entered the service as counselor and advisor to Peter the Great."

Karen stopped chewing. I had expected him to say something along those lines, but it still unnerved me to hear it out loud.

"Our family has spent generations in service to the Tsar and, later, the people of Russia," Maria added.

"And you are all…" Karen trailed off, searching for the word.

"Sorcerers. Yes." Dmitri dropped the word as blandly and casually as he dabbed his napkin at his mouth.

"How…how is that… How the hell are supernatural creatures running around Europe, and nobody ever noticed?" Karen demanded.

And now I choked on my food because Dmitri and Maria both burst out laughing. Okay, perhaps more of a subdued, academic chuckle, but still not the reaction I expected.

"We've had our fair share of unwanted publicity," Maria offered. Her mouth twisted up at the corner. "Maria Rasputina was my first cousin, twice removed." She stopped and looked up into space for a second. "Or my second cousin, once removed. Or my great aunt. I can never keep up with the genealogical categories." Her gaze returned to us.

Calix opened her mouth, then visibly halted herself and waited until it became apparent Maria and Dmitri were giving us time to react. "You're claiming that Grigori Rasputin—he was one of you? One of these advisors?"

Dmitri nodded. He brushed at the front of his sweater vest, almost in a gesture of embarrassment. "He was, perhaps, the wrong choice to shepherd the Romanovs into the new century."

"That's one way of putting it." I had been there for some of the shepherding the old regimes had attempted. It hadn't been pretty.

"My father led the group of nobles who assassinated him, which allowed us to reassert ourselves into the highest echelons of the revolution, and then the party," Maria continued.

"Is sorcery a talent or a skill?" Karen hunched forward, her arms crossed and resting on the table. Tension radiated off her, although her fingers tapping a frenetic pattern against her elbow was the only outward sign she made.

"If you're asking whether we are born or made," Maria answered, "the answer is yes."

Which one was it? I opened my mouth to interrupt anyway, just as the train slowed, the brakes squealing as we passed over an intersection. Outside the train, a line of cars waited patiently in the sunlight for us to pass. Bright, normal life. I felt like I'd been chasing it since I left my own family, and it remained ever outside a thick window of glass while circumstances kept me motoring on by.

"War is coming," Dmitri said into the silence. "It's been creeping up on us again, and the only way we can prepare for it is to make our alliances and consolidate our strengths."

I'd heard all this before, over a century ago.

"There are few others our family is willing to ally with," Maria continued. "Our strength cannot be the only one to hang an alliance upon."

Calix stayed silent. I wondered what she thought about all this. If there were things she hadn't told us about her family.

"Are you going to tell us your big reveal or just sit there and finish your coffee?" Karen took the words out of my mouth, which I'd filled with food again.

"My young friend, the organization you work with was, for a brief few decades, a worthy adversary and could have been a worthwhile ally," Dmitri said. "But it has wasted its time on unworthy goals."

"Unchecked, Black Mountain would roll over MONIKER and leave nothing standing," Maria added. "Perhaps the information you have shared will prolong that day, but it will not prevent it."

"That's why you dragged us into this mission." Karen's face betrayed her suspicions, her disgust at being used. "A pretext. You didn't need us to rescue your daughter; you wanted to get the data to MONIKER without it looking like it came from you."

"Yes." No more, no less of an answer than I expected.

"Why drag Rick into it?"

This time, Maria answered. "We decided the time was right to make our approach once we heard whispers that another wolf had achieved the *Überwechsel*."

I stopped chewing.

"You are the first wolf in centuries to call that Change to you," Dmitri continued where his daughter left off.

"That was Pushkin's drugs." At the thought, I clenched my hand tighter around the knife, willing my claws to sink back.

"You were not the first wolf they'd had on their table," Maria informed me. "Just the first to survive and call the Overchange."

Just like that, I lost my appetite.

"Strength." Dmitri nodded. "An ally with strength." He picked up his napkin, dabbed at a nonexistent piece of food on his chin. "An ally who owed a debt."

"And the rest of us?" Calix looked me in the eye, then glanced back to Dmitri. "Are we part of your alliance?"

"That is your decision to make," Maria answered. "We would never be so foolish as to invite Rick without the people he calls friends."

"Do I—we—get a choice in this?" I growled.

Dmitri's eyebrow lifted. He shrugged. "There are always choices. But the time is approaching when those choices will become harder, and the consequences higher." He put his napkin down as the train slowed again, this time in preparation for stopping. "Even now, your position remains unclear, even to you."

He and Maria stood, swaying slightly as the car came to a halt. Over the loudspeaker, the announcement informed us we would be at the station for ten minutes to allow passengers to depart and embark.

"If you have an answer for us, you know my home in Berlin," Dmitri said. He nodded to us and took his leave. Maria followed after, but not before handing Karen a small leather bag. Karen didn't say anything or acknowledge it other than nodding and tucking it away in one of her many pockets.

———

"Maria, wait." I'd followed her out of the car, not sure what I hoped for by going after her.

I caught up with her halfway through the train car. At the door, Dmitri looked back at his daughter, saw me, and disembarked without further comment.

"Rick." Maria stepped aside to let an older man pass us. "You've got your answer already?"

"Yes." No, wait. "No." Crap. "I mean, I wanted to ask how long you'll be in Berlin."

"Not very," she answered, ignoring my fumbling. "We want to follow up a rumor of a worldwalker operating out of New Orleans."

"Worldwalker?" I wasn't familiar with the term.

"First one in a couple of centuries." Maria shrugged. "My father thinks it will be worth the trip."

"Recruiting for your supernatural alliance?"

"Something like that." She looked straight at me, and once again, I lost my train of thought.

The whistle sounded, letting us know the moment was done. Maria bent over and brushed her lips on my cheek, an electric charge that jumped me back to myself. "If you wait too long, I will be in touch."

I didn't bother to ask how she would find me. She would. Everyone else always seemed to. I waited until she got off the train safely, then returned to where Karen and Calix were polishing off the remains of the breakfast spread.

With Dmitri and Maria's departure, the table seemed larger and the atmosphere more bleak. I'd never imagined I would see him leave with anything but relief, but now I kind of wanted to follow him off the train.

The only thing that kept me in my seat was knowing that once we got back to MONIKER, nothing would stand in my way. I didn't care if Dmitri and Maria had some elaborate scheme to achieve balance among supernatural agencies by keeping them and Black Mountain at each other's throats. I would burn the agency to the ground.

## 22

I thought we would fly out of Rhein-Main military base, but time and history have a way of conspiring to throw you off when you least expect it. While I'd been someplace else, the military had shut down the base. I'd last flown out of the Rhein-Main airport almost a century ago, strapped to a medical gurney, snatched from Dmitri's Soviet hands by Gunnery Sergeant Victor Wieleski.

This time, instead of the noisy metal and nylon webbing of a military cargo hop, we took off out of Nürnberg airport on a passenger plane, surrounded by a mix of German and American citizens. About half the Americans had the haircuts and bearing of troops heading home on rotation. The other half had the wannabe haircuts, tacticool pants, and faux military gear of contractors and the military adjacent. From snatches of overheard conversation, I gleaned they were heading back to the States after attending an arms conference in Nürnberg. Times really have changed.

Even on a crowded plane full of noisy people, Dmitri's absence made it feel like something was missing. I hadn't exactly gotten used to him being around. But I definitely noticed it, now that he wasn't.

And Maria. I missed her, too. I kept replaying the moment in the room together, wondering why I hadn't taken advantage of her offer. She'd caught me, embarrassed and unaware, but hadn't pressed or laughed. She'd said she would call me, and maybe she would. And yes, I realize that makes me sound like a founding member of the Lonely Hearts Club for Torch-Bearing Werewolves. Piss off.

Calix had fallen asleep the minute the plane took off. Sitting between us, Karen stared straight ahead, breathing evenly, barely blinking. She had fallen asleep with her eyes open, and by the way, that's every bit as unnerving as it sounds.

I couldn't stop fidgeting. Sleep was out of the question. Getting comfortable next to impossible. Even with the noise and the draft and the cold metal, at least military hops usually had space for me to change and curl up.

"Rick, quit moving around; you're driving me nuts." Karen hadn't shifted her position or her gaze.

In answer, I growled a little, more of a grunt than anything with aggression behind it. "I can't get comfortable."

"Same."

Startled, my body stilled for a moment. Karen wasn't the sharing confidences type, and the person who'd shared the sort of history that would allow us to meet in casual talk had been gone since I came back.

"There's a question I've been meaning to ask you." She flitted her gaze over some of the more military-looking haircuts, avoiding turning to look at me.

"Shoot."

"When did you know it was time to leave?"

I didn't know how to answer her question, so I waited to see if she had anything else.

"What was it that made you decide to draw a line and get out?"

"Of MONIKER?"

"MONIKER. The uniform. Germany. I don't know." She shook her head. "Never mind. Forget it."

Most of the time, the things I want to say come out with a thick layer of wisecracks and sarcasm. But even I knew this was not the time. Which was, I thought, some more personal growth and development on my part, and it left me choosing my words carefully.

"I've spent my life searching for a greater purpose," I began. "Which, if you look at it a different way, means I've also spent my life leaving things behind." She didn't give me an answer, so I kept going. "I left my family. My country. My adopted country."

The words retreated, just out of reach. I shivered. The ghosts of Aleksy and Shin hovered over my shoulder as if, turning, I might glimpse their presence.

"Times change," I continued. "People change. Even the ones you love become strangers. One day, you realize your home has become a strange place." I shrugged. "Or, they drug you, toss you on a lab table, and start slicing you into pieces while your friends watch from across the room and don't do anything to stop them."

Karen blushed deeply, her face going blotchy.

Okay, that came out kind of an asshole comment, but I thought it was slightly justified. But her question—how do you know when to leave—isn't a one-size-answer-fits-all kind of thing. What I didn't tell her—couldn't find the words at the time—was: that kind of decision is different for everyone. And the answer changes every time you ask the question.

In my experience—and at this point, I've had over a hundred years of leaving to try to find a new home, a new pack—you never really know it's the right time at the time. That's something you figure out only after the fact, or in hindsight, and then when you *do* figure it out, you just have to cut slingload and move on. Any regrets are up to you, how you want to deal with them.

I opened my mouth to try to explain, to try to give my friend some sort of comfort. The pilot's announcement we were landing shortly in Las Vegas interrupted any further conversation.

---

We made it through customs and the rental car counter without incident. Thank you, Dmitri. When it comes to getting people and papers from one place to the other with no hassle or questions asked, he remained the best.

Karen didn't say anything other than a few brief exchanges as we went through the routine. Even Calix kept quiet. I followed along obediently, not even making a joke about riding shotgun, even though it was my turn and it would have been easy with everyone not speaking to each other.

I wasn't overly familiar with the city of Las Vegas, but we'd driven around it enough on this adventure that I started to recognize the roads we took away from the airport. Karen, driving, wasn't taking us back to MONIKER. We were headed for the heart of the city.

None of us spoke a word until Karen stopped outside a hotel about three blocks off the main strip. She killed the engine and popped the locks.

"What's going on?" Calix asked the question I'd been thinking.

Karen twisted around in her seat to face me. "I've got a contact inside, room three-oh-four. You can head in through the front; stay to the left near the lounge and keep your head down, and you'll be out of view of the cameras."

"What contact?" I bent down to peer through the windshield. The hotel looked like a standard tourist trap.

"I'm not taking you back to the agency," Karen said. Calix went to say something, but Karen kept going. "Now that we've helped your friend Dmitri out with the rescue that wasn't, MONIKER will swallow you whole. You walk into that facility, and you won't be walking back out."

"I know that."

"Then get out of the car, go to room three-oh-four, and get the hell out of here." Karen turned back around, waiting. "I've got one favor stockpiled with this woman. After she helps you, she won't be taking any more of my calls, so MONIKER won't be able to use me to get to you."

I tried to keep the stupid grin off my face, but lost that struggle. "And what will happen when you and Calix just waltz back in without me? How are you going to explain that?"

Karen shrugged. "We'll think of something. Maybe a heroic death fighting the minions of Black Mountain."

"Think MONIKER will buy it?"

"I have no idea, Rick, but if you don't get out of this car so we can start heading back, we'll never find out."

I leaned back in the seat and crossed my arms. "And what about you?" This question for Calix. "You're all right with this plan?"

Calix narrowed her eyes. "It would help to know about the play before I'm supposed to back it, but yeah. Get out of the car. We'll figure some shit out."

"Nope."

"Rick. Get out of the car." Karen's hands tightened on the wheel, knuckles white.

"No way." Now I didn't bother trying to hide my glee. "I've been waiting for you to wake up or at least get out of my way. MONIKER is going down—I'm taking it down—one way or another. You two can get in on this if you want—or you can stay the fuck out of my way." I grinned, letting just the hint of the change sharpen my teeth. "Either way, I'm not walking there, so you might as well drive."

Karen and Calix exchanged looks, an unspoken question passing between them. Calix glanced back at me, and her face split into a broad smile, almost terrifying in its eagerness.

"Was wondering when you were going to come to your senses," she said to Karen. "I'm in."

"Then let's do this." Karen started the vehicle, threw it in gear, and peeled out. "But if we're going in together, we need some sort of plan."

Of course we did.

"What were you planning?" Karen directed the question to me, even though she kept her eyes on the road. She drove about twenty-five miles over the speed limit, causing my stomach to lurch with every lane change.

"They're expecting us back," I answered, trying not to flinch as she blew by two lumbering tractor-trailers, swerving in and out of them with inches to spare. "I was going to walk in, kill Doctor Strangelove, and…"

"That's as far as you got?" Calix asked. She, too, actively avoided staring directly out the window.

"Yep," I admitted.

"Your plan needs a little work." Calix's voice was as dry as the surrounding desert. Seriously, how do people live so far away from rain?

"That's because Rick doesn't have plans; he just Leroy Jenkinses his way through life-threatening situations."

Huh? Calix must have gotten the reference because she chuckled. "All right, so what's the real plan?"

"We'll walk Rick in," Karen answered. "Tug his sleeve down, and no one will notice right away that he's not wearing the cuff."

"The place is like one giant cuff," I offered. "Silver everywhere."

"And what about the tracker?" Calix asked. She turned to me. "It's toast, right? With all the changing and the—" She lifted her hands in the air and made a lurching movement that I guessed was supposed to be me when I'm furry.

"Don't quit your day job," I muttered. "But yes."

"The full moon rises in about three hours." Karen slowed to make a turn off the highway. We were heading into the mountains, not far away now from the facility. "We'll rely on nature to take its course. Anyway, Calix takes you down to the lab. You take care of business. I'll head to the data center."

We hit a bump in the road. At the speed we were going, it wrenched the wheel to the side. Karen fought momentarily to get the vehicle back under control.

"If we survive the Karen 500, what next?" I muttered.

"I still have access to the server, including the remote connections." Karen stepped her foot down even further on the gas. "I've got a little something a friend coded for me that should turn their networks into giant bricks."

"And what am I doing while you're playing girl hacker?" Calix broke in. "Tell me I'm not just babysitting MONIKER's pet werewolf while he pisses on their carpet."

"Of course not." Karen momentarily took her eyes off the road to catch my glance in the rearview mirror. "I'm going to give you the combination to the arms room and explosives locker."

"This is the best plan ever." Calix cackled with glee, a profoundly unsettling sound.

I still didn't think Karen's plan had any more details than mine, but I still got to kill Gratuszcak and fuck up MONIKER's life. Karen and Calix were going to help me burn the place down—all the basics were there.

And in any case, we found ourselves out of time. With a screech of the brakes that threw us all against our seatbelts, Karen stopped in front of the facility.

We were home. Time to get to work.

23

We made it just past the front door, and then everyone's plans turned to shit.

The welcome committee, for one, consisted of Ramirez and about a dozen really large things that looked human, but gave off the scent of rank otherness that did more than remind me of the creatures in the Black Mountain lab. My eyes were telling me they were human, but my other senses told me my eyes were lying.

Then again, Calix and I didn't show and tell on the first date, either.

"Dr. Willet." Ramirez didn't bother to acknowledge me. Or Calix.

"Ramirez." Karen nodded at the troops surrounding her boss, each of which overshadowed her by at least three or four inches. Now I knew what a hobbit felt like. "What's with the shock troops?"

"Standardizing our security protocol." Ramirez turned on his heel and started heading down the hallway. Karen fell into step behind him, and we fell into step behind them, mostly because the giant walking brute squad fell into step around *us*. "Based on the data you pulled from Black Mountain, we're upping our anti-incursion measures."

"Wait," I interrupted, forced to skip a step to keep pace with the inhuman basketball team Ramirez fielded. "We were the ones who incursioned them."

Ramirez didn't even roll his eyes. Or acknowledge me. "We've got a debriefing room ready for you."

"I was hoping to stop by the analysts," Karen said evenly. "See where they were with the data we sent."

By now we were drawing closer to the conference room where, the first time I'd been introduced to the facility, Dmitri had been waiting. Ramirez didn't answer right away. Instead, he drew near the door, then paused and gestured for Karen to go first.

"There'll be plenty of time for that after, Dr. Willet."

After what? Didn't sound like anything I wanted to wait around for to find out.

I growled, and the change came rushing toward me, faster than usual as the moon rose outside.

But not faster than the sledgehammer fist that descended on the back of my neck, shutting out the lights.

I didn't dream, although I wouldn't have minded a little mystic vision spirit advice from Aleksy if he'd been lurking about. Instead, I opened my eyes and vomited my brains out. Strapped down to the lab table as I found myself to be, this mostly meant I spewed all over myself and choked on it. Not the most auspicious start to facing down the bad guys.

Gratusczak regarded me with a sneer, one corner of his mouth wrinkled in a mien of disgust.

Another wave of nausea bowled me over. Spots danced in front of my eyes. I recognized the symptoms. Wasn't the first time I'd had a concussion.

Yanking against the chains only brought on a fit of heaving. This time, I turned my head as far to the side as I could, aiming as best under the circumstances at Dr. G's shoes as possible. He stepped back, out of harm's way.

"Fascinating."

"Mild head trauma will do that, Mister Spock." The words sat thick in the back of my throat. It had gone bone dry. How long had I been out? Couldn't have been more than a few minutes. With the moonrise imminent...

The realization hit. The real reason I felt twisted at both ends like a wet shop rag. The moon had risen, but something blocked the change. The *Überwechsel*.

After five minutes, I guess Gratuszczak felt safe enough to risk stepping up to the table without the chance of getting splashed by barf. He rolled a cart up next to the bed, a multi-tiered extravaganza of things to do science with.

The doctor poked and prodded, focusing on an intravenous line that had been run into my left arm. Someone had done a sloppy job; instead of a neat loop and clean entry, the tube was secured with a piece of medical tape stained dark with the blood that pooled around the entry site. The good doctor palpated my arm around the needle, then tapped on the line. Whatever the saline bag dripped into me, it wasn't hastening any sort of healing process.

"The silver-benzotriazole compound shows great effectiveness at stabilizing this form," Gratuszczak explained, almost absent-mindedly, as if he were making a note to himself rather than telling me anything. "Compound shows promise as a morpho-inhibitor." Here, he checked his watch, then continued in a less formal tone. "Note, the moonrise of the full phase occurred exactly thirty-five minutes ago, and he still shows no signs of change."

I twisted my head around, trying to look around the lab, figure out who he was talking to. I didn't find anyone else there. Either he really enjoyed talking to himself, or the good doctor had set up a recorder.

Sure enough, at the edge of the bed, I spotted a spindly tripod with a small video recorder perched atop. And I had been worried about Dmitri's notebook. My guess, with the cat—or dog—out of the bag, and MONIKER's shiny new shock troops all buff and ready to go, they weren't too concerned about their favorite mad scientist documenting his experiments.

Speaking of which, the last time he'd had me strapped to his lab table, there'd been a guard at the door. They'd at least not let him roam around unsupervised.

Perhaps those things that had met us at the door were his goodwill token. Perhaps with some shiny new supernatural toys, MONIKER had decided on Dr. Gratusczak as their new point man.

I reached once more for the change. Nothing. No buzzer, no pain, just—nothing. As if that part of me had been neatly excised.

"Those walking meatheads, I take it they were your invention?" I tried again.

Gratusczak didn't bother to even adjust his gaze from his work. "Of course, Rick."

"So, MONIKER sucks your cock and you give them supermen?"

This time, the palest of flushes on his dead cheeks rewarded my crudeness. He didn't reply, simply met my eyes with his intense gaze. The emptiness in there frightened me. The blood running from the rough IV site slicked around my left wrist, chafing under the silver-laced steel of the manacle.

"Once upon a time, you held great interest for this organization." Gratusczak's voice remained mild. He could have been discussing the weather. "Now you are an obsolete toy, broken, with all the shine rubbed off."

"Ouch. I must have touched a nerve."

Gratusczak chuckled, a thin, humorless sound. "You have sworn oaths to so many, and yet kept so few." He ignored my reaction, reaching for a thin, sharp knife that rested with several similar objects on a tray on the top tier of the cart standing to the left of the lab table. "Are you then so surprised when those you serve do not keep faith with you?"

The doctor rested the blade against the skin of my upper arm, then sliced cleanly and precisely.

At first, I felt nothing. Then, a burning sensation arose around the wound. My vision blurred with the pain.

"As expected, the solution dampens both the change reaction, as well as the subject's rapid recuperative powers."

Thrashing, I pulled against the chains, seeking some give or play in the restraints. Gratusczak ignored my efforts, until they threatened to dislodge the IV line. Then, he shook his head and gently placed his hand along my ribcage. Without any leverage or sign of outward exertion, he pressed down with his fingers and cracked two of my ribs.

Holy crap. The pain had screwed up my perception, but no way should the good doctor have been strong enough to do that. I ceased my flailing and concentrated on trying not to scream from the pain.

"Good boy."

I would have growled, but I had no fight left in me. Gratusczak had the right of it. I hadn't kept my oaths.

MONIKER had been a refuge, and more so, Karen's friendship, and I had left them both behind without thinking twice. I had forsaken my family—my flesh and fur—and risked their discovery and extermination in order to join in the service of a country. A country that offered not much more than a chance to die for a scratchy uniform and perhaps this new dream of a unified Germany.

I'd stayed far longer than I should have, taking and re-taking oaths. It wasn't long until I couldn't tell if I were fighting for my country, my comrades, or because fighting turned out to be all I knew. And then, one year, as the uniformed men around me shucked off their oaths to the bloated Weimar Republic, and pledged allegiance to the rise of a strong man who promised glory and power, I chose to break ranks with the last tatters of honor rather than take that oath.

First had come the whispers. Then the burning of the Institute. Then usurpation of the military by the Nazi Party, and Hitler. By that time, I'd discarded my uniform, and spent my time seeking ways to assist any shred of resistance I could find, trying to get the few friends still alive to safety. And that one night a month...

"Yes, you were some big hero."

By this time, I'd almost gotten used to Aleksy popping in whenever my consciousness went paisley.

But it wasn't my partisan friend sitting next to me, cracking wise. Instead, Shin stood over the table, arms crossed. His skin had an unnatural, deathly pallor, but he showed no sign of the wound that had ended his life.

"So?" He raised an eyebrow.

I didn't know what he wanted me to do. I couldn't do anything. I didn't want to. I simply wanted to curl up around the pain in my arm and go to sleep. And wake up back in the pack I'd abandoned.

My friend did nothing, said nothing, just shrugged. I turned away from his gaze. His eyes continued to burn into the back of my head.

Well, fuck him. If he wasn't going to help, he was as useless as he was dead at the bottom of a foxhole in the winter.

"It took me some time to fully decipher your friend's text." Gratusczak returned to my side, notebook in hand. "He was very clever, Dmitri Pietrovitch."

Did my complete lack of giving a shit show in my face? Obviously not.

"Every word of this notebook is in plain Russian," the man continued. "His handwriting is...perfection." He smiled, self-deprecating. "I read this from cover to cover, admiring the gall he had to write without concealment or cryptography."

I coughed, and something in my lungs burbled. If I were going to die strapped to this table, I wish they would just go ahead and put a bullet in my brain now.

Without further ado, Gratusczak turned back to his work table, taking a few steps to close the distance. His gait had lengthened. A half-hitch marred his left mid-step.

At the work station, he flicked on one of the several Bunsen burners that stood sentry along the desk. The bright blue flame leapt up, casting light that flickered through the dark lab.

"Did you know, the man who sold this to me was struggling to find a buyer?" Dr. Gratusczak gestured with the book. "Everyone he showed it to thought it was some kind of joke." He thumbed through the pages, pausing every now and then to run the tip of his index finger over a note. "At one time, I believe he even tried to sell it to a movie producer."

Was he talking about John Tell?

"What he didn't realize was that your friend had buried the true science behind an elaborate scheme of deception." Gratusczak smiled, his lips pulling back into yet another death's head grin. In the dark, the flame from the burner caught his eyes, giving them an intense, internal glow. His teeth glinted, showing just the tips. "Instead of telling *what* you are, this journal tells us *who* you are...if we just know how to read it."

And with that pronouncement, he held the leather-bound journal over the burner. The flames licked the cover for a few minutes before the fire caught and flared.

My mouth opened to protest. I shut it firmly. Just because I hated that Gratusczak had read the journal, didn't mean it wasn't a good thing someone was finally burning the thing.

"They don't need you anymore."

The words were plain as coffin nails. Thank you, Shin. My old buddy continued to survey the scene impassively, but his words hit me like an electric shock.

MONIKER no longer needed me as an agent—they had bigger and better supernatural creatures to do their bidding. They no longer feared me as a free agent—the silver cage and cuffs and whatever solution Gratusczak pumped into me at the moment proved that. And now, they no longer needed me as a lab experiment. Their resident mad scientist had just proved it by burning the journal.

Might as well put a silver bullet in my brain and be done with it.

"That's the lesson you choose to learn?" Shin spat, disgust wrinkling his forehead.

In my defense, I've always been a little slow when something disrupts my entire physiobiology. Shin shook his head slowly. It reminded me of Dmitri, showing his disappointment in me.

No. MONIKER didn't need me. Gratusczak didn't need me.

But somewhere in this facility, Karen and Calix were carrying out their part of the MONIKER takedown plan. Of that I had no doubt. And they might not need me, either, but I wasn't going to mope around on this lab table and wait to find out. They were my teammates, like Aleksy, and Shin, and Gunny Wieleski had all been, and I wasn't going to lie down and hope they'd be able to overcome this facility of monsters by themselves.

I'd spent more than half my life contained in my human skin, with only the brief moments of the full moon to escape its constraints. My time with MONIKER had lulled me into complacency, and the discovery of the *Überwechsel* had likewise led me down the path of thinking my wolf skin to be the more powerful. And it was. Sometimes.

But I'd been a soldier for more than a century with nothing more than my lovably sarcastic attitude and an occasional craving for raw meat, and I was still here. Motherfucker.

Shin rolled his eyes.

I tried reaching for the tray of sharp tools Gratusczak had left temptingly just out of reach. Shin snorted. If at first you don't succeed, aim lower. In this case, for the second tier of the cart with the trays. The top with the really sharp toys might not be reachable, but if I squirmed my body just right, the second tier came within biting distance.

I flailed a little more, clanking the chains, just to keep Gratusczak from getting suspicious. He frowned, busy at his work table, dusting the ashes of the notebook into a little garbage can and puttering around. Whether or not he planned to end me when he turned around, or when he tired of his little games, was not something I wanted to wait around to find out.

A towel laid across the top of the first tier of the cart hung down and obscured the second tier. But what lay there I found even more helpful. There were about five intravenous kits, complete with saline bags, tubing, and long, thin needles.

I angled my upper body, reaching for the nearest IV kit. I almost had it in my teeth, when Gratusczak, staring at his computer screen, grunted loudly. I froze. Darting back would only tip off his peripheral vision. Luckily, he simply commenced to swearing under his breath at whatever he'd seen.

Finagling the IV kit out of the cart, I dropped it into my waiting hand. The awkward angle made things more complicated, but then it became a matter of remembering only slightly rusty skills.

Fishing for the needle, I flipped off the protective cap from the sharp end and aimed it at the handcuff where the rotating arm locked into the ratchet. Here, I found out that MONIKER had spent more money than I could imagine in the silver defenses lining this supernatural prison, but had cheapened out in the worst possible way. Perhaps they were relying on the silver content of the cuffs, and the shit Gratusczak pumped through my veins, but the model of handcuff that secured me to the bed had apparently been built by the lowest bidder.

I found it a simple matter to slip the IV insertion needle into the ratchet area, slowly and gently, worried every moment I might break it off in there. Hardly breathing, I shimmed the teeth, giving myself just enough space to slip the rotating arm out and free my wrist. Ha!

Now the race began. How many of my limbs could I get free before Gratusczak came back to do whatever he planned to do? Working quickly, and yet so very carefully, I managed to free my other wrist and work almost all of my right leg free.

My luck chose that moment to reassert itself, and before the leg manacle came completely free, the sharp click of the needle breaking stalled my progress. *Scheisse.*

It would be painful, but I could still squeeze my foot out from the manacle. I reached over to the tray for another needle.

Too much movement. The motion caught Dr. Gratusczak's eye.

He turned and found me sitting up, three limbs free, working frantically to shim the final cuff around my left ankle. I had to give it to him, the man showed no sign of emotion or alarm as he stepped toward me. Warning bells rang in my head. The doctor had shown me his strength—had shown himself to be far stronger than he should have been. Almost free...

He took another step, bringing him just barely within reach. In a single motion, I turned, swiped a knife from the tray, and plunged it between his ribs.

Expecting Gratusczak to stagger back, fall down, bleed a little bit, I went back to working the needle into the left cuff. I had just shimmed myself free, when movement caught my eye.

Gratusczak stood, unbothered by the wound to his internal organs. The good doctor smiled, and this time, I could not mistake the light that glowed in his pupils.

"Thank you for finding such a unique method of escape." The words slurred in his mouth, forced out around teeth that were changing, rearranging themselves in a narrowing jaw. "I have been looking forward to this challenge for such a long time."

A year ago, he had synthesized the change, injecting himself with an experimental serum and transforming himself into a deformed, deadly miscreation. At the time, I thought it was a one-time thing. I also thought he'd died. Wrong on both counts.

Ripping the IV catheter out of my arm, I jumped off the bed to the right, leaving the empty fixture between us. The blood ran free as I crouched, darting my eyes around, scanning in vain for an exit.

In front of me, the doctor grew in stature, spindly arms and legs thinning and narrowing like some horrific perversion of the Change. His teeth shone, sharp at the points. The nails on his fingers grew, long and yellow. A stench wafted over me. Something was rotten in the state of the good doctor.

I've never been ashamed of fear, but I've also never let it immobilize me. Until now. I couldn't move my feet. My thighs were wet where I couldn't contain my terror. *Move*, I screamed internally, trying to jar myself out of my frozen state.

The thing that had been Dr. Gratusczak roared and leapt up from a standing position, vaulting across the lab table I'd recently vacated. His long fingers reached for my neck, aiming straight for the beating pulse of my carotid.

<h1 style="text-align:center">24</h1>

The only thing saving me from Gratusczak's onslaught was about a century and a half of reflexes, carefully honed by flinching whenever something sharp hurtled at me. His questing fingernails, keen as knives, barely missed sinking into my neck. They sliced shallow grooves in passing, opening my skin just enough to slick blood down my shoulder.

G's momentum carried him past me. He landed on his shoulder, rolling to his feet.

The man—thing—came at me again, faster than my eye could track. I got my arms and hands up to protect my neck. He cut and slashed at them with his claws and teeth, bearing me to the ground.

I curled up like a cockroach under him, trying to protect all my vulnerable parts. My breath came short. The pounding in my ears drowned everything out except for the soft grunts and shallow cuts as he tried to get inside my guard, turn me out.

With my legs and hips, I squirmed and kicked until I could grapple him around the midsection. I don't know if the man had ever been in an actual fight in his life, or ever fought a short person before. He kept trying to muscle me down and failed. The biting and the slashing, on the other hand, made ribbons of the flesh on my hands and arms. If I couldn't get the change—either one—to come around soon, I would be very seriously screwed.

I tried scratching back, but his long lab coat and pants protected most of him. Arching up with my back, I tried to dislodge him from me, get some space, but he followed my movements.

Every time I reached out, he attacked again.

Something incomprehensible dribbled out from his mouth. Saliva? Blood? It burned where it landed, and I closed my eyes, twitching and wriggling, trying to get positioned to try to roll him over under me. He was too big, too strong.

A hard object rapped my knuckles. I opened my eyes. And immediately screamed, as Gratusczak's acid drool dripped across my right eye.

Just that moment's glance had done its job. The hard object turned out to be the handle of the knife I'd plunged into his chest. The weapon still protruded from his skin.

In my distracting moment of realization, Gratusczak stabbed the claws of his right hand through the flesh of my left forearm, yanked my hand down, and buried his teeth in my neck. I screamed again. Hot pokers, needles, knives, and the fear of infection all crowded what brain cells I had left.

With my right hand, I grabbed the knife in the doctor's chest. I wrenched at it, trying to dislodge it from between his ribs.

He pierced my arm with the claws of his free hand, pulling back, trying to loosen my grip. I gritted my teeth and sobbed but held on until I twisted the knife out.

*Fuck.* I almost dropped it as I turned the blade to the side, slashing at Gratusczak's neck, trying to ignore the pain as his claws remained buried in my arms, his teeth in my neck.

I slashed, again and again. On the third or fourth pass, he opened his jaw, releasing my neck, and reared back, snapping at the knife.

It gave me just the slight change in his balance I needed. Sweeping my hips, I rolled him over flat on his back. Not giving him a chance to re-adjust, I stabbed the knife down, slipping the point under his sternum and in and out of the soft tissue of his abdomen.

He hesitated, just for a moment, the smallest hint of pain in the grimace on his rictus face. I jumped up, scrambling to get away, conscious of the fact that I was moving nowhere near as fast as I used to.

I had just made it to his work table when Gratusczak caught me from behind, his claws digging into my side. I reared back, screaming, and grabbed the still-lit Bunsen burner from the table. The smallest amount of play in the tubing allowed me to aim the thing over my shoulder without looking.

I got lucky, or as close to lucky as I get. The burner got him in the eye. He screamed and pawed at it, releasing me.

The door to the lab was too far to reach. I thought of the tray of knives, but so far he outnumbered me there; his claws would take me down before I even got close. He straightened and reached for me again, so I threw a coffee cup at him. He flinched, and I missed, but I didn't stick around to see how fast he recovered. That few seconds gave me the time I needed to reach the cabinet and shelves he used to stock his lab.

I have no idea what liquid resided in the large, plastic container I pulled out of there, but it had a big, dark gray diamond plastered on the side with a little white flame in the top corner. I grabbed it, popped the top and spun, splashing it indiscriminately, but mostly at Gratusczak.

Flammable chemicals plus hanging Bunsen burner equaled a crispy Gratusczak-critter, en flambé. He screamed, and the flames whooshed up, sucking in the air as they turned him into a pillar of fire.

He turned and staggered one step toward me. A burning spark landed on my pants, igniting them. I stumbled back, edging away, slapping at my leg as the rest of the liquid that had spilled around the room caught fire.

This time, I didn't look behind me as the creature that had been Gratusczak screamed and screamed, then whimpered, and finally went silent.

I frantically tried the door. Locked. *Slow down, Rick, there's got to be a release here somewhere.* Finally, I spotted a square panel to the side of the door and pressed it. A hand-shaped glow lit up in the center of the panel, flashing at me a few times. I tried again, and the same thing happened. Gratusczak had set the door to lock from the inside, keyed to his handprint.

The fire continued to rage, finding ever new sources of fuel. The basement lab wasn't small, but in the next twenty seconds I would be in a lot of trouble if I didn't get out of there.

I gave up and simply pounded on the door, shouting. Deep inside, the shackled wolf said a prayer to the Green Man, but on the outside, I cursed to find this would be how I would meet my end.

A click. A turn. The door swung open.

I stumbled through, hacking and coughing, trying to clear the door and push it shut behind me.

A strong hand pushed me none-too-gently out of the way and closed the door against the inferno reaching out for us. Cinnamon and old blood washed over me.

"Damn, wolf." Calix raised an eyebrow. "You look like the car missed you and the train got you."

---

We made it to the stairs before the aftereffects hit me. No matter Calix's urging, I couldn't take another step. My body, pushed beyond its limits, chose that moment to spontaneously purge itself of everything Gratusczak and his science had polluted it with.

I heaved until my body could empty no more. A cold sweat covered my body, the impurities leaking from my pores. At my neck, the acid from the doctor's bite burned ever more intensely as it consumed itself, taking part of my flesh with it.

"Damn, wolf, they did a number on you." Concern flashed in Calix's eyes. Not sure if it was meant for me, or for the impact an incapacitated teammate would have on their escape plan.

The nooks and crannies of my stomach finished emptying in one massive heave, along with what looked like part of my lungs and entrails. Lightheaded, I leaned against the staircase railing and waited. After three long seconds, I finally stood with my own legs steady under me.

"Okay, I think I'm—"

The Change barreled into me, just as the stairwell echoed with the screech of an alarm. The strobing lights kept time with the strident sound, messing with my vision.

Was I going blind? Were my eyes even open? Instead of the fast, yet methodical, sequence of the Change, the moon pulled it out of me almost at once. The pain of my bones and skin re-conforming stabbed and crunched through my nerve endings—even after the Change had completed.

I howled and screamed, the colors of my change vision washing over me in red and white.

"Feel better now?" Calix, unphased, raised an eyebrow.

I growled a low response in return. The pain faded, and I felt amazing. Strong. Ready to rip the heart out of anyone who stood in our way and suck the marrow from their bones.

"*Los!*" The German came out sounding like "*Ros,*" but Calix ignored the Scooby Doo sound effects and picked up on the context clues.

"Follow me." She took the lead up the stairs, bounding two at a time.

I didn't stop to ask how she got loose. I didn't stop to ask where we were going. If there were ever a moment to trust my teammate, it was now. As long as she led me toward the enemy, I would follow her.

---

Our progress through the facility came oddly easy, as if all the troops had been called away to another part of the building. The alarm continued to blare, but with all the urgency of a mechanical clock.

Calix, stalking ahead of me, stilled. She motioned me against the wall, and I flattened as much as I could against the side of the corridor. Giant werewolves blend in more in the woods, not corporate décor, but we rarely get to choose our own battlefields.

The moment passed, and whatever had moved ahead of us disappeared. Calix waved at me to continue.

"Fire response team," she whispered, pitching her voice too low to be heard by anyone who wasn't a giant werewolf.

I'm normally short. I like referring to myself as a giant werewolf.

Calix stopped outside of a heavy, steel door and raised her fist to rap on the metal. Before she could knock, the door swung open, revealing another, barred door standing open behind the steel one. A harried man in a MONIKER polo shirt paused in the act of locking the door to give her an incredulous glance.

"What are you doing here?"

I understood his surprise. With a fire alarm blaring, the arms room should have been on total lockdown.

"You hear that?" he demanded, pointing at the alarm blinking on and off in the corner of the armory. "It means you should be evacuating. Let's go."

I growled and stepped out from the shadows behind her, revealing myself in full werewolf glory. Or so I'd like to think.

His jaw worked, but no sound came out. Calix shrugged and punched him in the solar plexus.

The man's eyes rolled into the top of his head, and he folded in half, down and out for the count.

Calix crouched to grab him under the armpits. "Grab his feet, will you?"

I complied, and we carried him back into the armory, closing the door behind us to allay suspicions.

Together, we set the unconscious armorer down on a wooden crate and looked around. Calix turned slowly, the smile on her face growing ever broader. The pure glee reminded me of Karen in a gun store. Or me in an Italian butcher shop.

On the other hand, many of the weapons, aside from the rows of M-4 rifles and pistols of various makes, were designed to threaten the health and welfare of supernatural creatures. A rack of swords sported blades of steel and silver alloys—I could almost taste the acrid stench of the metal. At the end of the rifle rack, a slew of tranq guns and TASERs stood stacked next to each other.

"Those bastards." Calix strode to the wall opposite the swords. Hanging by itself on a peg, her peculiar blade flashed in the still-strobing alarm light.

She grasped the handle of the weapon, lifting it from the peg and giving it a few swings. Satisfied they hadn't harmed her baby, she looked around at the rest of the toys.

"See anything that grabs your fancy?"

I gestured to the rifles, and she nodded. Not every rifle had a sling attached to it, but she picked out two that did.

As for me, remembering the hybrid creatures we faced in Black Mountain, as well as the strength and sharp teeth and claws of whatever Gratusczak had turned himself into, the last wall of the armory held the only weapon that appealed to me.

A heavy steel rack held a lineup of half a dozen flamethrowers. I pointed to one of them and gestured.

Calix didn't bat an eye, just adjusted the straps to their loosest setting, and helped sling them over my shoulders. They barely fit, the handle almost too small and intricate for my paws, but I'd manage.

I grinned. Best day ever.

At the end of the room stood a heavy, metal door with another of the handprint panels next to it. The various warning stickers pasted on the door proclaimed to the world—or anyone who could get into the armory—that this was where the good stuff had been deposited.

Calix handed me the weapons she'd collected, keeping her sword firmly grasped in her left hand, ready to use. She dragged the still-sleeping armorer over to the door and pressed his hand against the panel. The door whirred, clicked, then opened about an inch ajar. Calix unceremoniously dropped the armorer's hand and swung the door the rest of the way out.

"This is so beautiful." She smiled and stepped aside to show me the spoils.

We had just enough time to admire the impressive display of rows and boxes of ammunition, tranq darts, and explosive material, before the alarm shut off.

"Crap, let's get moving." Calix grabbed a quick and varied selection of full magazines for the rifles, explosives, detonators, and a few other choice objects of destruction.

At that moment, a new, insistent beeping started up. I tried to growl something along the lines of "Hey, that's the arms room alarm," but it mostly came out as a series of Rs and Grrs. Calix got the message.

We skedaddled on out of there, Calix with her arms full of weapons and ammo, me with my arms full of armorer. We had just enough time to close the door and slide down the hall to an empty conference room before the tramp of the goon squad blocked our way out.

I dumped the unconscious man behind the door and stared at Calix. "Rut rext?"

---

What came next was the goon squad realized no one would let them into the armory, and the troop of hybrid creatures started taking turns kicking the door. Just goes to show you could have strong soldiers, and you could have smart soldiers, and these things were bred for all muscle.

We waited until they were fully occupied with the door—and leaving little dents all over the reinforced steel surface—until we jumped out like two extremely unscary horror movie minions.

There's nothing more anticlimactic than jumping out at an enemy, ready to tear limbs and beat jerkoffs, and getting completely ignored.

"Hey, assholes!" Calix brandished her sword. None of the six creatures spared us a glance. Maybe we were too badass for them.

The hybrid that grabbed me from behind and threw me into the wall, crunching parts of me that shouldn't be crunched, put that thought to the lie.

I shook off the impact, rolling to my feet and launching myself at the incoming troops. Six to the front of us. About ten to our rear. Perfect odds.

Unfortunately for us, the hybrids didn't wait in a line to attack us, one by one like in the movies. Instead, they piled on, surrounding us and leaving me little room to swing my claws or Calix her sword.

A fist like iron thudded into the side of my head, followed by brutal attacks to my side, kidneys, anywhere they could get around my defenses. Even in my *Überwechsel* state, these fuckers were my equal in size and reach.

Calix swung, but her sword barely pierced skin, although it raised lacerations that quickly faded. A few made it inside her guard, and she staggered from the blows.

She attacked and pivoted, setting her back against mine. The movement pushed the tanks of the flamethrower against my spine.

I lashed out with one hand against the slavering crowd, even as they grabbed my legs. They pulled me in two directions at once by the arms, like kids fighting over an action figure. I started flashing back to the creatures under the Black Mountain facility.

The nozzle of the flamethrower swung with the motion of the fight. I grabbed it, even as the creature immediately in front of me made a play for it.

Pretty certain I was about to burn myself alive, I pointed the nozzle at the creature and depressed the trigger.

The gout of flame spurted out, engulfing the hybrid and filling the hall with the scent of burning flesh. Drool slavered from my jaws. I screamed as the creature fell back. I had ignited the fur along my front. But pain and I were old friends.

For the next few moments, the fighting intensified as the hybrids kicking in the armory door paused in that mission and turned on us.

I depressed the nozzle again, spreading flame in great fiery gushes that smelled of chemicals and caused the barbecue scent to intensify. It smelled like brisket but didn't stir my hunger. They were probably infected.

As I played Bradbury fireman, Calix swung her sword. Where the flamethrower incinerated flesh, it parted more easily beneath her blows.

In a matter of ten minutes or less, the smoking, bleeding remains of Gratusczak's finest scientific work lay scattered around us. I'm not proud. I'm not ashamed, either, of how satisfying I found it.

"Rick, let's go." Calix didn't leave me much time to enjoy my triumph, just picked up the stuff we'd raided from the armory and took the lead down the hall.

I followed slightly behind and to her left. We came upon several more squads of four or six hybrids, heading toward the armory, alerted to the fact the facility had come under attack.

With each new squad, I roasted them lightly on the outside, and let Calix carve out their tender, red insides.

I didn't bother asking Calix where we were going—I knew that we'd end up by Karen. I wasn't wrong. We rounded a few corners and found ourselves in front of the server room.

Calix motioned me back. The door stood ajar. From inside, the sound of raised voices reached us. I recognized them, matched them to their scent. Karen. Ramirez. Cordite and steel.

Ignoring Calix's sudden cry, I pushed the door back and charged in.

Before us, Ramirez and Karen faced off. In the split second of entry, I noticed three details.

First: Karen stood, blood smeared across her clothes, over the bodies of two of the MONIKER hybrids. Second: the screen of the computer in front of her had fragmented into a glowing, pixelated mess.

Third: Ramirez's finger squeezing the trigger of the gun he held, aimed straight for her head.

## 25

Ramirez wasn't a field guy. I don't know if he'd ever pointed a weapon at someone with lethal intention. His hand shook.

I froze. Karen had a pistol in her hand, but her arm hung at her side. Ramirez had gotten the drop on her.

The two of them faced each other. The chaos of the fighting around us seemed to fade away.

"Ken." Karen spoke calmly and evenly. "Please."

Something in Ramirez's face shifted.

The gunshots echoed around the small room.

In a blur faster than even I could track, Calix leapt on him, taking him to the floor even before the sound of the shot reached us.

As she tackled Ramirez, I darted in front of Karen, faster than I'd ever run before, but still too slow to keep a bullet from her.

With a snarl, Calix ripped Ramirez's throat wide open, spraying the room with a fine mist. He didn't gurgle or scream, already dead before she dropped his body to the floor. Karen's bullet had drilled a neat hole through his forehead, blowing out the back of his head all over the computer equipment stacked against the wall behind him.

Then Calix hovered next to me, face painted red with Ramirez's death. "Is she…?"

"I'm fine," Karen groaned. "Rick, get off me, I can't breathe."

I had to physically force myself to release my grip, and only did so by letting Calix take my place, cradling Karen in her arms.

The shot had grazed her temple, but aside from copious bleeding, there didn't appear to be any permanent damage.

Calix helped Karen to her feet, fussing at the wound until Karen pushed her hand away.

"I said, I'm fine." She blinked at us. "Thanks for the rescue. You bring the stuff?"

I stepped out the door to pick up the weapons, ammo, and explosives we'd brought with us, then hurriedly stepped back inside, slamming the door behind me. Just one more thing I like about this form—opposable thumbs.

"Chrompary." I handed the supplies to Calix and Karen. Opposable thumbs aside, I wasn't going to volunteer to rig explosives if I couldn't even pronounce it in this form.

"That still freaks me out," Karen said as they got busy. "Hearing you talk when you're furry."

"Chrompary," I reminded her. "Rots."

"Yes. Company. I heard you." She carefully set out the remaining explosives, handing them one brick by one brick to Calix, who set them around the server room. "One problem at a time."

While it did my heart good to see the means of MONIKER's destruction being arranged around the room, the thought of what awaited us on the other side of the door also concerned me.

The heavy kicks against the steel alerted us that our time had run out. The agency's hybrids had been heading to our position, and from the sounds of things out there, we were going to find it hard going to get out in one piece.

Frustrated, I kicked Ramirez's body. Even soaked in blood, his tie was still obnoxious.

I grasped the nozzle of the flamethrower. I couldn't read the gauge, but no way did I have enough fuel to take down the troops they were sending at us, troops that were knocking the hinges of the door askew. Karen and Calix were emplacing large amounts of explosive materiel, but blowing ourselves up to take down MONIKER didn't seem like the best plan ever.

"Ready?"

Calix's voice jerked my attention away from self-pity. I nodded, raised the nozzle of the flamethrower with one hand and displayed the claws of my other hand. Yeah, I was ready. Let's take down some of these hybrid assholes.

Karen inserted a loaded magazine into one of the rifles and slung it over her back, then loaded up another rifle, holding it at the ready. Her pockets were already stuffed with spare mags.

We turned as one to face the door, as one last heavy kick sent it flying.

I unloaded with the flamethrower. The first hybrid through the door threw up a forearm to shield his face, in vain. His skin bubbled and roasted, and the bullets Karen sent into his chest in a neat circle dropped him in front of the door.

His body caused the next few hybrids in line to pile up, leaving them easy targets for the three of us. For the shortest of eternities, we fell into a lethal rhythm. First, I blasted them with a gout of flame from my new favorite toy, and then either Calix cut them in half, or Karen shot them down.

One of the hybrids, a little too eager to get to us, clambered over the bodies of his fellows, as well as the one in front of him. He pushed the first one to the side, which broke our rhythm. Calix spun off, facing the first hybrid, while Karen and I dealt with Mr. Overachiever.

I both cursed and gave thanks for the narrow quarters of the server room. We were tripping over dead bodies, but while we had no room to maneuver, neither did our opponents. The hybrid reached out, slashing and clawing. I depressed the nozzle of the flamethrower.

The device belched out a hiccup of flame—then nothing. Stupid toy.

Karen fired a three-round burst. The bullets lodged in the skin of the hybrid, but without the fire to tenderize it first, it kept coming.

I dropped the nozzle and attacked, slashing and clawing. By sheer force of momentum, I pushed the thing back. Karen fired again.

This time, I got in her way, and one of the bullets grazed its way across my side.

"Sorry." She threw the apology at me. I ignored it. The round burned—contained some silver—but it wasn't even painful.

Slash-and-burn tactics were the only ones that had so far been effective against these guys.

Calix found another one.

"Dammit!"

I threw a quick look over Mr. Overachiever's shoulder as we wrestled for position. Calix had her booted foot on the first hybrid's neck, using it to brace herself as she tried to yank her sword out of its mouth. Looked like she had found another vulnerable point.

I roared and wrapped my arms around Overachiever's head, jamming my fingers into the sides of his mouth, opening it forcefully. He let go of my body and grabbed my hands, trying to force them away.

Ducking to the side, I left a line clear for Karen, and without hesitation, she stepped forward. Jammed the rifle in its mouth. Fired straight up into its brain cavity. Dead overachiever. Let that be a lesson.

A spray of bullets from the outside sent us ducking for cover, even though there wasn't any. I hoisted the body of the hybrid between the door and the three of us and let it absorb the spray of bullets.

Even with that barrier, several rounds stitched my side, and metal shrapnel pinged off the door, giving Karen a few more future badass scars. She shrugged it off and returned fire under my arm.

My brain had just enough time to wonder why hybrids were attacking us with rifles, when my other senses informed me that MONIKER had run out of hybrids and had sent their normal attack troops. Human troops.

For a fraction of a second, Calix and I froze, and Karen hesitated. The mistake almost cost us our teammate.

I roared and charged. After fighting the impossible, a few pesky humans weren't going to be any trouble. The nozzle of the now-useless flamethrower swung wildly as I plowed into the pack of MONIKER troops outside the door.

The first few I disemboweled. The next I grabbed their weapons, using the fact their rifles were attached to their bodies via slings to pull them in close and slash across a few vital organs and an artery or two.

MONIKER troops were disciplined, evident by the fact that they kept coming, even after being coated in arterial spray from their comrades.

The alarm still blared in the hall, adding to the din of weapons firing uselessly, men and women screaming, and general chaos and upheaval.

But even in the cacophony, I still managed to hear Karen's loud, clear voice ring out.

*"In nomine lunae—dormiunt."*

A green light shot from behind me, stabbing in long, sharp beams down the halls. The beams branched out into smaller, thinner beams, each of which sought one of the MONIKER troops, enveloping them.

The beams emanated from Karen's raised fist, held high over her head. Her voice didn't waver, but her eyes squinted and she half-turned her head. This was new for her, too.

Where the beams touched human skin, it looked like someone had turned off a switch. The well-trained ranks of MONIKER went out like a prizefighter someone paid off in the fourth round. Within seconds, the halls were full of snoring men and women.

The adrenaline coursing through me demanded more action, called to me to continue rending, clawing, slicing. But in this form, I had more control of who and what I was, and none of me included murdering unconscious human beings. Even if they did fight for the opposing team.

Next to me, Karen breathed heavily, panting. The effort of keeping her hand raised caused her to break out in a sweat. The scent of rosemary mingled with the smell of blood and another I couldn't quite place, but reminded me of Maria.

As the targets decreased, the beams faded away.

"Set the timer." Karen closed her hand around something and slipped it back in her pocket. "Twenty minutes."

Calix nodded and headed back into the server room.

I growled a question, not bothering to try to form words.

Karen shrugged and guessed what I wanted to know. "It gives us enough time to get these guys out of here and dump them far enough away to not get caught up in the blast."

Ugh. Of course. Not only do we get to save the enemy's life, but then we get to make sure they get a chance to come at us again another day. Stupid honor.

I turned and shrugged, growling again. Karen helped unstrap me from the flamethrower. I let the empty tanks clang on the ground. Muttering to myself, I slung a few of the troops over my shoulder and loped away.

Outside the facility, I found the deepest, dirtiest snowbank, and dropped my load into it. For a moment I thought about adding some yellow snow to the mix, but Karen and Calix would figure out who did it, and I didn't want to hear about it.

I headed back inside and met the two women heading back out. Calix had a similar load, while Karen carried one of her former comrades in a fireman's carry. I threw a mock salute as I passed them.

"I'll be right back in," Calix said as I loped by. I found it easier to move along on all four legs, even in this form.

Ha! If there is one man-rule out there that shall not be broken, it's that one never makes multiple trips if one can help it. True, I'd already broken this rule, but those are merely details.

There were six more bodies lying on the floor, and I'm pretty sure I strained something in my lower back, but I got everyone out before Karen and Calix had made it much past the lobby.

I dumped my load of sleeping humans with their comrades and threw myself down on a neighboring snowbank next to my teammates, just in time for the charges Calix had set to finally go off.

First came a *whoosh*, and then a thud. A section of the roof imploded, and some dust rose over the complex. Talk about an anticlimax. I'd hoped for at least some shooting flames and maybe an explosion or two.

"What time is it?" Calix asked no one in particular. She lay back, sprawled out, sword still clutched in her left hand.

"Almost ten." Karen, sitting with her arms wrapped around her knees, didn't bother looking at her wristwatch.

The entire ordeal had lasted fewer than two hours. That was the amount of time it had taken for me to put an end to Gratusczak, while Calix took care of MONIKER's nascent attempts to branch out into vampire research, and Karen created as much havoc with their data as she could reach.

"How much time do you estimate it'll take for the agency to recover from this attack?"

Karen shrugged off Calix's question. "An hour? A week? A year?"

Calix sat up next to Karen, snaking her arm around her waist and drawing her in close. She leaned her head against Karen's shoulder.

I can take a hint.

Besides, of all the things I wanted to do with this night, stick around and watch the remnants of MONIKER burn weren't very high on the list. Instead, the night wind had picked up, bringing with it all the desert smells of spring.

High overhead, the sky shone clear. A slight neon glow kissed the horizon. The moon called and, free of the agency and its silver pollution, I could finally answer.

## 26

The early sun rose over the desert as I shook off the last remnants of the Change. I scrounged up some pants and a shirt—don't ask, just trust that I've been doing this for a while—and headed into the outskirts of the city.

An older woman in a classic VW bug gave me a ride, dropping me off a few blocks from my final destination. She introduced herself as Luz and offered to continue the ride all the way to her hotel room, and I was sorely tempted. She had a wild energy, a kind of electric light to her aura that made me think we could have fun and forget about everything for a while.

I turned her down. I had places to go and couldn't enjoy the luxury of forgetting what had just happened, not even for a little while.

Besides, what I really needed was a shower.

I waved and smiled as the woman blew me a kiss and peeled out, leaving actual tracks on the asphalt. Then I turned and jogged around the corner and down the street to the diner where Calix and Karen waited for me.

We hadn't discussed meeting there, but I followed a thin, white line that stretched before me, the same link that had bound me to my pack. The same connection I'd once had, back when my family and my pack were one and the same.

It wasn't any giant, magical beacon. It might have just been a sort of sibling love, or me wanting to see something that wasn't there. But I had no doubt my steps were leading to the right place.

The inside of the diner was slightly too warm for comfort, and it smelled of booze, sex, and waffles.

Calix waved at me from a table in the back. Karen sat on the opposite side; the two of them had unobstructed lines of sight to the front, the back, and the side door.

I made my way over and slid into the seat next to Calix.

"Ladies."

"Rick." Calix grinned. "You look like hot shit."

"Your girlfriend's hitting on me," I told Karen, who rolled her eyes. The ghost of a grin played at the sides of her mouth.

"Where'd you get the clothes?" she asked.

"Donations," I explained.

"I just didn't see you as much of a *Star Wars* fan." She folded her arms on the table and raised an eyebrow.

I looked down at the front of my shirt. I had, indeed, swiped someone's fanboy—or girl, *Star Wars* fandom is a gender-neutral thing—T-shirt. "Chewbacca's my soulmate, leave me alone."

The waitress took that moment to arrive with cups of coffee, one for each of us. Apparently, I'd been expected.

We each took a minute to appreciate the caffeine. Around us, the diner slowly filled with other patrons who also looked like they had slept in their clothes—or swiped them from an unattended clothesline.

"How's your head?" I asked Karen. The wound had been mostly cleaned up, along with the shrapnel from the door, but the deep cut remained, surrounded by a growing purple bruise.

"It's fine," she said. "Nothing that a year's vacation won't fix."

She and Calix exchanged one of those couple glances.

"Is that where you're headed?" We hadn't talked at all about anything, including about what happened next.

Karen busied herself fidgeting with the cream and sugar, even though she took her coffee black. Calix pretended to study the menu.

Panic rose in me. On the one hand, I'd been freed of MONIKER and the organization's little machinations, and that meant I could head back into the wilderness and never see anyone ever again who wasn't furry and didn't run on four legs.

On the other hand, I'd finally found the people I could trust with my life, who might possibly be the ones I could now call pack. Were they about to politely tell me to get lost?

Instead of answering, Karen dug in the pocket of her pants and pulled something out. She placed it on the table and pushed it toward me with her fingertips.

The object turned out to be a stone medallion, carved in the shape of a wolf's head. I touched it lightly—the stone felt cool to the touch.

"Green jade," Karen said.

"I was going to guess something along those lines."

"Maria gave it to me, right before they took off."

Calix reached out and touched it. "Feels like we used up all the juice."

Karen shrugged. "Probably. She said it was for an emergency."

"Getting attacked by a bunch of humans isn't an emergency." I detected a touchy note in Calix's voice.

"Usually not," Karen replied. "But I knew some of them by their first names."

"Do you mind if I...?" I broke in.

"Go ahead." Karen sat back on the bench.

I closed my hand around the medallion, finding the coldness of the jade comforting. Also, the thought of Maria.

"Where are you heading?" Calix asked, switching topics.

"I'm heading back up north." Until I said it out loud, I wasn't sure. But that seemed like a good plan.

"Hiding out?" Karen asked.

"I don't 'hide out,'" I retorted. "I simply make it hard for assholes to find me."

Calix snorted. "It wasn't that hard."

I grinned. "So you admit it?" The look on her face. I laughed out loud, then sobered. "Nah, I'm not hiding out. MONIKER can kiss my ass." I finished the last of my coffee and set the empty cup down on the table. "I'm going to go up north, stay with Randall and Lara until after the baby comes, make sure they stay safe from Black Mountain or MONIKER or any other asshole trying to get to me through them."

"Fair enough." Calix shifted in her seat and met Karen's eyes, asking her a silent question.

Karen took a breath and leaned forward. "Rick, Calix and I have a proposition for you."

I grinned, not making any of a selection of juvenile responses. See? Personal growth. She rolled her eyes anyway and continued.

"We're going independent, starting our own thing."

"Choosing our own assholes to work with," Calix contributed.

"And for," Karen added. "You interested?"

I didn't even pretend I hadn't been waiting for them to ask. I extended my hand across the table to shake Karen's. "I'm in."

"Great," Calix said, slapping me on the shoulder. Ow. "We can write off breakfast as a business expense."

She grinned, and the shadow of my cousin, Markus, passed unexpectedly over my mind. Just another piece of my puzzle that didn't fit anymore.

I shook it off. "So, ladies, where are you heading for vacation?"

"California. Arizona. New Mexico." Calix gave Karen one of those couple smiles. "Going to meet the Family."

"Don't forget to invite me to the wedding."

Karen rolled her eyes at me. "You'll be our ring bearer. We'll get you one of those cushions to wear and everything."

The joke was at my expense, but I grinned anyway. Karen and Calix were family. They were pack. I was home.

# EPILOGUE

T he fire crackled and popped as the gray-haired woman stirred it back to life. Satisfied it wouldn't die yet, she stood the poker back in its stand and closed the grate against an errant spark.

"Your meeting went well?" She settled herself back in a leather chair and picked up the book she'd been reading before her visitor interrupted.

"Yes, ma'am." Markus tried to read the spine, but the title was written in Cyrillic, and he had no knowledge of the alphabet.

She raised an eyebrow, inviting him to elaborate.

"He wore a silver cuff." The large man tried to think of another way to describe it, but he didn't have the gift of eloquence, and the woman in front of him did not suffer fools gladly—or at all. "There was something else, underneath."

"Explain." The tone of her voice was drier than the white wine in the glass at her elbow.

"His scent had changed." Markus considered telling her of the shadow he had seen, the one that turned his bowels to ice and shrank his stomach in fear. No. Better not.

The woman closed her eyes and rubbed her temple with her right thumb. "Go. I'll read your report."

Markus nodded and turned to go. Her voice behind him stopped him in his tracks.

"Wait."

He turned.

"Tell me…" The firelight sparked in her eyes, turning them incandescent in shades of brown and yellow, just for a moment. "My son—is he a threat to our plans?"

# ABOUT THE AUTHOR

As a military journalist, Rachel A. Brune wrote and photographed the Army and its soldiers for five years. When she moved on, she didn't quit writing stories with soldiers in them, just added werewolves, sorcerers, a couple evil mad scientists, and a Fae or two. Now a full-time author and writing coach living in North Carolina, Rachel enjoys poking around old military posts and listening for the ghosts of old soldiers … or writing them into her latest short story. She lives with her spouse, two daughters, one reticent cat, and two flatulent rescue dogs.

# ALSO BY RACHEL A. BRUNE

Side Roads

The Amazing Stories of Detective Boudreaux & Sergeant Woodson

Cold Run

# FRIENDS OF FALSTAFF

Thank You to All our Falstaff Books Patrons, who get extra digital content each month! To be featured here and see what other great rewards we offer, go to www.patreon.com/falstaffbooks.

**PATRONS**

Dino Hicks
John Hooks
John Kilgallon
Larissa Lichty
Travis & Casey Schilling
Staci-Leigh Santore
Sheryl R. Hayes
Scott Norris
Samuel Montgomery-Blinn
Junkle
Vickie DeSantos
Quincy J. Allen
Allison Charlesworth

# Thank You for Supporting Independent Publishing!

We believe that you should be able
to read your books, your way.
That's why this Falstaff Books
print edition includes a digital copy
at no additional cost!

Just scan the QR code with your device,
follow the directions on Prolific Works,
and enjoy!
You can also join our newsletter when prompted,
and never miss an awesome Falstaff Release!

www.ingramcontent.com/pod-product-compliance
Lightning Source LLC
Chambersburg PA
CBHW050310110726
47899CB00007B/2184